EDEN UNVEILED

EDEN
UNVEILED

Maria del Rey

This book is a work of fiction.
In real life, make sure you practise safe sex.

First published in 1996 by
Nexus
332 Ladbroke Grove
London W10 5AH

Copyright © Maria del Rey 1996

Typeset by TW Typesetting, Plymouth, Devon

Printed and bound by
BPC Paperbacks Ltd, Aylesbury, Bucks

ISBN 0 352 33116 X

The right of Maria del Rey to be identified as the Author
of this Work has been asserted by her in accordance with
the Copyright Designs and Patents Act 1988.

One

She was studying the large canvas in the corner of the gallery when Louis spotted her. He waited for a moment, watching her struggle with the strange swirls of blue and brown that seemed to be fighting it out on the rectangular canvas framed against a white wall. She stared at it for a moment, perhaps attempting to find something figurative in the eddies and currents of colour, then she stepped back to look at the splashes of paint that had besmirched the virginal white wall.

'It's intense, isn't it?' Louis remarked, appearing at her side just as she was about to give up on the picture.

She looked at him for a moment, her dark blue eyes seeking out the true meaning in his words. 'Yes, very intense,' she agreed, smiling.

'It's reminiscent of an early Rothko,' he continued, offering a smile in return.

She looked at the swirling blues and browns again. 'Yes, very Rothko,' she agreed. 'The catalogue compared him to Ryman too,' she added.

He laughed. 'Rothko I'm familiar with,' he admitted, 'but who the hell is Ryman?'

She shrugged. 'It's a bit dull, really, even if the artist has daubed paint on the wall.'

'It's supposed to represent the struggle of the artist to fit his work into the traditional modes of expression represented by the canvas,' he explained. She didn't look like one of the usual arty crowd; there was no sign of her

1

taking the whole thing too seriously like many of the art groupies who flocked to shows.

'I think it's more to do with being drunk,' she suggested. 'Or being bored with the picture and then deciding to destroy it, but being too far gone to carry it through. I think the artist was bored to death with painting more than anything else.'

He smiled. 'I can't see that theory ever making it into the catalogue,' he replied. She was wearing a very seductive little black dress, very short, very tight and very sexy. She looked better than anything else at the gallery, far better. 'It is an interesting theory though.'

'It's not a theory,' she whispered, coming up close so that he could breathe her scent, 'I met the artist earlier and he explained it all himself.'

Had she had too much to drink? Her glass was almost empty and she sounded as though she'd decided to make an art statement herself. 'Another drink?' he suggested, staying in close to her, afraid that if he let her go she'd disappear and he'd never see her again.

She looked at her glass dubiously and pursed her lips as though thinking on the decision. 'Just one more.'

'Wait here,' he instructed, hiding his own glass which was untouched.

The gallery was buzzing, the murmur of conversation growing louder as the drink flowed. The usual faces were there: the arty crowd, kids from the university and the art school, a smattering of local celebrities. Louis manoeuvred his way to the front of the bar, practice having made perfect as regards getting a drink at these kinds of functions. He exchanged quick hellos with acquaintances, but was careful not to get into conversation. He poured his wine away and switched to mineral water; it was safer that way. For the woman, and he didn't even know her name yet, he grabbed a tall glass of white wine.

He felt grateful relief when he got back and she was still there, in the corner, still gazing at the blue and brown canvas. Long dark hair framed her face and fell softly over her bare shoulders. She was tall and slim and her dress was perfect, it moulded itself to the contours of her body: firm, round breasts, the curves of her backside and her belly, the long and enticing length of her legs.

'It's called 'Heat Death',' he informed her, passing the white wine. 'I'm Louis, by the way.'

'Emily,' she replied, turning to look at him properly.

'Pleased to meet you, Emily. I've not seen you here before. Do you live in the town, or are you just visiting?'

She seemed to hesitate for a moment. 'Just visiting,' she told him. 'And you?'

His answer was drowned out by a sudden burst of music. He raised his eyes to heaven and shook his head. 'I hate the music they play at these things,' he said, moving closer to her so that she could hear him above the pulsing beat that echoed through the cavernous gallery.

'It doesn't sound that bad,' she replied, leaning towards him.

He could feel the warmth of her body. When she moved even closer, he could breathe her perfume, enjoying the mingling of the senses as his arm accidentally brushed against her chest. Her nipples were pressing against the tight black material, and from looking at her earlier he was sure that she was wearing nothing but the dress.

'Yes, but when it's this loud, you can't talk,' he complained. He took her arm gently and guided her to the back of the gallery, steering her towards an alcove that shielded them from the direct force of the sound.

'This is a bit out of the way,' she said, without losing her smile.

'A bit of privacy helps things along,' he told her.

She nodded and leant back against the white wall, sipping her drink. 'You go to lots of art exhibitions?'

'You could say that,' he replied. 'I work for a gallery in London. I like to see what the colleges are turning out each season.'

'Do you like anything you've seen so far?'

He smiled. 'Apart from you, nothing.'

She giggled. 'I think I've had too much to drink,' she confessed, closing her eyes for a moment.

'Would you like to go somewhere to relax?'

'Your place, you mean?' she asked.

Louis hesitated. From the sound of her voice, he wasn't sure how she'd reacted. 'We could go for a meal,' he suggested, hopefully.

She made no reply. Her eyes were closed and she was resting her head against the wall. Her breasts were firm, jutting forward, her nipples poking hard against the constricting black material of her dress. She had raised one leg, lifting the short dress high against her thigh, bringing out the contrast between the whiteness of her skin and the blackness of her clothes.

'Where are you staying?' he asked, giving up on the idea of the meal.

'Near here,' she replied, vaguely waving a hand at the gallery around her. 'What about you?'

'I'm staying at a hotel a cab ride away,' he told her. He leant against the wall too, looking at her in profile, admiring the shape of her body as it was outlined in black. She turned and looked at him directly, her blue eyes piercing, a neutral expression on her face. 'I told you,' he explained with a sly smile, 'you're the best thing I've seen all night.'

For a second there was no reaction and then she smiled. 'Flattery and drinks,' she said. 'I guess that means you like me.'

He reached out with his free hand and touched her thigh, letting his fingers stroke the contact point between bare flesh and the hem of her dress. 'You don't really want to stay here, do you?'

She turned towards him slightly, not moving his hand away, letting his fingers stroke higher so that his hand lifted the front of her dress. 'That feels good,' she whispered.

He let his hand linger and then moved towards her,

4

tilting his face so that his mouth came to hers swiftly. They kissed slowly, deeply; she let him explore her mouth with his tongue, let him breathe her hot breath. He moved away, his heart beating with excitement, his prick aroused to hardness by the responsiveness of her body.

'Let's go back to my place,' he suggested again, stroking her inner thigh persuasively, up and down slowly, inching ever closer to the heat of her sex but never quite getting there. Her nipples were hardening, clearly displayed by the tightness of her dress. She made no reply and they kissed again, harder, more passionate, her fingers brushing lightly against the hardness of his cock.

'Why wait?' he insisted. He was aware of her excitement; he could see it in her eyes, in the response of her body and her breathlessness. His own excitement was obvious, he had pressed his erection against her belly, letting her know just how physical his desire was. She kissed him again, inviting his fingers to stray under her dress again. He held her with both hands and pulled her closer, away from the wall, so that he could feel the outline of her backside with his fingers.

'Here you are, Emily!'

The male voice startled them. Emily pulled away suddenly, almost panicky. Louis turned quickly, the beat of his heart switching from passion to irritation that they had been disturbed. He faced two men, one of them fairly young, about the same age as Emily, and the other considerably older, probably in his middle to late 40's.

'We've been looking for you everywhere,' the older man exclaimed.

'I was just ... just talking about the exhibition with Louis,' she explained hurriedly, smoothing her dress down guiltily.

'Hi, I'm Alex,' the younger man said, offering his hand to Louis, 'Emily's husband.'

Louis groaned inwardly. It was obvious what he and Emily had been up to – there was no other explanation for the state she was in – and he guessed that Alex and the other man must have seen everything. 'Louis Anthony,' he said, shaking Alex's hand.

'Robert King,' the older man introduced himself.

There was silence for a moment, an awkward, uncomfortable silence that nobody seemed inclined to break. Louis damned his luck for not getting Emily out earlier; he was certain that she would have joined him back at his hotel if her husband had not arrived. The young man seemed ill at ease, as though he did not know how to react to catching his pretty young wife in another man's arms.

'Do you like the exhibition, Mr Anthony?' Robert asked finally.

'No, not really,' Louis replied. He glanced at his watch. It was getting late and he knew that he'd missed out on finding someone else that night.

'I don't think it's that bad,' Alex said, glancing at Emily.

'Louis is an art dealer,' Emily told him.

'Really? With which gallery?' Robert asked.

'I work for an auction house in London,' Louis replied. He looked again at his watch. 'I really must be going now,' he said, apologetically. 'It's been nice meeting you all.'

'Do you really have to go?' Emily asked, her disappointment openly expressed.

'Yes, there are a few calls I have to make,' he lied, hoping that Alex and Robert hadn't picked up on Emily's disappointment.

'What a shame you can't stay longer,' Alex said, putting an arm around his wife. 'I'm sure Emily would have enjoyed your company a little more.'

Louis swallowed hard. Alex was speaking calmly, a half-smile on his face, his arm casually around Emily's waist.

Emily smiled. 'Are you sure you can't stay a little longer?'

Louis wasn't sure what was going on. Alex seemed to be on the level; the smile on his face didn't fit with any feelings of anger or jealousy.

6

'Perhaps it's the surroundings?' Robert suggested. 'The music's just a little too raucous for me. You're a stranger here, Mr Anthony?'

'Call me Louis, please. Yes, I'm just here for the exhibition. I'll be returning to London tomorrow morning.'

'Can we all go back to your place, Robert?' Emily asked, smiling sweetly. 'Please?'

Robert laughed. 'You'd charm the angels from the heavens,' he told her. 'Why not? Louis, would you care to join us?'

Louis felt drawn to Emily, she was looking at him with wide open eyes and a pleading smile. Her scent still lingered and the feel of her smooth pale skin had been pure pleasure under his fingers. But what of her husband? The situation was strange, and he wasn't sure whether he wanted to get involved in whatever was going on between the couple.

'It's okay,' Alex assured him. 'I know exactly what Emily was doing. There's no problem with that on my part. Darling?'

Emily turned and kissed Alex on the mouth quickly, and then walked to Louis. 'It's okay,' she whispered. 'You can kiss me again.' She reached out, put her arms around his neck and allowed him to draw her to his body. They kissed again, mouth to mouth, breathless and passionate. His hands wandered down, instinctively moving to caress her sinuously sexy body. When he released her, she looked flushed, her cheeks red and her eyes sparkling with desire. Behind her, Alex was smiling, looking relaxed, almost as though he were proud of his wife.

'Louis?' Robert asked.

'I don't know what the hell's going on here,' Louis admitted. 'But I'd be a fool to say no.'

Alex smiled. 'A wise choice,' he remarked. 'Emily makes love beautifully. You won't be disappointed.'

* * *

Robert's car had been parked a good distance from the gallery, much farther than Louis had expected. Emily waited for Alex and Robert to go ahead so that she could follow on with Louis, who still seemed perplexed by the situation.

'It's okay, really it is,' she told him, falling into step and then clinging to his arm.

'This is a weirder situation than I'm used to,' he replied, doing nothing to hold her close.

'Just relax and enjoy it,' she told him.

Robert and Alex were already in the car; Robert was driving, with Alex beside him. Louis held the rear door open and Emily slid on to the seat, her dress riding up to show an expanse of smooth white thigh. He got in beside her, but made no move to get close.

'She's got such lovely smooth skin, don't you agree?' Alex remarked, twisting round in his seat to address Louis, who nodded without saying a word.

Emily leant back in the seat and then flipped her long legs on to Louis's lap, making no attempt to smooth down her dress. She smiled, enjoying the look of confusion on his face, as he struggled with his natural inclinations and the social rules that he imagined still bound them.

'It's okay,' Alex continued. 'Why don't you touch her again?'

Louis looked blank for a moment, pure incomprehension marked in his expression. Emily took his hand and placed it on her knee, smiling encouragingly. She loved the way Alex was talking about her, making her sound cheap and slutty, talking almost as though she weren't there. She remembered the feel of Louis's fingers sliding back and forth across her inner thigh, exciting her each time his fingers brushed towards the swollen lips of her sex.

It was only when Alex turned back to look at the road ahead that Louis began to touch her again, his hand stroking down from her knee to the most sensitive flesh of her upper thigh.

'You like this, don't you?' he murmured, managing a smile despite the obvious discomfort the situation was causing him.

'I like this, too,' she replied, leaning forward to kiss him on the mouth at the same time as she moved her hand to his crotch. His cock was hard, flexing as she closed her fingers around it, trapped in the thickness of his trousers.

She parted her thighs slightly as his fingers brushed against the sensitive lips of her pussy, making her moan as he withdrew again. She ached for him to stroke her pussy, to tease the swollen lips aside and touch a finger to the wetness that oozed inside her.

Instead, he used his hands to squeeze her breasts, cupping them in his palms and then flicking his thumbs over the erect points that strained against the tightness of her dress. He teased her for a while, sucking at her mouth and playing with her nipples. He stopped suddenly.

'You really don't mind?' he asked Alex, who had been watching silently.

'Why should I mind? It turns me on to see my wife with another man,' Alex replied.

'You're not happy with the situation?' Robert asked, glancing quickly over his shoulder.

'It's just – it's just that if she were my wife,' Louis explained, 'I think I'd keep her away from other men. I mean, I just couldn't handle seeing her being kissed or touched by another man.'

'It excites us both like this,' Emily assured him, taking his hand and putting it on her thigh again. He shook his head, as though admitting that he couldn't understand it.

The car turned off the road and on to a gravel drive which led to a large detached house set well back from view. The house was in darkness but for orange lights that were triggered by the sound of the car; they shed a soft, unfocused glow over the entrance.

Emily kissed Louis on the mouth quickly, her excitement growing in intensity now that they had arrived at

Robert's house. She watched Alex and Robert get out first, but Louis seemed to be holding back. 'We're here now,' she said, encouraging him.

Alex went in first – going straight for the room at the front of the house – switching on the light and making way for Louis to pass him. Emily followed, nerves now starting to tingle deep inside her.

Robert came in last. 'Drinks everyone?' he asked, heading straight for the drinks cabinet at one side of the room.

'Scotch for me, please,' Louis murmured. He walked to the centre of the large room, looking around approvingly. 'Are you a collector?' he asked, waving a hand at the canvas which dominated one side of the room.

Robert chuckled. 'A dabbler rather than a collector,' he said. 'That one's by a young artist friend. I let her use my place to hang her work sometimes. Do you like it?'

Emily took the drink from Robert and walked over to the Louis. 'It is good, don't you think?'

Louis took the drink, absently. His attention was focused on the explicit painting before him: bodies entwined, male and female, exquisitely detailed genitalia, expressions of ecstasy etched on their faces. 'It's good,' he agreed. 'She's very talented. That's quite an academic style for such a – an intense image.'

Alex laughed. 'An intense image,' he repeated. 'I'll mention that to her. She was happy to call it pornographic.'

Louis turned and smiled. 'I like it a lot,' he admitted. 'It's the sort of thing that would sell well to rich Americans or jaded Europeans.'

Emily stopped the conversation dead by kissing him again, putting her mouth to his. This time there was no holding back. He put his hands to her waist and held her in place. The heat was building up in her sex, adding to the excitement until she could stand it no longer.

She moved herself against him, enjoying the feel of his erect cock pressed into her belly. Her fingers stroked him, playing with his cock so that he sighed into her mouth. He reached behind her and pulled her dress up until she could feel cool air on her fully exposed backside. She ached for his touch, wanting him to take her there and then; to fuck her hard in full view of Alex and Robert.

Louis eased her dress higher, up past her belly and then, when she stepped back, he pulled it over her head. Her hair fell back, long dark strands of it covering her face and falling untidily over her shoulders. It didn't matter. She was naked now and enjoying it.

'You look gorgeous,' Louis murmured, feasting his eyes on the swell of her breasts, her large round nipples hard and erect, her long thighs meeting at the dark triangle of hair that covered her pussy. She turned to Robert who smiled encouragingly, and to Alex, whose eyes were full of desire. She knelt down in front of Louis, waiting expectantly to see what he wanted of her. He looked down, his eyes wider than she had ever seen them.

'Fuck her in the mouth,' Alex suggested, his voice a low whisper that did nothing to break the tension.

Louis walked backwards to the heavy leather chair under the painting on the wall. She made no move until he motioned for her to come forward, and then she crawled on all fours, aware of the sway of her breasts and the twisting of her hips. On hands and knees she felt beautiful: a creature destined for nothing but sex and pleasure.

'Your mouth,' Louis told her, his voice a command that made her flush with pleasure. She worked to free his cock, holding it with her delicate fingers, sensing for the first time the power that she ached for. He sighed as she stroked him, working her fingers the length of his stiffness, exciting him as she moved her head closer.

She arched her back, pushing her backside higher so that her bottom was best displayed for Alex and Robert to enjoy. The heat in her sex was growing; a wet, sticky heat that seemed to suffuse her whole body. She touched her lips to Louis's hardness, pressing her mouth to the

11

underside of the glans, savouring the feel of it against the softness of her lips. She traced her tongue under it, tantalising him with the pleasure only she could give.

The pleasure in her sex could no longer be denied. Very slowly, knowing that every move was being enjoyed by the two men standing behind her, she slid her hand down from her chest, across her tummy and then between her thighs. She closed her mouth around the hard flesh, sucking on it gently, while pressing her fingers through the moist-laden petals of her sex. His sigh of ecstasy was echoed by her own as she wet her fingers deep in the heart of her sex.

Slowly she worked her mouth up and down Louis's cock, cascading her tongue and lips across the hard length of his flesh until he was panting softly. She withdrew his erect prick completely, looked at the glistening flesh and the glans soaked by her tongue and the rivulet of fluid that welled at the slit. He urged her on impatiently, his eyes filled with longing.

She closed her lips and then forced his hardness into her mouth, knowing that the exquisite pleasure would be redoubled by the resistance of her lips. He bucked upward, pushing his cock deeper into her mouth, pressing it all the way in. She took his length, letting her tongue lash the underside of it, holding it then moving up and down, the pace growing faster and faster. Her fingers echoed the movement of his body, so that she was fucking herself furiously, penetrating her wet pussy with hard thrusts. Spurred on by the double pleasure of a cock in her mouth and fingers in her sex, she arched her back for climax, lingering on the edge for as long as possible, prolonging the pleasure until she felt him gasping.

Her fingers moved upwards, pressing on her clit so that she climaxed suddenly, just as the white essence spurted from Louis's cock into her mouth. She sucked down on it, taking every drop of the spurting fluid and savouring it as she felt it slip down her throat.

She drew back and smiled at Louis, who smiled in

return, his penis still hard and glistening. Her fingers were coated with the sticky honey from her own orgasm; she turned to Alex and smiled before licking her fingers clean.

Robert, seated nearest the drinks cabinet, motioned for her to come to him. There was no need to speak. His intentions were clear; he had already undone his trousers and he was holding his erect cock in his hand. She was on all fours again, delighting in the idea that now Louis was going to be watching her from behind. She moved slowly, languorously, knowing that every sinuous movement excited her audience.

Robert touched her face with the tips of his fingers, caressing her smooth skin before opening her lips. She sucked at his fingers, lashing her tongue to let him know what she was going to do with his cock. Her own fingers sought her pussy again, reaching for the velvet wetness, and teased her clit slightly, making her shiver with pleasure. She alternated between pressing her fingers into her sex and then playing with her bud, until she was close to orgasm.

Her fingers were wet with her own juices as she stroked Robert's cock, making the thickly veined rod glisten enticingly. When she put her lips to his hardness she tasted herself first; tasted the essence of her sex, the liquid evidence of her pleasure. She sucked harder, her tongue probing, seeking out every last taste of her pussy on his flesh. He stroked her hair, running his fingers through the dark strands as she worked her mouth deliriously over his cock. Her fingers were playing faster and faster with her pussy, building up the pleasure – a pleasure heightened by the fact that she knew Alex and Louis could see her fingers slipping in and out of her wetness.

Robert pressed her head down sharply, using both hands to hold her in place as his orgasm burst forth, cascading thick come into her mouth. She held it there, waiting for him to spurt his seed until he was done. When he released her she sat back, lingering on the verge of her own climax.

Alex was there, waiting for her; naked, erect, ready. She reached back and they kissed mouth to mouth, Robert's come slipping from her mouth to his. They kissed long and hard, tongues touching, sliding with semen. When he let go she saw the trail of semen dripping from the corner of his mouth. It turned her on immensely, excited her like no other image to see another man's seed dripping from Alex's mouth, knowing that she had passed it to him in a passionate kiss.

When they kissed again she licked away the come from his face and tasted it still on his breath. He turned her round and she understood. She pressed her face and chest to the carpeted floor, lifting her behind high and opening her pussy lips with her fingers. She cried out blissfully when he thrust his cock deep into her sex. It felt so good; she pressed back, opening herself more so that he could thrust hard and deep into her pussy. Her fingers teased her sex bud, pushing herself closer and closer, until she cried out her climax for all to hear.

She pulled away, greedy now to taste herself again. Alex's hard flesh was coated with her wetness, glistening with the thickness of her sex honey. He thrust into her mouth, unable to hold back. She sucked him hard, riding up and down his cock, her mouth fluid and wet like her pussy; faster and faster, she let his glans escape her lips only to plunge deep again, making him moan softly.

He gasped and she swallowed his spunk, feasting on it, wanting it all. She continued to suck him even when he lay back, exhausted and bathed in sweat. She held his hard prick in her fingers and licked away the last drops that seeped from the reddened glans. As she sucked, she was aware of movement behind her.

'I want you again,' Louis informed her hotly, stripping his clothes off quickly. His excitement was there to see; his cock was still hard and seeping drops of silvery fluid.

'Fuck her here,' Alex suggested, 'while she's still over me.'

Louis needed no second bidding. He took her by the

waist and kissed her pussy gently, letting his tongue stroke the swollen lips that were flecked with her come. She sighed and moved over so that she could kiss Alex on the mouth again, gratefully.

She closed her eyes when Louis pressed his cock to her sex. She wanted him to take her softly, sensitively. She held her breath as he slid his hardness into her, easing it in slowly, letting the sensations build up gradually. She opened her eyes and smiled to Robert, who was watching with interest.

'That's good,' she sighed, as Louis began to fuck her properly, pushing himself deep into her pussy in a slow, even motion.

The pleasure grew in intensity when Alex cupped her breasts, closing his hands over the erect nipples as if to hold in the exquisite sensations. He held her for a moment, letting her body sway back and forth, while Louis took her from behind. She sighed again when her nipples were squeezed, Alex's fingers closing on the swollen nubs of flesh.

Robert joined them, his naked body connecting with the melee on the floor. He took her chin and forced his tongue into her mouth, sucking at her breath, kissing her forcefully. She cried into his mouth, uttering a strangled sigh when she felt Alex's fingers brush roughly against her pussy bud.

Robert was hard again, and she knew what he desired most of all. She opened her mouth and tasted his cock again, holding the glans between her lips so that she could tease the fluid with the tip of her tongue. The pleasure was everywhere: on her breasts, inside her cunt, electric on her clit and in the hardness in her mouth. She felt more desirable, more sexual than at any other time, knowing that there were three naked men worshipping her body.

They fucked endlessly, the three men changing positions at random, so that Alex was fucking her with harsh, rough strokes while Louis sucked hard on her breasts; or

15

Robert sucked her pussy while she played with the other two cocks with her mouth and hands. She climaxed repeatedly, not counting, not caring; wanting only for the pleasure to go on and on.

Her body was bathed in sweat and spunk: Robert covered her breasts with his white jism as Louis came deep in her pussy, with finally Alex climaxing and spurting his come into her freshly fucked pussy.

Sleep, when it came, was deep and dreamy; the high of her orgasms carrying her forwards through the night.

TWO

Patrick waited for the young woman to come into the room before he closed the door behind her. The sharp sound of the door slamming shut seemed to startle her. She turned and looked at him, with eyes so wide and innocent it almost brought a smile to his face.

'You look nervous,' he remarked, taking her by the hand and leading her through the narrow ante-chamber and then out into the wider space of the conservatory.

'I'm sorry,' Amanda apologised quietly, doing her best to keep up with him.

'Don't talk,' he told her. 'There's no need. You're here to listen and learn. If you speak out of turn again, I'll punish you for it.'

Her eyes widened still more and she bit her lower lip, and although she wanted to, she did not speak. He could see the questions in her eyes – could see her looking to him for answers, for directions, but there was nothing. His face was cold, unsmiling, unrevealing. When he put his hand on her shoulder he could feel her tensing, the fear in her expression becoming physical.

'What do you see?' he asked, the wide sweep of his hand taking in the spread of buildings arrayed across the hilly landscape before them. The conservatory offered the best view of Eden, Patrick's house being higher than any of the others. The girl hesitated, not knowing whether the question demanded a reply or not. He waited a moment, but she made no response, guessing correctly that the question was both his to ask and his to answer.

'This is the future,' he told her. 'Our small community is a model, a template for others to study and emulate. We want to show that there's a different way to live, a better way. Ours is the most modern mode of existence; free of the traditions of the past that have strait-jacketed society; free of the mistakes that have all but destroyed any hope for the future.'

Amanda listened intently, her eyes fixed on the loosely clustered houses on the hillside below them. Each house was self-contained and spacious; individually designed, but with a similar look and feel to the others. There were no gardens or fences demarcating the borders between each property; rather the land around them was shared, common to all of them.

'People have been building alternative communities since the nineteenth century, all of them fired up with some idealistic vision of how life should be, rather than how it is. However, each of those experiments has failed in some way; the reality never coming close to the vision. But we are different. Very different, in fact.'

The girl continued to stare through the twin layers of glass at the community below. In the distance, barely visible from the conservatory, lay the high walls which ringed Eden; high stone walls, tipped with wire, that were scanned automatically by security cameras. From the outside, the effect was forbidding; from within the community, the effect was innocuous, the high walls being sufficiently far from the houses to remain unobtrusive. Patrick and Katerina had designed it to be so. They wanted to engender a feeling of security, without any attendant paranoia setting in.

'As you well know,' he continued, wondering for a moment just how much she did know, 'many of the alternative communities of the past have floundered due to social problems between the inhabitants. An enclosed society is a breeding ground for petty jealousies and factional squabbles. Do you understand?'

When she failed to answer, he tightened his grip on her shoulder for a moment. 'Yes, Patrick. I know what you mean,' she answered, her voice eager to please, but revealing the full extent of her nervousness.

'Good,' he said, letting go of her. 'It is for this reason that anyone taken on to help us, even for a short while, has to fit in exactly. It's simple, really. We're looking for the sort of person who'd fit in for a much longer period, the sort of person whom we could imagine staying with us permanently.'

'I'm sure I –' she began, but fell silent as she noticed Patrick watching her.

The thick layer of cloud above the hilly landscape parted slightly, the sudden flash of white light filling the conservatory with its welcoming warmth. The rays of light seemed to be amplified by the layers of glass, the warmth spreading quickly, triggering panels and solar cells all over the building.

Patrick turned and walked to the padded bench against the far wall of the conservatory, his footsteps clicking hard on the solid stone floor. He sat down and waited, making himself comfortable, secure in the knowledge that he was fully in control. When the girl turned away from the panoramic view of Eden, her face was flushed a bright pink. Her eyes met his for a moment and then she lowered them, unable to hold his gaze.

'You do want to work with us?' he asked, his voice level and emotionless.

She stood rooted to the spot, standing with ankles together, hands held in front of her, and her head slightly bowed. 'Yes,' she whispered. 'Very much.'

'Good. Your course finishes when?'

'My finals are in late spring,' she replied.

'And then?'

She shrugged. 'I might spend some time travelling. Or I might look for work straight away.'

'You understand that if,' – and he stressed the word 'if' – 'you join us for the summer, you'll not be able to leave until your work here is finished?'

'Yes, I know.'

'Are you sure that's acceptable to you? It means no contact with boyfriends, girlfriends, family, potential employers and so on.'

The girl seemed to grow more confident. 'I know. Katerina has explained all that to me already.'

'And it's acceptable?'

'Yes.'

He nodded, gravely. Was she beginning to show signs of life at last? Her eyes met his again, lingered a moment longer and then she turned away again.

'Undress for me,' he ordered, using the same neutral tone as before. He noted her look of shock, the slight widening of the eyes again, the reddening of her face. She was still standing in front of the glass, in full view of anyone who happened to look towards the house. The sunlight filtering through the glass was casting an orange glow over her, highlighting her figure even more.

She closed her eyes for a moment, and when she opened them, tears welled there, sparkling in the bright light. Her hands were shaking; he could see her fumbling with the loose wraparound skirt which covered her long legs. She faced him, but dared not look at him. Her skirt came down first, the flimsy fabric falling softly to her ankles, and then she pulled the loose T-shirt over her head. She wore skimpy white briefs and matching bra, her dark nipples visible under the lacy fabric.

'Completely,' he told her, when she paused.

Again, there was a single moment of hesitation before she reached round to unclip her bra, letting it fall to the ground. Next came her panties; she slipped them down to her ankles quickly and stepped out of them. She glanced back at the window, aware that her nakedness was on display to whoever might look. When she straightened up, he could see that her face was bright red and her eyes were still filled with tears.

'You don't want to do this?' he asked, motioning for her to turn full circle.

'Katerina told me. She explained –'

He ignored her words. Her body language told him everything. Her nipples were puckering up, becoming erect slowly; she moved her long limbs awkwardly, her face was flushed with shame. And yet she obeyed when even a single word would have sufficed as refusal. He noted the fullness of her behind, the tuft of golden hair that fringed her sex, the pert breasts that were pointed hard by erect nipples. And her face: sweet innocence itself, with blue eyes that filled with tears so easily, making him hard just looking at her.

'Here,' he said, pointing to the space at his feet. 'Kneel down.'

She obeyed again, without question. She strode across the room away from the glass front, away from prying eyes but closer to him. He liked the way she walked; there was a certain feline elegance about it that even her nervousness could not hide.

He reached out and stroked her back, running his hand firmly from her shoulder to her waist, enjoying the warmth of her flawlessly pale skin. She shivered under him, a shrinking flower, an innocent untouched. He enjoyed the feel of her thighs, and sought out the inner thigh to caress intimately. Her breasts he touched casually, flicking her nipples with his fingers until she uttered a half-cry of complaint, or pleasure, or both combined.

He unbuttoned his trousers and freed his erection, keeping her face by his lap so that she could see everything. She looked even more embarrassed: cheeks hot to the touch, bottom lip quivering nervously. With one hand, he pulled her closer, looking intensely into her confused eyes. She parted her lips and took his cock nervously, letting it slide into her mouth slowly. He pushed himself deep and lingered for a second, feeling her breath on his sensitive flesh, her tongue resting under the throbbing shaft.

She began to fellate him, moving her head across his lap gently, closing her mouth so that it was tight over his

21

hardness. He let her move with her own rhythm while he continued to fondle her breasts, teasing her nipples so that her breathing quickened even more.

He pulled her to her knees in front of him and made her cup her breasts for his pleasure. His cock was wet with her saliva and the fluid that leaked from the glans. She inched forward and closed her breasts around his erect flesh, using her hands to masturbate him with her breasts, letting her nipples rub against him. He made her move faster, pressing himself upwards as she forced herself down, increasing the pressure and the pleasure.

He stood over her, making her rub herself harder as he fucked the valley between her beautiful breasts, now slick with the fluid from his glans. Faster and faster, he made her massage her breasts, holding her in place until he uttered a single cry, and climaxed. He was breathing hard as the jism arced from his cock on to her face and down over her reddened breasts, thick rivulets of fluid sliding over her skin to drip sensuously from her erect nipples.

While his cock was still hard, he urged her forward to suck away the last few drops of fluid, making her cleanse his body with her tongue. She obeyed again, sucking at the glans, lapping at it with her tongue to take up every trace of his salty fluid.

'Wait here,' he ordered, buttoning himself up.

'Can I get dressed?' she asked, making no move to get up. Her chest was still patterned with thick splashes of his semen; the fluid glistening on her skin, pouring down between her breasts, or lingering on her nipples as though she had secreted it herself.

'No, just wait.'

It was almost lunch time when Emily finally decided to get up. The miserable weather seemed to have cleared up; drawing the curtains, she was surprised by the blast of orange light on her naked body. She decided against getting dressed; instead she donned a baggy T-shirt, and made her way downstairs.

Robert and Alex were in the kitchen, chatting quietly as Alex fixed some lunch. She listened at the door for a moment, wondering whether Louis had spent the night with them at Robert's house or whether he had indeed returned to his hotel room.

'Hi, darling,' she said, pushing the door open when she was certain that Louis wasn't there. She kissed Alex on the mouth and then did the same with Robert, letting the older man hold her close so that he would know that she was naked under the loose cotton garment.

'Well?' she asked, excitedly. 'What's the verdict?'

'You don't have to ask, do you?' Alex countered, smiling broadly.

'I think it's pretty safe to say that your friend Louis enjoyed an encounter he's unlikely to forget for a very long time,' Robert told her.

'We were just saying,' Alex continued, 'that pretending we were married really freaked him out a bit. You should have seen the look on his face when I encouraged him to touch my wife.'

Emily giggled. 'To be honest, it turned me on as well,' she admitted. 'I kept imagining that you really were my husband. It's strange, isn't it, how that made everything seem more exciting.'

'There's nothing strange about that,' Robert told her. 'It's the breaking of taboos. It's one of the biggest aphrodisiacs of all.'

Alex dished up three plates of steaming pasta and then passed each in turn to Robert at the table. A bottle of red wine was already open; Emily poured herself a glass and sat at the table. Breakfast or lunch, she couldn't decide what the meal was. She still felt radiant, her body tingling with the after-glow of her ecstatic climaxes the night before.

Alex came up behind her, put his hands on her waist and kissed her on the back of the neck. 'You really got off on being my married slut,' he teased, bringing his hands up to cup her breasts in the soft folds of her T-shirt.

She turned slightly, meeting his mouth and enjoying a soft, sensual kiss. 'It was fun, definitely,' she whispered.

'Alex and I were discussing the summer vacation,' Robert said, when she and Alex had stopped kissing. 'Do you have anything planned?'

Emily sighed as Alex sat down beside her; she felt excited by his touch and by the vivid memories of enjoying three hard cocks at the same time. 'Nothing. We haven't really talked about it, have we, Alex?'

'We'd talked about doing Europe,' Alex explained, 'but there are no definite plans. I've got my finals to worry about, and Emily's still got her first year project to complete.'

Robert listened while he ate. 'How is the course?' he asked Emily, between mouthfuls.

'It's okay,' she said, not sounding terribly excited by it. 'It's a bit hard to concentrate on social anthropology when there's a whole world out there waiting to be discovered.'

'She means sex,' Alex teased, putting his hand to her thigh as he spoke. 'I don't know, Robert. Meeting you sometimes seems like the best thing that ever happened, but sometimes –'

'Yes?' Robert asked, when the sentence trailed to a stop. He was looking serious, studying Alex's reactions minutely. Emily caught him looking and was reminded that Robert was a psychologist first and foremost. Everything they did together seemed to be part of an on-going experiment, no matter how pleasurable it was.

'It's just that sometimes it's hard to concentrate on other things,' she explained. 'Studying, and doing course work; well, it can seem so dead compared to the things we get up to with you.'

Robert mused on the remark for a while before replying. 'Life is about balance,' he said, 'and perhaps what we're experiencing here is a slight tipping of the scales. Don't make the mistake of letting everything else slip, just because the sex is so enjoyable. Try to see it as part of a far larger vision.'

'Tell her about Eden,' Alex suggested a few minutes later. 'It sounds pretty interesting.'

'Eden? As in "the garden of"?'

'As in paradise,' Robert said, breaking into a smile again. 'It's a small community set up by some friends of mine. They've got together with a few like-minded souls and built themselves a sort of village up in the hills somewhere. It's not a commune exactly, nor is it one of those new age communities. It's quite difficult to describe, really.'

'What's the point of it?' Emily asked.

'To see if they can find a different way of living to the rest of us,' Robert told her.

'It's not a religious thing, is it?' Alex asked, looking as though the idea horrified him.

Robert smiled. 'No, nothing like that. They're all very worldly, if that's what you're worried about. No, I think they just grew sick of the daily grind of urban life, the careerist rat race and all that. It's quite high-tech; they decided that looking after sheep and cabbage patches wasn't what they wanted to do either. I've only been up there a few times, but they're an interesting group of people. And, as I explained to Alex, they're looking for a couple of helpers during the summer. Would you be interested?'

Emily looked at Alex. 'I said I'd talk to you first,' Alex told her.

'It all sounds a bit – a bit serious. You know; very earnest and boring,' she said.

Robert smiled. 'One of the things they're doing is experimenting with new kinds of relationships,' he explained. 'They're looking at everything afresh.'

'It'll just be for a couple of months,' Alex added. 'It'll be our chance to get away from it all as well. It'll be something different.'

Emily was undecided. It still sounded a bit worthy, a bit tedious. 'Can we go up there to see them first?'

'I'll arrange it as soon as I can,' Robert agreed. 'In the

meantime, it's a glorious day, too good to cover yourself up like that.'

The sun was streaming in through the kitchen window. Alex was looking at her encouragingly, knowing that she would not be able to resist flaunting herself. He was right, of course. She loved showing herself off; it always excited her to know that she could excite others. The T-shirt came off in one swift movement and the sunlight warmed her naked body.

Amanda was dozing when Katerina entered the conservatory. She was just as Patrick had left her: naked, and sitting on the floor by the bench, on which she was now resting her head. Luckily, the conservatory was comfortably warm, and it was that warmth, Katerina surmised, that had helped the poor girl doze off. Patrick had described her perfectly: long limbs, full breasts and a pretty, innocent young face.

'Katerina?' the girl whispered, waking suddenly as the other woman approached her.

'Patrick has gone now,' Katerina assured her, wishing to allay the fear that sparkled in the girl's clear, blue eyes.

'Did I please him?' she asked urgently. 'Did I do everything the way he wanted me to?'

Katerina evaded the question by asking one of her own. 'Did you do as well as you wanted to?'

The girl shook her head sadly. 'No, I just couldn't let myself relax enough. I wanted to please him so much.'

Katerina sat on the bench and pulled Amanda towards her, resting the girl's head on her lap. 'Did you enjoy it?'

The girl took a moment to answer, as though the experience had been so puzzling that she needed time to work it all out. 'It excited me,' she confessed, hiding her embarrassment in Katerina's lap. 'It excited me, but "enjoy" doesn't seem like the right word to describe what I felt.'

'I understand,' Katerina told her, passing her hand through the girl's long blonde hair, softly.

'Do you really understand?' Amanda wondered. 'I felt like I was there to do exactly what he wanted, to serve him no matter what –'

'And the experience was arousing,' Katerina said, finishing the sentence for the girl.

'Yes.'

Katerina lifted the girl slightly, making her sit up on her knees until they were face to face. She brushed the hair clear of the girl's face and gazed into her eyes, seeking the tears that Patrick had found so arousing. She tilted her head slightly, parted her lips, breathed softly and the girl came towards her. They touched lips softly, tentatively, afraid of the contact and yet unable to resist. They kissed again, Katerina parting the younger woman's lips, pressing her mouth hard, taking control. When she pulled away, the tears were there; the same tears of confusion and fear that threatened to rain down the girl's virtuous, young face.

Katerina kissed her again, pressing her mouth to the girl's lips, pushing her tongue all the way in, voraciously, like a man. She stroked her hands down the girl's back and then round to the belly and up again, stopping when her fingers closed over sensitive nipples that were hard to the touch. Amanda held her breath as her nipples were squeezed, and Katerina pulled her up on to the bench. They sat side by side, kissing again and again, whilst Katerina caressed the girl's body as she liked.

'You're so wet,' she whispered, when her fingers pressed into the tightness of the younger woman's pussy.

The reply was a moan and then the tears began to fall, cascading down the high cheek bones and red flushed skin, rippling down to her naked breasts. Katerina kissed the tears away, flicking her tongue over the girl's face and then scooping down to suck softly on a hardened nipple. The girl moaned softly, cradling Katerina's head in hands that trembled.

'Shall I stop?' Katerina asked, able to breathe the musky scent of the girl's pussy.

The girl shook her head vigorously, but could not trust herself to speak. Katerina smiled and put her lips to the girl's open slit, flicking her tongue between the sensitive folds of skin to suck deep on the wetness within. She tasted the girl's sex, wet her tongue deep inside her pussy, before turning her attention to the girl's swollen bud. Katerina kissed and sucked and teased the girl's clitoris until the girl heaved forward, arched her back and cried wordlessly as the orgasm took her.

'Lay back now,' Katerina instructed, softly. She kissed Amanda on the mouth, knowing that the girl would be able to taste her own juices. The girl obeyed, trembling and wide eyed, but seemingly unable to resist.

'Shall I stop?' Katerina repeated the question.

'No. Don't stop.'

Katerina stood, pulled her skirt up around her waist, and climbed onto the bench. She sat astride the younger woman, positioning herself over the girl's mouth, slowly sitting lower. She felt the girl's breath on her inner thigh and then the cool touch of the girl's lips. Silently, she reached down to pull her pussy lips open, to show the girl what it was she wanted. The girl understood; she began to lick and suck and probe with her tongue. Katerina closed her eyes to the pleasure that swept through her, a pleasure so strong that she knew she was going to climax directly over the young girl's mouth.

'Where is she now?' Patrick asked, looking up from his desk when Katerina arrived.

'I took her back to my room,' Katerina replied, taking the seat on the other side of the desk. 'I said she could rest there until we wanted her again.'

'Well?' Patrick asked, putting his pen down and leaning forward.

'She cried for me,' Katerina stated, allowing the faintest trace of a smile to lighten her dark features.

'And?' Patrick said, easily able to picture Katerina's dark body beside the pale skin and golden hair of the younger woman. It was a contrast that he always found exciting; knowing that Katerina's dark beauty implied a fiery temperament which wasn't always apparent – she could be as cold and as commanding as the iciest blonde.

'I agree with you,' she told him. 'She's simply not right for us.'

'Too precious?' he guessed.

'It's not so much that. There's something very docile about her. The emotional vulnerability is fine; it adds some fire to her.'

He knew exactly what she meant. 'I know,' he agreed. 'It's always interesting to watch that struggle between her desires and her feelings of what she should and shouldn't be doing.'

'So what do we do?'

Patrick leaned back in his seat. 'Have you spoken to Robert about the couple that he's found?'

'Not yet,' she said. 'I'm not sure that a couple is a good idea; it might be too complicated.'

He knew she was right but time was moving on and the first twinges of desperation were making themselves felt. 'We have to do something,' he pointed out. 'He said he'd be calling this week. If he does call, arrange to go down to meet them as soon as you can.'

Katerina looked at him sharply. 'And you?'

'I've got things to do here,' he said. He waited for an argument that never came, and, when he realised that there was going to be no discussion, he resisted the smile of satisfaction which was his natural reaction. 'I'd better talk to her,' he added, thinking of Amanda. 'I'll break the news gently.'

'Treat her well,' Katerina suggested. 'It's been a tough time for her here.'

'I know, but we've taken her as far as she wants to go now,' he explained. 'She's at her limit as it is. It's going to take her a while to adjust to the things she's learnt about herself as it is.'

'It is a pity, though,' Katerina sighed. 'She looks so perfectly innocent that it's a pleasure just looking at her.'

* * *

29

Amanda was curled up on the bed when Patrick arrived later. The sun had started to go down and now a soft pink glow suffused the deep blue of the sky. She was clothed in the velvet softness of shadows as she sat on the bed, gazing through the large square window opposite, watching the setting sun and the way the light danced over the sparse scattering of buildings below.

Patrick sat at the foot of the bed. 'Have you had a chance to think now?' he asked, allowing a note of genuine concern to colour his voice.

'I still don't want to leave,' the girl replied softly, pursing her lips sulkily. She wore only a short satin robe that did nothing to hide her long bare legs, the shiny black satin setting off her pale limbs.

'You feel that there's more for you here?'

'Yes,' she replied emphatically. 'It's not fair, you didn't give me enough chance. Please, if I could try again.'

Patrick smiled; her eagerness was pleasing, but it made no difference: he and Katerina had already made the decision. It was hard to define exactly why she did not fit in with their plans – there was much that they both liked about her – but in the end she lacked a certain spark, a certain wilfulness that they both desired.

'I'm sorry, the decision has been made,' he informed her apologetically. He waited for the tears but there were none, instead she dared to glare at him defiantly.

'You didn't give me time!' she accused. 'Everything happened so quickly. If I could have one more chance . . .'

He watched her get up onto her knees, slowly loosen the robe and then let it slip gently from her shoulders. She was naked, her body on offer, his to do with as he wished. This was her second chance, her calculated move to get him to change his mind. He smiled approvingly; for the first time since her arrival, she was showing signs of defiance and initiative.

'Here,' he told her, pointing to the space beside him. She crawled on hands and knees towards him, keeping

30

her eyes fixed on him, her rouged lips parted enticingly. When she was beside him he pulled her across his lap, pushing her off the edge of the bed so that she had to reach to the floor to stop herself falling over. Across his knee, prone, her bottom was displayed perfectly; her long legs kicking slightly added to the impression of vulnerability.

It wasn't what she had been expecting. He could see the confusion returning to her expression, replacing the defiance with a mixture of disquiet and excitement. He smoothed a hand along her thighs, enjoying the silky smooth feeling of her skin; pulled her bottom cheeks slightly apart to gaze adoringly at the pinkness of her sex and the dark button of her anus.

He raised his hand suddenly and brought it down forcefully, the sharp slap making her cry out with pain and horror. Again; hand high and then brought down swiftly to make contact with her taut backside. Again. The third heavy stroke landed on the right side of her bottom, leaving another red oval on her white flesh.

He paused and saw the sting of tears in her eyes again – the look of sweet innocence was there once more, arousing in him the desire to beat her harder. He smacked her again and again, until her bottom was patterned red and her cries were echoing round the room. Tears splashed to the floor but when he cruelly pushed two fingers into her sex she was wet and her cries became low moans of sensual pleasure.

'What did Katerina ask you about me?' he demanded, holding her in place while he worked his fingers in and out of her welcoming pussy.

'Nothing . . .' she gasped, trying to move herself to the rhythm of his fingers.

He raised his hand again and resumed the spanking, beating hard, flat strokes against her punished flesh. She wailed and cried, trying to wriggle free but to no avail.

'Did she ask about me?' he repeated, pushing his fingers into her pussy again, making her cry out with orgasmic pleasure.

31

'Nothing, nothing, nothing,' she cried.

He pushed her to the floor, and then pulled her on to her hands and knees. He strode to the mirrored wardrobe and retrieved something from within. She looked up at him in horror – her eyes fixed on the wide leather belt that he held.

'She asked nothing,' she told him, crawling backwards, moving away from him.

'Come here!'

She hesitated, but her will to obey was stronger than her fear. He watched her crawling towards him and understood that she was telling the truth – and that he and Katerina had made the right decision after all.

He raised the belt and brought it down hard across her bottom cheeks, imprinting a thick red band on her pink flesh. She cried, her squeal of pain too real to have been faked. He beat her again, the leather snapping hard on her chastised backside. A third stroke, and then he tested her sex with his fingers; she shuddered and climaxed violently when he penetrated roughly.

He put the belt around her chest, pulling it so the thick leather band was tight across her nipples. He buckled it up, encircling her chest, forcing her nipples to rub against it. She made no move to get away. She was dazed; almost delirious with pleasure and pain. He forced her to the floor, face down, pressing her hard so that the leather belt rubbed against her swollen nipples.

She waited as he undressed, her backside smarting and her nipples throbbing with pleasure. He knelt down beside her and began to spank her again, making her squirm and wriggle against the floor, creating endless sensations on her backside and her tightly bound nipples.

'What did Katerina ask you?' he asked once more.

'Nothing . . .' she whispered.

He mounted her suddenly; pulling her waist to him, he forced his cock into her cunt so that she screamed her climax into the darkness of the night that engulfed them.

Three

Emily had been expecting Katerina to be on her own. When Robert returned to the room in the company of two women, she was more than a little surprised. There was no doubting which of the two women was Katerina. Robert's description had been precise: tall, olive skinned, dark eyes and jet black hair; there was no mistaking her. In contrast, the other woman was younger: definitely not past twenty, with pale skin that matched her blue eyes and long blonde hair brushed straight to the small of her back.

'Katerina, this is Emily,' Robert said, introducing the two of them formally.

Emily, wearing fashionable knee-length leather boots, short denim skirt and a very tight cotton top, stood up and shook Katerina's hand quickly. She wanted to smile but felt inhibited by the presence of the other young woman, who matched her so closely in age. Who was she? Emily had been expecting a very private meeting with Katerina; no one had spoken of spectators.

'This is Amanda,' Katerina explained to Robert, turning away from Emily. 'She has been with us at Eden for a short while. However, unfortunately, she's unable to work with us through the summer.'

'Other commitments?' Robert asked, looking not at Amanda, who was staring fixedly at the ground, but at Katerina. She half smiled and he seemed to understand well enough.

33

They were in Robert's book-lined room at the university; there were places to sit but the effect was cramped all the same. Having half a dozen students in for a tutorial was one thing, but Emily could sense that this was going to be an altogether different meeting of minds. She sat down again on the tatty sofa, sinking comfortably into place. Katerina sat in Robert's padded armchair, leaving Amanda to stand awkwardly to one side.

'On the floor,' Robert told Amanda, pointing to a space next to the armchair. Amanda, wearing tight jeans, trainers and a loose shirt, sat down immediately, shuffling so that she could sit next to Katerina. Robert came over to the sofa and sat down beside Emily, leaving a noticably empty space in the middle of the room.

'Alex is giving a presentation this morning,' Robert explained. 'If he finishes in time he'll be joining us.'

'He's completing his finals this semester?' Katerina asked, casually reaching out to stroke Amanda's hair.

'Yes, that's right.' Emily answered quickly, unwilling to be left out of the conversation. She was aware of the other young woman; disturbed by her silence and the brooding manner with which she regarded those sitting opposite her.

'And you?' Katerina asked in turn.

'I'm just coming to the end of my first year,' Emily told her. 'The exams are no problem. I've done those. I've just the project to complete and then that's it.'

Katerina smiled, her full, sensuous lips parting slightly, somehow lighting up her dark eyes. 'And what of your studies with Dr King?'

Emily smiled. She always thought of Robert as Robert. Hearing him referred to as Dr King, especially when he was sitting beside her, felt a bit strange. 'I've been enjoying Robert's games very much,' she admitted, turning to smile at Robert. When she looked back there was no matching smile from Katerina, and Amanda was looking even more depressed than when she had arrived.

'Describe to me what you mean by "Robert's games" ',

Katerina suggested, sounding as though she were conducting a university lecture or giving an academic tutorial.

Emily's face coloured suddenly, a red flush of embarrassment making her face burn. Games were games and she had assumed that Katerina was in the know, that she knew precisely the kind of things that Robert had been teaching Alex and herself. 'I mean sexual experiments,' she announced, trying to sound cool and collected, hoping that the others hadn't noticed her embarrassment.

'What kind of sexual experiments?' Katerina persisted.

Emily turned to Robert. 'I'm sorry, Robert,' she said quietly, 'but I thought you'd already explained all that to Katerina.'

Katerina spoke before Robert had a chance to reply. 'I want to hear you describe it, in your own words,' she stated.

'I see,' Emily sighed. 'In that case, we've been exploring different sexual scenarios, playing sex games, adopting different roles. Sometimes I've pretended to be married to my boyfriend, Alex, and then we've flirted or had sex in public or in front of others. Recently, we pretended to be married and invited another man to make love to me whilst Alex and Robert watched. Once, at a party in London, I pretended I was married to Robert and that Alex was my lover. It was fun to see how people handled the situation, especially when it became clear that Robert was encouraging me to have sex with Alex. That's the sort of thing we've been doing.'

'And how does it make you feel?'

Emily smiled. 'Very aroused,' she admitted proudly. 'It turns me on playing these different games, stretching people's expectations. I liked being a slutty young wife and having three men make love to me at once.'

Katerina nodded; approvingly, Emily hoped. Amanda looked up at Katerina, with questioning in her eyes, but Katerina seemed to ignore the girl. Robert picked up on it, though. 'Does what Emily has described interest you, Amanda?' he asked.

There was a pause, and then Amanda spoke for the first time. 'Yes, I think so,' she replied quietly, not daring to look up from the dull grey of the carpet.

'And why have you been playing these games?' Katerina continued, her questions delivered in an even, almost emotionless voice. 'What is the reason for it all?'

Emily paused. It was a good question, one that she hadn't ever really asked herself. 'I'd be lying if I said that it was purely for intellectual interest,' she admitted finally. 'I mean there is an element of that, it's interesting to see how people react, to find out what society dictates in each situation. It's also interesting to watch the reaction when we behave inappropriately, when we screw up society's expectations. But all that's the icing on the cake, really. I like it because it turns me on,' she continued, warming to her subject. 'I want the pleasure. I want the ecstasy and the fun and the humour and the sex. We're not exactly encouraged to enjoy sex for its own sake, are we? This is a chance to explore the different avenues for pleasure, it's a real hedonistic thing with me, I think.'

Katerina smiled, obviously happy with the answer. She was dressed sexlessly, clad in a long skirt that extended to her ankles and a thick baggy top that obscured the contours of her body. Yet there was an obvious sensuality which she communicated with her eyes. They could be expressive one moment and opaque the next.

'What about obedience?' was her next question.

'Obedience?' Emily repeated, looking from Katerina to Robert and then back again.

'Yes, obedience,' Katerina confirmed. 'Have you played those sort of games yet?'

'I don't think I quite understand,' Emily replied.

'Perhaps Amanda would care to demonstrate,' Robert suggested, helpfully.

The suggestion was greeted with a smile from Katerina and a look of anguish from Amanda. The atmosphere in the room underwent a sudden change, as though Robert's suggestion was enough to raise the temperature above freezing point – where it had hovered since Katerina's arrival.

'Amanda, undress for me,' Katerina ordered, stroking Amanda's face softly with the back of her hand. Amanda looked up sharply, her lips closing tight, making her seem even more nervous. She glanced towards the window and then back towards the door. It was an obvious gesture and one not lost on Robert.

'This room is overlooked by half a dozen offices and at least one lecture theatre,' he told her. 'I am also in the habit of encouraging my students to drop by if they have any problems with their work or if they need to deliver essays and so on. If somebody knocks, then I am under an obligation to allow them to enter, no matter what is going on in here.'

It was the sort of answer designed to cause greater uncertainty and fear, and, judging by the horrified expression on Amanda's face, it had worked well. Emily was shocked; the calculated answer seemed so cruel. She would never have imagined that Robert could be so cold. She wanted to say something, to stop the proceedings going further but she realised that this was precisely why Katerina had brought Amanda with her.

Despite her silent nervousness, Amanda began to obey. She kicked her trainers off first and then she crawled to the centre of the room. Her long hair fell forward completely obscuring her red faced expression. She stopped and faced Robert, though she made sure her eyes stayed at ground level. Katerina was watching excitedly, enjoying the younger woman's obedient display. Amanda unzipped her jeans and then tugged them down sharply, revealing that she was naked underneath. She sat on her backside and pulled the jeans off completely, dropping the crumpled blue denims beside her. Next she removed her top, exposing her bare breasts.

'Now,' Katerina continued, once Amanda had stripped completely, 'show Dr King what a good girl you can be.'

Amanda looked beseechingly at Katerina, her blue eyes

37

filled with silent pleading. There was not a flicker of mercy from the dark-haired woman; she merely waited for her orders to be obeyed. Reluctantly, Amanda crawled towards Robert, keeping her head bowed all the while.

'Let me touch you,' Robert instructed, reaching towards the naked young woman. His hands seemed massive against her pale skin as he caressed her long limbs, felt the fullness of her breasts, and then stroked her taut, round backside. Emily watched, fascinated by the way Amanda submitted to the examination; by the way she let herself be touched intimately without betraying a glimmer of emotion.

'Emily, I think you should undress also,' Robert decided, talking to her in a tone of voice she had never heard him use before. Her initial reaction was to laugh. It was such a silly request to make. She had been naked in front of strangers any number of times – except now things had changed. She stood up and unclasped her denim skirt, letting it fall to the floor. She stepped out of it and then wriggled free of her top. She stood for a moment, dressed only in black G-string, lacy bra and her long boots.

'Here now,' Katerina ordered. 'As you are.'

Emily looked at Robert, his fingers toying with Amanda's reddening nipples, and decided that there was no way she was going to crawl across the floor. She strode confidently across the room, allowing herself a swagger of arrogance, swinging her hips as she went, knowing that she was stronger than Amanda in some way. She stopped in front of Katerina and crossed her arms, waiting for the next order with a playful smile on her lips.

'On the floor,' Katerina ordered sharply.

Emily looked at her for a moment, smiled sweetly and then knelt down, knowing that her smile was worth more than Amanda's abject silence. She stretched, pushing her backside higher and her tummy down, presenting the best view of her rear, aware that the slip of material between her thighs added to the alluring image she presented.

Her smile vanished when she felt Katerina's fingers on the inside of her thigh, stroking smoothly in the same way that Robert was handling Amanda. She froze as Katerina's fingers brushed against the tight, black material that pressed against the bulge of her sex. She moved away instinctively, unwilling to let the other woman touch her there.

'You don't like that?' Katerina observed, pushing her fingers directly on to the silky material, pressing it into the soft folds of Emily's sex.

'No,' Emily replied gruffly, looking towards Robert for support. Amanda had her eyes closed, and was breathing sharply as Robert slid his fingers between her pussy lips whilst squeezing a nipple with the fingers of his other hand. He had no time for Emily; his attention, and his excitement, were directed towards the submissive young woman at his feet.

'Then you have much to learn,' Katerina told her. She stopped, removed her fingers and began to caress Emily's backside, moulding her hands to the firm bottom cheeks, pulling them slightly apart and looking down at the intimate scene she had created.

'Nor there,' Emily informed her coldly. She tried to move away but Katerina suddenly had a hand entwined in her hair and was using it to reign her back.

'Hey!' Emily cried. 'That hurts!'

'Stay still,' Robert instructed from the other side of the room. His voice was hard, no longer the voice that Emily knew and trusted. It was as though Katerina's presence had invoked a new person: a Robert who was far colder and more cruel than Emily had imagined possible.

'And here?' Katerina asked, slipping a finger under the thin strip of lacy material to touch a fingertip directly to Emily's rear hole.

'Stop that!' Emily cried, her panic rising.

'You do have much still to learn,' Katerina told her

calmly, releasing her at last. 'Remain where you are,' she added threateningly.

The discreet knocking at the door silenced Emily. She knew that the pounding fear in her chest was a pale echo of what Amanda was feeling. The fear of being discovered – a fear that had always been the source of erotic thrills in the three-way games she enjoyed with Alex and Robert – was surprisingly real. Amanda had opened her eyes, she was looking to the door with unconcealed trepidation.

'Enter!' Robert called sharply, not even bothering to ask who it might be.

The door opened and Alex came in. His welcoming smile gave way to confusion when he saw Emily on her hands and knees in front of Katerina, and Amanda, completely naked, and being fingered by Robert.

Emily pushed away from Katerina; she got to her feet and ran to Alex's welcoming arms. 'What's wrong?' he asked, holding her tightly and looking around the room angrily.

'You've arrived at an opportune moment,' Robert told him. 'Katerina was beginning to put Emily to the test.'

'What sort of test? And who's she?' Alex demanded, pointing to Amanda, who had shrunk back, trying to hide behind Robert's legs.

'That is Amanda,' Katerina informed him. 'She was just showing Emily the virtue of obedience, something Emily has yet to discover. And you,' she added, 'what do you know of obedience?'

'She means treating you like a piece of meat,' Emily said, turning to glare angrily at Katerina.

'Emily! That's not what I expected of you,' Robert cried. 'I'm sorry, Katerina. I had thought that they were both ready, but perhaps I've been too hasty in my judgement.'

'Hold on,' Alex intervened. 'I've just walked in on this. Give me a chance to get my bearings, okay?'

'She was doing things to me,' Emily complained sulkily.

'What sort of things?' he asked quietly, holding her by the shoulders and gazing into her eyes.

'She was . . . she was making me do things, testing me to see how far I'd go.'

'Perhaps you both need another example of obedience,' Katerina said. She reached into her bag and produced a long velvet slip case, which she placed neatly by her heels. 'Amanda, I think you ought to present this gift to Dr King.'

Emily watched Amanda's eyes; every emotion, every misgiving was clearly expressed. The naked girl crawled slowly across the room, using her hair to obscure her face once more. Her body was beautifully toned; her long slender legs and slim waist in perfect proportion to her round breasts tipped with dark red nipples that seemed always aroused. In absolute silence, she crawled to Katerina's feet, meekly kissed the other woman's black heels and then took the velvet case in her hand and crawled obediently back to Robert.

'Thank you,' he said, smiling as he took the gift. He opened the case to reveal a long black dildo sitting in red satin, suggesting a hard cock in the blood red flesh of a woman's body. He wrapped his fingers around the base of the dildo and prised it out of the case. Amanda was wide eyed with horror; her eyes fixed on the shiny black phallus.

Robert reached out and motioned for her to move forward and to turn, so that her backside was visible to Katerina, Alex and Emily. Amanda cried out softly when Robert eased the black dildo into her sex, pushing through the swollen pussy lips and into the heat of her body. She sighed softly as he worked it in and out slowly. He was careful to build the pleasure slowly, almost teasing her with the slow, steady penetration.

'Emily, here,' he ordered, pushing the dildo hard into Amanda's sex, making her cry out with undisguised pleasure.

'Only if you want to,' Alex whispered.

Emily felt her face burning again, embarrassed by the sudden desire to be where Amanda was. She looked at Alex and he smiled to her, letting her know that the choice was hers to make. Reluctantly she knelt down on all fours; she wanted to get up and storm out of the room almost as much as she wanted to have Robert fuck her with the dildo. She crawled forwards lithely, putting on a show as she had in front of Louis a few nights previously. For a moment it was possible to imagine that Katerina was a bad dream and that the only people in the room were Alex and Robert.

She moved forward beside Amanda and felt the heat of the other woman's body so very close. Their eyes met for a moment and all that Emily could see was the look of pure unbridled pleasure in the other young woman's expressive eyes. Robert moved her into place, making sure that her body was on display to the excited onlookers. The dildo was wet; she felt the other woman's moisture brush against her thigh. She turned and smiled to Alex just as Robert pulled her panties aside and pushed the hardness into the wetness of her pussy. He pushed it in nice and slow, moving it inch by inch so that her pleasure seemed to last an age.

'Undress now,' Katerina ordered, speaking to Alex in the same imperious tone she used on the others.

Emily held her breath, her eyes fluttering as Robert quickened the pace, fucking her expertly with the black dildo. When she looked at Alex again, she saw that he was naked too, and making no attempt to cover his erect penis; instead, he faced Katerina wearing little more than an insolent grin.

Alex was ordered on to his hands and knees, and then made to crawl to Katerina just like the young woman had been. Emily moaned disappointedly when Robert began to use the dildo on Amanda again, fucking her much harder this time, making her gasp with pleasure and move her body with each stroke. Emily turned away and directed her attention to Alex and Katerina.

'Obedience you have yet to learn,' she was telling him, a slight smile on her face. 'Punishment you also do not understand,' she stated with the same coolness.

'I don't see what punishment's got to do with sex,' Alex replied, still on all fours in front of her. He sounded less sure of himself than usual, as though being naked on hands and knees had robbed him of his confidence.

Katerina smiled. 'They both imagine themselves to be so liberated, and so adventurous,' she said, speaking to Robert, 'and yet they have so much to discover. Are you sure they are willing to go further?'

'We are,' Alex replied, daring to speak to her directly.

Katerina smiled. 'You'll be punished for speaking out of turn,' she told Alex. 'I expect complete obedience at all times. You'll speak only when commanded to speak.'

Emily could see Alex's excitement; it showed on his face and in the thick erection of his cock, hanging stiffly between his thighs as he knelt on all fours. Alex turned to her for a second and she saw the look of helplessness in his eyes, an expression that was new, as though Katerina had suddenly revealed a side to his character that Emily had never suspected.

Katerina lifted her hand high, smiled sensuously, and then brought it down in a swift arcing movement to land on Alex's right side. The stinging slap filled the room, the sound of flesh on flesh echoing louder than the sharp exhalation of Alex's breath. The red imprint of Katerina's hand marked Alex's right buttock, leaving an imprint of each finger and the half circle of her palm on his tanned flesh.

There was no way Emily could see Alex's expression – he was staring directly at Katerina – but his hardness flexed powerfully, as though the excitement he felt was growing stronger. Several more sharp slaps of the hand served to spread the pink flush across his backside, each stroke making him breathe harder, faster. There was no diminishing of his arousal; his cock was just as hard and just as enticing.

Emily was bumped by Amanda. She turned and saw that the other girl was mouthing Robert's cock, her head rising and falling over his lap. Amanda's eyes were closed but there was no mistaking the delirious expression, the rapt and attentive delight as she sucked on the hard pole of flesh in her mouth. Robert leant back, using both hands to guide Amanda's head, holding her down, positioning her so that his pleasure was perfect.

'Take this to Katerina,' he managed to say, handing Emily the dildo, still smeared with the liquid essence of hers and Amanda's sex.

Emily took the dildo and stood up. She knew that Robert wanted her to crawl across the room on all fours, to demonstrate again what he and Katerina termed obedience, but it didn't feel right to do it. Her pussy was soaked, her wetness seeping through to saturate her panties which were pulled tightly into her pussy lips. She strode across the room, feeling so sexy in her knee-length boots and lacy black lingerie.

Alex's face was down at ground level, his reddened backside raising even higher, presenting a taut round target for Katerina to inflict her hard punishment. Emily stood and watched, fascinated by the way Alex's skin changed colour, by the way he responded to each hard stroke with a gasp of breath that could have been pleasure had it not been tinged with pain.

Katerina paused for a moment, then looked at Emily and smiled enigmatically. She lifted her skirt a little to reveal black ankle boots which were strapped tightly, high heeled, narrow tipped and polished to a fine shine. 'Worship them with your mouth,' she told Alex.

Alex glanced towards Emily and then turned away quickly, unable to meet her eyes, a look of pure shame on his face. He obeyed without question, pressing his lips to the shiny heels, kissing and then licking the pure leather with his tongue. He seemed lost in the action, concentrating on worshipping Katerina's heels in the same way that Amanda was worshipping Robert's cock.

'Make love to yourself,' was Katerina's order to Emily. 'Show me how you can give yourself pleasure.'

Emily smiled and shook her head. 'Why should I?' she teased, waving the black dildo in front of her. It wasn't that she was not turned on; watching Alex submit himself was more arousing than she cared to admit, but she also liked the idea of pushing Katerina. She wanted to test her in the way she was testing all of them.

'Then you'll leave me no option but to use that thing on Alex,' Katerina warned coldly. She moved her finger between Alex's spanked bottom cheeks, tracing the line from the underside of his balls, along the crease between the punished globes of his backside until she rested her finger directly over the tightness of his rear hole. Emily saw Alex wince. He faltered for the first time and looked at her in mute horror.

Emily succumbed, allowing the excitement to break through everything else. She lay on the floor, on her back, and pulled her panties to one side, roughly opening herself, exposing the pink moistness of her pussy. Katerina began to spank Alex again, admonishing him for faltering in his task of licking her heels. Emily slid the dildo into her sex and felt the pleasure burn like fire inside her. She gripped the delicate lace strip of her panties tightly in her fist, twisting it into a taut thin band which she rubbed against her throbbing clitoral bud while thrusting the dildo in and out of her sex with hard, deliciously blissful strokes.

The pleasure was too much; soon she was squirming, gasping for breath as she fucked herself for her audience. Vaguely, she was aware of being watched by both Robert and Katerina, each of them busy with an abject slave but still excited by her lewd display. Harder and harder, until her moans were loud and delirious, she forced the dildo in and out of her soaking cunt, keeping a steady rhythm of caresses on her clitoral bud.

'Here! Under Alex,' Katerina ordered suddenly. Emily climaxed instantly; the sound of command, the special tone of voice making her peak her pleasure. She rested a moment but her body cried out for more. She wanted to feel the pleasure endlessly, to climax repeatedly until she could take no more. Quickly she edged back, pushing herself along the floor until her panties were trailing down her thighs and her pretty black bra had worked loose. She looked like a slut, bathed in sweat and her underwear in tatters, her fingers still soaked with the pure honey from her pussy.

She inched under Alex, placing her head directly under his erection, eyeing the deliciously hard flesh that was smeared with fluid which had worked itself from his glans. She began to fuck herself again, using the dildo with total abandon, not caring any more what she did or why. Alex was moaning softly, his body quivering and moving with its own ecstatic rhythm. The spanking had ceased and it took Emily a moment to understood why Alex was writhing with such pleasure.

Alex cried out once and then the seed spurted in thick, white arcs from his cock, raining down directly onto Emily's face and into her open mouth. She reached up to suck the fluid from his hardness, greedy for the taste of his pleasure. It was then, on the cusp of her own climax, that she saw it. Alex had climaxed whilst Katerina's finger was thrusting in and out of his anal hole. She had finger-fucked him to orgasm despite the redness that stung his backside.

Emily closed her eyes and shuddered to orgasm, the taste of Alex's spunk deep in her throat. Her mind was filled with one image – her boyfriend being penetrated anally by another woman. It was an image that excited her beyond words.

Emily watched from the window as Robert, Katerina and Amanda walked across the square towards the university gates. She turned to Alex, who was still getting dressed, and sighed. 'Well, what do you think?' she asked, sitting back on the sofa. She was still dressed in her knee-length boots and black underwear; she enjoyed the look of herself like that and was in no hurry to cover up again.

'I want to go there,' he admitted, slumping down in the seat that Katerina had occupied. 'But I'm not so sure it's for the two of us.'

'What? What do you mean not good for the two of us?' Emily demanded. 'If it's good enough for you, why isn't it good enough for me?'

Alex stared up at the ceiling. 'I don't know. I think that you need to be a certain age before you get into anything ... anything too weird.'

'Huh! A certain age? Christ, Alex, there's only two years between us, not twenty. You liked what she did to you, didn't you?'

'It's not that,' he insisted, though Emily knew him well enough to recognise that he was lying.

'What else is it then?' she demanded. She recalled the image of Alex being spanked by Katerina; of Alex licking her heels; of Alex being fucked by her. Emily knew he had loved the experience but she could also sense his helplessness; she knew that he had been unable to resist Katerina at all.

'You heard what they expect at Eden,' he replied. 'Total obedience and regular punishment. I mean, is that really what you want?'

'No, but it's obviously what you want,' she responded angrily. She felt the first flush of jealousy, an emotion that had been alien to them throughout their games and explorations with Robert. What was it about Katerina that engendered such passion?

Alex fell silent for a moment, pondering his next move, not daring to look at her directly. 'Do you want to be like Amanda?' he asked finally. 'She hardly dared speak. She did as she was told without question. Is that really you?'

Emily smiled. Alex knew her well enough to seize the weak points in her arguments. There was no way she was an Amanda; abject obedience could never be hers, never. 'How do you know that's how I'll end

47

up?' she responded. 'And besides, it applies to you as well. Is that how you want to be?'

He shrugged. 'I want to see what it's like,' he confessed quietly. 'Just for a while, only to find out what it's like . . .'

Emily laughed curtly. 'You'll be claiming it as an intellectual exercise next,' she said bitterly. 'Admit it, Alex, you just want to go off with Katerina!'

'That's not it at all,' he told her angrily. 'You see, I told you you wouldn't understand!'

'Well I want to understand. I want to see what happens at Eden. I'm as curious as you are.'

'No you're not,' he said. 'You just want to see what I get up to.'

She smiled sweetly. 'That's true,' she admitted. 'But don't worry, I don't plan on getting in the way. There'll be no guilt trips from me, I promise. I just want to see how far we can both go.'

'What if you don't like it?'

'No,' she replied, turning it around again, 'what if you don't like it? It's something we both have to do; the two of us, individually.'

He mused on it for a while. 'You're right,' he agreed, finally. 'Now we've just got to wait and see if Katerina's happy with us. She's still the one who's going to make the decision. It might be either of us or neither of us.'

'Or both of us,' Emily added, knowing that they were both destined to travel to Eden that summer.

Four

Robert decided that it was going to be *Il Capriccio* for lunch; he and Katerina always enjoyed the food and the smoky ambience of the cramped but homely *trattoria*. When they arrived, with Amanda, the atmosphere was pleasantly convivial; most of the tables were taken, the buzz of conversation was rising and the aromas from the kitchen were enough to whet even the most reluctant of appetites. Lunch times were invariably busy, as the excellent food and friendly service attracted a loyal clientele from the university.

Robert's heart sank as he surveyed the scene. He had hoped for a little privacy, but the waiters were already having to weave their way through the closely packed tables. He was on the point of suggesting an alternative, when a place in the corner became free. While one of the staff quickly cleared the table, he and Katerina exchanged polite greetings with the elderly proprietor, a wizened old Italian whose expressive gestures made up for his lack of English.

By the time they sat down, in the most secluded corner of the restaurant, even Amanda's dour mood seemed to have improved. Certainly the colour had returned to her face and she had even smiled shyly when they took their places. Robert thought that Katerina also seemed more relaxed, as though she were pleased with the way Alex and Emily had performed for her.

He waited for the Italian waiters to finish fussing

around the table before speaking. 'You liked Alex and Emily,' he declared confidently, addressing Katerina.

She laughed, her dark eyes brimming with good humour. 'Am I that transparent, Robert?' she replied.

He noted the way she reached out for Amanda's hand without looking at her, knowing that the younger woman was always attentive. 'Not at all,' he replied with a smile. 'It's just that I can't imagine anyone not being taken by them. Except, perhaps, for Patrick.'

'Amanda, what did you think of them?' Katerina asked, squeezing the girl's hand tightly.

Amanda paused for a moment, lowering her eyes shyly. 'I'm not sure,' she whispered. 'Emily seems too full of herself – I mean, she's probably very nice and everything, but . . .'

Robert nodded. It was true, Emily certainly had more than a little self-confidence, and she took great pride in her appearance and the power it afforded her. 'What about Alex?' he asked, interested to see what impression he had made.

Again there was a slight pause, as though Amanda was afraid to speak too hastily. Robert saw was another contrast between the girl and Emily, who was often too impulsive for her own good. 'Well, what did you think of Alex?' Katerina asked, prompting for an answer.

'I felt jealous of him,' Amanda replied softly, her face colouring slightly.

'Jealous?' Robert responded.

'Yes, because I know that he's going to spend the summer at Eden and I'm not.'

'Does that mean you don't think that Emily's going to be accepted?' he asked, intrigued by the girl's answer.

'No, she's not right for it,' came the honest reply.

The conversation was interrupted while they ordered. Robert had no need to look at the menu, he knew it by heart. Amanda ordered last, her hesitant voice barely audible above the background buzz of conversation.

'Do you agree, Katerina?' Robert asked, after the wine

had been poured. ' Do you think that Emily's not going to be accepted?'

'If I were not convinced that they both had a chance I wouldn't bother with either of them,' she replied. 'However, I can't presume to speak for Patrick. You both know what he's like.'

Robert thought he detected some flicker of emotion in Amanda, as though the mere mention of Patrick's name made her feel uncomfortable. Or perhaps, he thought, it was another reflection of the envy that she was feeling, now that she was to leave Eden for good. 'And what are your plans for the summer?' he asked her.

She shrugged. 'I don't know,' she admitted forlornly.

Katerina seemed to understand and her eyes widened just enough for Robert to get the message. 'You seemed very interested in what Emily was saying earlier,' he said, switching tack. 'Do the sort of explorations she described excite you?'

'I think so,' Amanda murmured, casting a questioning glance at Katerina.

'What do you like about them?' Katerina asked softly.

Again Amanda hesitated before speaking. 'I don't know,' she admitted. 'I liked the idea of playing games in public, sort of.'

'What excites you about it the most?' Katerina persisted.

Robert spoke when no answer was forthcoming. 'Are you excited by the exhibitionism?'

'No,' Amanda answered, too quickly. 'No, I liked the idea of pretending to be different people.'

Katerina laughed softly. 'If I were to ask you to pretend to be my niece, would you do it?'

'Would you call her Auntie?' Robert asked, joining in. 'Do you think you can slip into that role and act it out in public?'

'I think so,' Amanda said, though there was no confidence in her voice.

'And would you let your Aunt touch you in public?'

51

Katerina asked, smiling sweetly. 'Would you let me stroke your thigh, or caress your nipples or slip my hand under your skirt?'

Amanda fell silent, her face flushed with embarrassment. 'Would you let your Aunt touch you in public?' Robert asked softly. He didn't want to cajole the girl; he could see that she was genuinely torn between her desire for pleasure and her desire for conformity.

'Here?' she asked, hardly daring to voice the question.

'Yes, what if it was here?' Katerina responded. 'What if I introduced you to Mr Dadamo as my niece and then stroked your thigh in front of him? Would that excite you?'

Amanda shivered. 'Yes,' she replied breathlessly. 'It excites me just thinking about it. But,' she looked at Robert directly, 'I don't think I'm ready to play yet. I'm frightened . . .'

'Of what?'

Amanda sighed softly. 'Frightened of me, I think,' she explained. 'I mean, I do have an aunt that I had a crush on once and – well, it would be confusing to play that particular game.'

Katerina nodded. 'I understand,' she said. 'The game then becomes too real, and it would be difficult to divorce yourself from it. Is that what you mean?'

'Yes,' Amanda agreed gratefully. 'That's it precisely.'

'Would you consider staying with me for a while?' Robert suggested.

'For the summer?'

'If that's what you want,' he replied.

Amanda turned to Katerina. 'If I stay with Robert do you think you'll have a chance to come back down and see me?' she asked.

Katerina smiled. 'Of course,' she said, and then, just as the waiter approached, she pulled Amanda closer and kissed her softly on the mouth. Amanda parted her lips for the kiss and closed her eyes for a moment.

When Amanda sat back her face was blazing and she

kept her gaze averted while the waiter served the food in
absolute, shocked silence. Katerina was smiling, ignoring
the waiter's unvoiced disapproval and Amanda's stunned
embarrassment.

'Are you shocked?' Katerina asked, after the waiter
had departed to convey the news to the rest of the staff.

'Surprised, that's all,' Amanda murmured, staring at
her food without any apparent appetite. In the background they could hear the waiter reporting on what he
had seen and, although he spoke in Italian, the excitement was clear in his voice.

'Why don't you return the kiss on the way out,' Robert
suggested.

'Yes,' Katerina agreed. 'Let them have something to
really talk about.'

Amanda leaned across the table and kissed Katerina
immediately; a passionate kiss that was entirely sexual, a
kiss between two lovers. Robert smiled approvingly; the
buzz of conversation in the restaurant had been effectively silenced.

Katerina glanced over her shoulder at the curled up figure
of Amanda, sleeping soundly on the back seat of the car.
She had changed out of her jeans into a long, loose skirt
which she had pulled aside so that the bright sunlight
could warm her sleek, elegant thighs. She slept with her
hands tucked under her face, her knees curled up towards
her tummy and her eyes closed tight. Her expression was
at once peaceful and innocent, turning her from an adult
into a child, bathed in warm orange light.

Katerina turned back to the road. They were almost
home and the countryside through which they were
driving was alive with the light and colours of late spring.
It hadn't been until she had moved from the city that the
seasons had made sense to her. Now she delighted in the
unfolding of time, in the way the world around her
changed day to day without really changing at all. Her
first year away from the grime of central London had

been a revelation: the changing of the colours in the fields around them, the ebb and flow of seasonal crops, the flowering of blossom and the harvesting of the hay; it was a delight to watch and understand the turning of the earth.

Amanda stirred for a moment, her breath exhaled from her dream, and then she fell silent once more. Katerina glanced back again, taking great pleasure in the younger woman's sleep, enjoying the vision of innocence in the same way that she enjoyed the view of the countryside around them. She and Patrick were making the right decision, she realised; for all her willingness to learn, there was a core of innocence in Amanda that they had not touched.

Even now Amanda still did not understand what it was that Patrick wanted from her. She assumed that what he wanted was obedience, but in her own naive way she confused obedience with docility. It was, perhaps, an easy mistake to make; Katerina knew that Amanda had not been the first to travel that particular path. In her confusion Amanda could not see that Emily was perfectly suited to Eden; she could not see that Emily's impulsiveness and haughty disdain were precisely the qualities that Patrick desired most of all.

The sign pointing to Eden had been removed, leaving the track unmarked and unremarkable. Was it more evidence of Patrick's paranoia, Katerina wondered. She turned off the narrow road and on to the track that wound through the dense copse towards the gently rolling hills that lay hidden from view. The trees shielded the car from the sun so that it was dappled with shadows and Katerina caught only glimpses of the blue sky.

As the car approached the high perimeter wall, Katerina's pulse quickened. For all the problems and the heartache, Eden was home and she loved it more than any other place she had ever put her name to. It had risen from nothing; a casual conversation with Patrick, an idea to play with when things were getting tough and she longed for escape. The idea had grown slowly: the casual conversation giving way to a set of sketches, which turned into a set of designs, which became ever more detailed until – and then Patrick had found a site. Somehow, he had located the perfect place to found the paradise they both desired.

The wrought iron gates loomed up ahead, cameras swivelling round silently to track the car as it approached. She slowed the car – it normally took a few moments for the sensors to work – and then the gates parted silently for her to drive in. The view ahead still took her breath away: a sea of lush green grass enclosed by the straggling line of the perimeter wall, eight solid houses dotted at random across the landscape and, in the distance, the shimmering silver of a lake nestling under a thick line of trees.

It was everything she had envisaged and more. Each house was unique and yet part of the greater whole, built with the same strong lines in wood and stone and glass. They had used the latest technology to fashion homes that were solid, comfortable, efficient and yet still at one with the land around them. She had wanted each home to be perfect and nothing had been spared, thanks to Patrick, in ensuring the construction matched the elegance of her designs. The plan had been to found a community that utilised the best in technology to create a quality of life not available in the cramped, grey streets of the city.

In retrospect, she realised, the technological problems had been the easiest to solve. Those sorts of problems had solutions that were either right or wrong and compromise was always easy when differing factors had to be balanced up. The real problems she had been naive enough to discount in the beginning, much to her continuing regret.

The real problems were human, and hence intractable. This had been apparent from the beginning. She had concentrated on the designs and had relied on Patrick to sort everything else out. Getting planning permission, for example, had been an absolute nightmare, far worse than she had anticipated. It had taken longer to work through the maze of bureaucracy than it had to come up with the plans and designs. Patrick had somehow steered everything through, taking all the flak along the way until he had succeeded.

In addition to taking on the bureaucrats, Patrick had been organising the funding of the project. They had agreed that Eden – the name had suggested itself – was to be a community of equals. In practice, this meant that the costs of the project were equally divided between the eight households, each buying an eighth of the company which owned the lands and the buildings. The division by household and not by individual had been based on financial equity, though it meant that a house full of people had no more say than a household of one.

Katerina and Patrick shared the house at the highest point in Eden; it had been the first to be built but the symbolism was clear for all to see. She drove along the narrow road, passing several of the other houses along the way. The serene quiet was just as she had imagined it would be; it had been a central point in her vision of the perfect community.

Amanda awoke just as the car came to a gentle halt outside the house.

'Why don't you go straight up to your room,' Katerina suggested, turning back to face her. 'Patrick and I have a lot to discuss.'

'Are you going to tell him about me going to stay with Robert?' Amanda asked, sitting up properly.

'Yes, amongst other things. You haven't changed your mind, have you?'

'No, I don't think so,' Amanda replied hesitantly. 'Do you think I should wait until the two of you decide on Alex and Emily?'

Katerina shook her head. 'No, I don't think so,' she said, hoping that Amanda wouldn't take offence.

'In that case I'll start to pack my things,' she decided, simply.

Patrick was waiting for them inside, an impatient expression marking his features. Katerina could sense the anger in the air as soon as she walked through the door; a cold, hard feeling that filled the house like an unpleasant aroma. Amanda sensed it too; she mumbled a quick greeting to Patrick and then disappeared upstairs to her room.

'That bloody woman!' Patrick hissed even before Katerina had had a chance to sit down.

She inhaled sharply to control her own nerves. Patrick could only be talking about Helen. 'What's happened?' she asked, slumping into the nearest comfortable seat. The sun shone brightly above the horizon, filling the room with a light that nevertheless failed to lift the angry atmosphere.

'She was here earlier,' he explained, barely able to contain his anger. 'She demanded to know what our plans are for the future, as if it's any bloody business of hers.'

'What did you tell her?'

'I told her to go to hell,' he replied, smiling grimly. 'What we plan for the future has nothing to do with her or anyone else.'

'Did she talk about the board meeting?' Katerina asked.

'No, the bitch didn't mention it once. She just kept going on about how we had no right to make plans behind everyone's backs. As if they've got any bloody rights to stop us doing what the hell we like.'

Katerina listened in silence. She felt drained of emotion, suddenly tired by the whole business of making Eden work. That was the one thing she missed about living in London; the chance to close her doors on the rest of the city, to just sit back and let everything pass her by. Paradoxically, Eden, the perfect community, had turned into one constant struggle to keep things going.

Far from everyone living in peace and harmony, things had descended to mutual suspicion and vindictive re-crimination.

'I had a good meeting with Robert's young protégés,' she said, realising that there was nothing to be gained in talking about Patrick's argument with Helen.

'What did you think?' he asked sullenly. 'Will they make the grade?'

'I think so. The girl, Emily, is impulsive, slightly arrogant and extremely attractive. Her boyfriend is a natural born submissive, though he doesn't know it yet. I think they'll both do well for us.'

'How do you think the girl would take to us?' he asked, the edge of anger blunted by his sudden interest.

Katerina smiled at the images forming in her head. 'Both of them are total innocents when it comes to the sort of games we like to play,' she explained. 'But the best part is that they both imagine themselves to be enormously sophisticated, and they have that strong sense of pride that goes with it.'

'What about Amanda?' he asked, instinctively looking to the door to make sure she wasn't listening in.

'She has agreed to stay with Robert for a while,' Katerina reported. 'I think she'll flower with his guidance; you know how much he enjoys having innocent young women to play with.'

Patrick seemed satisfied with the arrangement. 'Excellent. When can the other two join us?'

'A week or ten days at the most. But,' she added, 'I think it best that Amanda leave sooner, tomorrow perhaps.'

'Agreed, agreed,' Patrick murmured. 'But see if you can't get Emily and her friend here sooner.'

It was dark when Patrick finally went up to Amanda's room. Now that it had been agreed that she should leave he began to wonder whether he had not been too hasty in his judgement of her. It couldn't have been easy for her; he knew that it took time to adjust to life at Eden. Unfortunately for Amanda, time was the one luxury that he could not afford.

He listened for a moment at her door but heard nothing. He knew that she had finished packing earlier and he had expected her to come down afterwards. He knocked gently and waited for her to answer before going in.

'How are you feeling?' he asked, standing in the doorway. She was sitting up on her bed reading but put her book down as he watched.

'Okay . . . I'm a bit nervous, I suppose,' she admitted. As she moved slightly away from her lamp, shadows were cast across her face, shielding her eyes from his gaze.

'There's no need. You can trust Robert; he knows exactly what he's doing,' he told her, trying to reassure.

'Yeah, I think he's nice,' she murmured nervously.

'And what about me?' he asked, smiling darkly. 'Am I very nice, or do you still think I'm a complete bastard?'

He had half expected her to laugh, as if he had just let slip an outrageous lie, but her silence told its own story. It couldn't be helped; sometimes cruelty was the only way. He stepped into the room completely and closed the door behind him. 'Does that mean if I ask you to stay you'll refuse?' he asked, keeping the emotion from his voice as far as possible. He wanted the question to disturb her; he wanted to see the hesitation and confusion in her eyes.

'But you're not going to reconsider,' she replied softly. He could sense her disappointment and it felt good. In spite of everything some part of her still wanted to stay with him.

'No, I'm not,' he stated flatly, smiling.

She picked her book up again. 'You *are* a bastard,' she said coldly.

He walked to the bed and took the book from her hands and let it drop on the floor. If she had wanted to resist it would have been easy enough; she would only

59

have needed to have held on to the book instead of letting it slip away with the whisper of his touch.

'I might be a bastard,' he told her, sitting down on the edge of the bed, 'but I'm an interesting bastard.'

'That's what you think,' she responded, an edge of anger seeping into her voice. He put his hand to her thigh and felt her tremble. She was excited, the way she was always excited when he was strict with her.

'You'll miss me,' he whispered, as he lifted her tight white T-shirt to expose her breasts. He loved the way her excitement was always communicated by her body, so that her words were exposed as lies the second he exposed her breasts or fingered her sex.

She made no verbal reply to his comment, instead she sucked in her breath as he slowly stroked her hardening nipples with his thumbs. The growing darkness cast shadows across them both, but he was close enough to sense the colour that flooded her cheeks as her excitement grew. He kissed a nipple softly, closing his lips around the fleshy nub and then tracing the circle with the tip of his tongue until she sighed softly. He kissed the other nipple, putting his lips to it gently, almost reverently, before closing his teeth around it and squeezing hard. She tensed momentarily as he pulled at her erect nipple; he could feel her moving towards him to lessen the pain.

'I'll miss you,' he told her, sitting back to admire her body. He delighted in the swell of her breasts, framed by the constricting tightness of her T-shirt, and her hard nipples pointing upwards slightly. She doubted him; her silence filled the room, adding to its heavy, tense atmosphere.

When he stroked her nipples again they were still wet where he had kissed her. He pinched her lightly, making the tips of her breasts ever more sensitive, rubbing his thumbs back and forth insistently. He kissed her breasts again, letting his tongue slide from nipple to nipple, wetting her warm skin thoroughly with his tongue.

'Will you? Will you really miss me?' she asked finally, her voice a delicate whisper that begged for an answer.

He pulled her skirt aside and slid his hand between her long legs. 'Of course,' he replied, working his fingers across the soft flesh of her inner thighs. He could tell that she was waiting for the punch line; she expected him to deny that he'd miss her, but he was telling the truth all the same. She parted her thighs for him and thrust her chest forward, not daring to pull her T-shirt down to cover up her breasts.

'Then why can't I stay here?' she asked, inevitably.

He kissed her breasts in reply, flicking his tongue across the aroused nipples as he stroked her inner thigh. Each time his hand brushed against her sex he could feel the wet heat that made her panties moist and sticky. He concentrated on her breasts for a while, sucking hard, enjoying the contrast of hard nipple and soft skin. She leant back, using her hands to support herself, thrusting her breasts forward so that he could devour her hungrily.

Her panties were drawn back between the swollen lips of her sex, the thin strip of material pushed into her body. He pressed his finger against the wet garment, forcing her pussy lips open but using the tautly stretched fabric to stop himself from penetrating her fully. She inched forward, trying to push herself open even more, wanting him to push his fingers deep into her cunt.

She lay back on the bed, cupping her breasts so that he could continue to suck on her tumescent nipples. Her knees were bent, thighs parted fully, her skirt an untidy bundle around her waist. He pressed the flat of his hand against her vulva, using the pressure of his middle fingers to force her panties further into her sex. She moaned softly and tried to push his hand into her sex but he moved her own hand away.

'Please . . . Fuck me now,' she whispered urgently.

He smiled and slid his hand up her thigh, away from the heat of her pussy. She looked at him with dark desire in her eyes, her disappointment fringed with the certainty

61

that he was driving her mad with a deep, animal want. He tugged at her nipples again, biting hard so that she uttered her pain with the same breath as her pleasure. He moved away from her breasts, sliding slowly down her body towards her sex.

He ignored her pleas and the way in which her hands were now caressing the bulging peaks of her breasts. He kissed her thighs with slow deliberation, her skin cool to his lips. Her panties were pulled deep into her cleft, he could see the swollen lips of her sex on either side of the damp sliver of material. He kissed her pussy lips, passing his tongue across the sensitive folds of skin, tasting the sweetness of her juices for the first time.

'Please . . .' she begged once more, her desire expressed in the urgency of her pleading. He pressed his tongue directly at the opening of her sex, pushing her panties deep into her cunt, using the garment to delay the moment that she ached for. She jerked forward, lifting herself up to his mouth, desperate to feel his tongue slipping into the wet heat of her slit.

Very slowly he teased the material aside and pressed his tongue into the velvet welcome of her sex as he lightly stroked her clit with his finger. She arched her back suddenly, her body tense as she climaxed, a stifled cry of pleasure escaping from her open mouth.

He sat up for a moment and leant across the bed to the cabinet beside it. She lay back, eyes half closed, and watched. He opened the bottom drawer and retrieved the long white dildo that he knew she kept there. He smiled as her eyes widened.

'How did you know?' she asked softly, staring up at the ceiling as the red flush of shame rushed to her face.

He hesitated for a moment. It had been a stupid mistake to make; he wasn't supposed to know what she kept in her room. 'I guessed,' he told her, his voice calm and as confident, as though it were natural to be aware of such things.

Any further questions were stifled when he traced the

smoothly rounded tip of the dildo across her breasts, touching each nipple in turn before tracing the line down towards her parted thighs. She inched up and pulled her panties down quickly, unwilling to let the soiled garment get in the way of her pleasure again. He smiled at the gesture; it pleased him to see her acknowledge her appetite so openly.

She let out a low, animal moan of pleasure as he pushed the dildo deep into her pussy. He let it linger for a moment, fascinated by the way she moved her body with her pleasure. It was always a delight to watch her when she let go, when she finally gave way to the pure essence of sex and discarded the lies and pretence that normally cloaked her. He moved the dildo in and out slowly, penetrating her with long, smooth strokes as he watched with cool disinterest.

Amanda's fingers fluttered across the bed as the pleasure grew in intensity with the speed of the strokes into her pussy. He fucked her harder, driving the dildo into the velvety wetness of her sex then pulling back slowly. With his other hand he pressed against her clit, making her squirm and moan and sigh deliriously. He lay beside her and began to play with her breasts, timing the hard thrusts of the dildo with the play of his lips on her nipples. She climaxed again, her body shuddering with waves of pure electric bliss, but continued relentlessly.

He turned her over on to her belly and began to smother her backside with wet, seductive kisses while continuing to stimulate her with the dildo. She bent forward, raising her backside towards his face, wanting him to carry on. Her hands were now between her thighs, playing with her pussy bud as her sex was expertly fucked with the long, smooth dildo.

Patrick took her hand and placed it at her sex, letting her take hold of the object which had driven her to climax already. She gripped it and began to fuck herself, moving it with a speed that matched the movement at the apex of her pleasure. He watched for a moment, his eyes fixed on the white hardness that slipped in and out of the moist opening of her vagina. It took only a moment for him to undress completely, and then he resumed his exploration of her body with his tongue. He pressed his lips to her sex, licking at the juices that coated her bulging pussy lips and the white smoothness of the dildo.

He guessed that she was on the edge of climax; her breath was shallow, ragged, her hands were moving with a swift, urgent rhythm. He pushed her on to her back again and pressed his mouth to hers, sucking at her breath and feeding her the taste of her pussy juices. She answered his passionate kiss with a stifled sigh of pleasure and then a gasp as he swapped the dildo for the hardness of his cock.

He moved with a strong, urgent rhythm, holding her body to his own as he took her over the edge: she cried out her orgasm and dug her long nails into his back. When she fell back he slowed, savouring the wetness of her body, taking pleasure from each slow thrust into her sex. They moved together so that they faced each other, side by side, mouths locked in a long, tender kiss.

'Tell me . . .' he began, whispering his words to her mouth, his eyes fixed on hers.

'Why can't I stay?' she asked, confusion and hurt clear in her voice.

'Because it's better that you go,' he replied. 'Tell me, when you were with Katerina and Robert . . .'

'They didn't say anything about you,' she replied instantly, her eyes clouding with tears.

'Did they tell you to say that?' he demanded. He was wrong; he could see it in her expression, in the blank incomprehension which greeted his question. Anger swelled inside him; anger directed at himself for being so stupid, so distrustful, so bloody paranoid.

He fucked her harder, suddenly pushing her flat on her back and pressing into her with a violence that made her open herself even more. Her long limbs were wrapped around him, holding on to him as he pounded into her, his erection pushing deep into her body. He held her tightly and lifted her from the bed, supporting her with his hands under her backside so that he could take her as he desired. Moments later he turned her over, pushed her flat on to her belly and plunged his stiff rod into her pussy from behind.

With one hand he held her in place – bearing down on her back so that she could not move – and with the other he rubbed the slick juices from her cunt on to the dark button of her rear hole. She arched her back and offered up her bottom, using her hands to pull her bottom cheeks apart. He eased the wetness into her anus, pressing his finger against the tightness but refusing to invade it.

When her anal opening was wet enough, he gripped her tightly with one hand. She looked back over her shoulder; her hair was in disarray and covering her eyes, but he could see the sudden look of anticipation and fear. Her rear cheeks were pulled apart allowing him to enjoy the sight of his hardness plunging deep into the folds of her sex, its shaft smeared with the glistening reward of her pleasure. He lingered for a moment longer, delighting in the vision of her anal bud glistening with the moisture he had rubbed from her pussy.

Surreptitiously he reached for the dildo, still wet but lying discarded beside her. She had turned away, perhaps readying herself to accept his hardness entering her anal hole, her eyes were closed and her mouth was half open as though ready to suck away the pain. Instead he bucked forward, driving his cock into her pussy, going in as deep as he could so that her bottom was pressed flat on to his abdomen.

The perfect globes of her backside were widely parted and he pushed the tip of the dildo directly against the tight rear opening. It went in slowly, slipping smoothly into Amanda's body and she thrashed around with a look of horror on her face as the cool, hard object penetrated her fully. She cried out at once, a loud scream of pleasure and pain that filled the house with its intensity. He pressed down on her body, pushing his cock deep into her sex as he climaxed, spurting thick waves of come. The dildo pressed against him, filling her anal hole as he pushed it deep into her with his abdomen.

Five

Emily had been as surprised as Alex at being summoned to Eden the day after their first meeting with Katerina. She had imagined that things would move slowly, that perhaps Katerina was going to take her time in talking things through with her partner. Instead, the call had come through on the same evening as Katerina had returned to Eden. It was as though she had issued a command; Alex had no problem with that, he was willing to drop everything to drive up to Eden with Robert.

Emily had agreed, too, though not with the same enthusiasm, and now she lay in the back of the car as Robert drove through the countryside towards their strange destination. It was an unusually quiet journey; all her attempts at conversation had been stifled by Alex's pensive mood. His stream of questions to Robert had run dry as soon as they had left the familiar streets of the city and taken to the motorway for the longest part of the trip. Much to her disappointment, Alex had chosen to sit in the front of the car, next to Robert, as if to emphasise how keen he was to get there.

The motorway was behind them now. They had turned off at a busy junction, sped through a small town of dull-looking terraces and then turned on to a narrow single lane road which meandered through the country-side. At first Emily was taken by the pretty view, marvelling at the endless gradations of green and yellow, and at the patterns the clouds cast on the distant hills.

There were few other cars on the road, and hardly any pedestrians, even in the tiny villages they drove through.

She closed her eyes and let the sunlight filter through, the patterns dancing and dappling as they passed under trees and out to open road once more. Now that they were nearer, she felt the butterflies of excitement waking in her belly and she smiled to herself. She looked forward to seeing Katerina's face when the car pulled up and she got out. That morning, she had gone out and got her hair cut; she had been acting on a whim but that had only added to the sense of delighted anticipation she felt. Her long black hair had been cropped short, almost as short as Alex's, but she was pleased with the result. Far from making her look boyish, short hair seemed to make her look younger and more innocent, or so she hoped.

'How much further?' Alex asked impatiently, repeating the question for the third or fourth time.

'We're nearly there now,' Robert assured him. 'You're not nervous, I hope,' he added.

Alex grinned. 'Of course I'm nervous,' he admitted. 'Wouldn't you be?'

'Is it the thought of meeting your darling Katerina again?' Emily teased, sitting up again. She saw the flicker of emotion in his eyes and knew she'd scored a direct hit.

'It's more than that,' he told her, unable to deny the basic fact.

'Look, across those hills. You can just see an outline of the place,' Robert said, slowing the car.

Emily followed his line of vision. There were sheep in the fields closest to them. Beyond that the land curved upwards slightly and she could make out the large enclosed area that had to be Eden. The place was far larger than she had imagined, the straggling perimeter wall closing off an area the size of a village. The distance was too great to make out much detail; there were a number of buildings set in the grounds, a dense copse at the farthest corner, and what might have been a road linking the buildings together.

Robert drove on a little further, speeding up to get through a tiny village before he slowed to a stop. He turned to his passengers and smiled. 'There it is,' he said, waving an arm in the general direction of their destination.

Alex was struck dumb. He opened the door, climbed out of the car and crossed the road to lean on a slate grey wall so that he could get a better look. They were much closer and could see more detail: low-slung buildings that seemed to have grown organically from the soil; well-tended gardens; a shimmer of silver that might have been a lake or a pool nestling under the trees. Emily followed suit, crossing the road to join Alex.

'It looks brilliant,' he exclaimed softly, his eyes filled with a glowing excitement. 'I sort of expected a run-down little village; you know, converted cottages, old barns, that sort of thing.'

Emily pressed herself close to him, letting him put his arm casually around her waist. 'It must have cost a fortune,' she realised, tracking the long perimeter walls with her eyes.

'It's perfect, isn't it?' Alex remarked enthusiastically. 'I mean, if you want to create an alternative vision of life then you've got to go for it in a big way.'

Emily could understand his excitement; the sheer scale of the place was impressive. A whole chunk of country-side had been taken over, enclosed and transformed. Her pulse quickened at the realisation that this was a place cut off from the surrounding countryside, the physical reality of the high stone walls creating a space that was free of the constraints that governed the rest of the land.

She turned back to the car, letting the sun warm her long legs and her bare midriff exposed by her short, cropped top. The fresh air felt cool and refreshing after the stale heat of the car. Robert was leaning against the bonnet of the vehicle, obviously enjoying the excitement that the panoramic view generated in his two protégés.

'Come on, we'd better get going,' he said, glancing at his watch.

Alex and Emily walked back together, his arm around her waist slipping down to gently caress her bottom over her loose skirt. 'We're going to learn a lot here,' he promised.

She leaned across and kissed him softly on the mouth. 'What if we don't like what we learn?' she asked, voicing a sudden fear.

'I'm sure that won't happen,' he told her, squeezing her backside reassuringly. 'I mean, we're here through choice. No one's forcing us to do anything we don't want.'

Emily nodded, pretending to be reassured for his sake. She glanced again at the distant enclosure and felt the unease still inside her, part and parcel of the feeling of excitement.

'Is everything alright?' Robert asked, picking up on the sudden change of mood.

'Yes, we're fine,' Alex told him, putting on a smile. He leaned across the front seat and patted Emily's hand reassuringly.

They arrived at the wrought iron gates a few minutes later, the car stopping in front of the imposing entrance to Eden. Emily stared up at the cameras that were tracking them, wondering why Katerina and Patrick felt the need for such high security. The obvious question asked itself: was it to keep people out or to keep people in?

'Why do they need so much security?' she asked Robert, as the gates began to open electronically.

'You said it yourself, Em,' Alex replied instantly. 'There's obviously a lot of money involved in a place like this; it's bound to be a tempting target,' he said, speaking like an over-enthusiastic child. 'Isn't that right, Robert?'

'Perhaps,' Robert replied cautiously.

They drove through the gates and on to the private road which led to the individual houses. There was little in the way of obvious activity and the overwhelming impression was one of peace and serenity. As they passed the nearest of the houses it struck Emily that they seemed

70

to combine the homely structure of Alpine chalets with the grace of a Japanese pagoda.

It was only when they were moving up the slope towards the highest house that they saw signs of life. A young woman was walking across the grass, possibly going from one house to the next. She was wearing cut-down jeans and a denim top; her long limbs sported an even tan and her long hair seemed bleached by the sun. She stopped and waved at the car for a moment – Emily smiled to her and waved back – before she continued on her way.

'How do you feel?' Robert asked, once they had pulled up outside Patrick and Katerina's house.

'Nervous,' Emily replied, knowing that she was speaking for Alex too.

'Good,' Robert told them, 'we want you nervous.'

Emily noted his use of 'we' to define himself, Patrick and Katerina as a single entity, in which case she and Alex were outside the charmed circle. She wondered if Alex had noticed it too, but saw that his attention was already focused on the house.

Robert was out of the car first, followed quickly by a nervous-looking Alex. Emily waited for a moment, her heart beating faster as the apprehension flooded through her. She looked back down the hill, towards the iron gates which were now closed, locking them in, away from the rest of the world. What had she let herself in for? Alex had been the one with the nerves, but now that they had arrived his nerves seemed to have been transformed into excited anticipation. It was her turn now to suffer the uneasy apprehension.

When she turned back to the house she saw that Amanda was at the door greeting Robert with a shy smile. Wearing a cotton slip dress that was moulded to her curves by the soft breeze, she looked utterly relaxed, a person transformed from the acquiescent creature they had seen before. Her smile was there for Alex too as they exchanged a quick greeting.

71

'Your hair looks great,' Amanda said, coming over to the car as Emily got out.

'Thanks, I had it done this morning,' she explained. They walked towards the house together, not quite knowing what to say or how to act.

'The others are out on the terrace,' Amanda explained, leading them through the house. Despite the heat and the sun directly overhead, the interior of the house was cool and airy. Emily wanted to see more but Amanda was taking them directly to meet Patrick and Katerina. It seemed rude to want to wander through the house uninvited.

They had to walk through the conservatory to reach the terrace and the profusion of flowers and plants under glass was startling. Emily had expected something lifeless; an arid, dry atmosphere that was divorced from the nature around them. The sliding glass doors had been opened to reveal the smooth marble floor of the terrace at the back of the house. The terrace itself was bordered on three sides by a low wall which overlooked the landscaped garden behind the house.

A simple canopy had been pulled down from the upper storey to cover one side of the terrace, creating a large shaded area from which to escape the glare of the sun. Patrick and Katerina were there, waiting in the shade for their visitors. Emily stayed back for a moment, wanting to get a good first look at Patrick – a man whom she had imagined to be a male version of Katerina. Amanda excused herself and returned to the main house.

Robert and Patrick shook hands heartily; old friends who had not seen each other for too long. Patrick put his arm around Robert's shoulder and held him close as they swapped a few words in private before both gave a low chuckle of laughter. Emily's expectations had been confounded once more; far from being a male version of the dark and icy Katerina, at first glance Patrick was fair haired and possessed of an easy, charming nature. Patrick's blue eyes were flecked with grey and their

72

expression was at once clear and good humoured, matching the relaxed smile with which he greeted Alex.

'And this is Emily,' Robert was saying, steering Patrick away from Alex and towards her. She smiled and took his hand, delighted by the way his eyes seemed to light up when he returned her smile.

'I've been looking forward to meeting you very much,' he told her, his voice carried just a hint of accent, a faint murmur of some Celtic heritage.

'Thank you,' she replied softly, looking directly into his blue grey eyes and finding that her heart was racing once more. She held his gaze for a moment longer then looked away, a slight flush colouring her face. He was holding her hand still and she knew that he could feel the excitement that pulsed in her veins.

Katerina came over. She had already spoken a few words to Alex and now she came over to join Emily and Patrick. 'Short hair suits you very much,' she remarked pleasantly.

Emily smiled. Cutting her hair so short had been something of a declaration of independence; her way of telling Katerina that she was still in control of the situation. Now that Katerina approved, she felt pleased.

'I agree,' Patrick said. It looks most attractive. 'But,' he added with a charming smile, 'I suspect that you looked equally beautiful when your hair was longer.'

Katerina looked towards Robert. 'Cutting her hair was a message, don't you think?' she asked.

'Very obviously a message,' Robert agreed. 'However, its meaning is open to discussion.'

'Is it?' Emily asked, certain that it had only one clear meaning.

'Why, yes,' Katerina told her. 'You are telling us that you remain in control, but it also represents a new start, does it not?'

'That's right,' Alex said, rushing to agree. 'A new look for a new start.'

'That's not why I cut my hair,' Emily insisted, annoyed

by Alex's obvious desire to ingratiate himself with Katerina. 'I cut my hair because I wanted to; it's that simple.'

Robert touched her arm softly. 'Things are never that simple,' he told her softly, 'as you are going to discover shortly.'

The conversation was cut short when Amanda reappeared with a tray of long, cool drinks. She offered a drink to Robert first, flashing him a shy smile once more before turning to Patrick, Katerina, Alex and, finally, Emily. That order had been chosen deliberately, Emily was sure of it. She was last and it rankled; despite the casual and relaxed atmosphere there were things going on below the surface and it annoyed her because she was uncertain what they were.

With all the drinks distributed, Amanda placed the tray on the white aluminium table that occupied one corner of the shaded area and came over to join the others. In the sudden silence, her presence seemed to draw the most attention; she could even sense it herself. Emily saw the way she shrank back from view.

It was Katerina who broke the silence. 'Are you afraid, Amanda?' she asked softly. The question was enough to change the atmosphere completely. Whatever had been lurking in the background was suddenly, menacingly, made clear.

'I know what's going to happen,' Amanda murmured quietly, looking not at Katerina but at Patrick.

'And do you want it to happen?' Patrick asked casually, losing none of his charm.

'Surely that's unfair,' Robert intervened. 'How can she answer such a question?' Amanda looked relieved, as though in answering for her Robert had put a stop to whatever was going to happen.

'Perhaps so,' Patrick replied agreeably, walking over to Amanda. He put his arm around her waist and pulled her closer. 'I'm sure that you're going to be in good hands with Robert,' he told her. 'But while you're here you still abide by our rules.'

The colour drained from Amanda's face, the nervous smile replaced with an expression of pure trepidation. She remained where she was, her blue eyes lowered respectfully, her arms hanging limply at her sides. Patrick turned her towards Robert, so that she had her back to everyone else. 'Robert,' he suggested quietly, 'perhaps you'll show our young friends what happens when rules are transgressed.'

Emily watched, fascinated by the strange game being played for her benefit. Robert pulled one of the heavy white chairs from the patio table to a space in front of Amanda, while Patrick retreated back towards Katerina. Robert sat on the chair and motioned for Amanda to move closer. If there was hesitation on her part it was a fleeting, momentary thing that was dispelled when Amanda obeyed and stepped towards Robert.

Amanda's thin whisp of a dress was pulled up to her waist, exposing her long, bare thighs and the naked curves of her backside. Robert's expression was emotionless, his eyes assessing the exposed body displayed in front of him without a flicker of pleasure or desire, as though he were engaged in some sexless task that required total concentration. He stroked the outside of Amanda's thighs, running a hand against the smooth flesh of each in turn. This he followed with a similar exploration of the inner thigh, his fingers travelling across the creamy expanse of flesh from the knee to the join of her thighs.

Emily thought she heard a sharp intake of breath from the other young woman, but then it might have been the soft breeze that cooled the terrace. Amanda parted her thighs on command, pushing her feet apart and bending towards Robert so that her backside jutted roundly towards her silent audience. Robert's fingers traversed the inner thigh again, making a slow, deliberate exploration that made Emily shiver with vicarious excitement. Robert's touch was familiar to her; she knew how he could tantalise with the skilful play of his fingers, drawing excitement and desire with his soft caresses.

Amanda uttered a simple 'oh' when Robert's fingers brushed between her thighs. Her backside was sticking out further, exposing to view the curves of her bottom and the deep, enticing rear cleft. Robert's fingers hovered about her pussy lips, stroking nonchalantly, making her sigh softly with an unsatisfied want.

'Across my knee,' Robert told her suddenly, taking her arms and pulling her across his lap. Her dress was still bunched up about her waist, a loose, fluttering curtain of thin cotton that did nothing to hide her. In moments, her backside was raised high; rounded bottom cheeks offered temptingly to view. She glanced back towards her audience. Her face was still red but her eyes sparkled with excitement.

Her eyes met Emily's and lingered; she seemed to be telling her something. Emily could not smile, but stared into the deep blue of the other woman's eyes and wondered how she would cope in similar circumstances. Amanda turned away suddenly, just as Robert's upraised hand came swinging in a smooth arc to smack down on her bottom. The sharp slap seemed to echo across the landscape; a sharp retort that did nothing to disturb the heat and the silence of the afternoon.

A second stroke followed the first, Robert's hand beating down on the other side of Amanda's rear. This time the sharp snap of sound was followed by a moan from her full, red lips. Stroke followed stroke and soon a pattern of pink and red was imprinted on her curved backside. The colour of her punishment stood out angrily against the pale skin of her thighs and back. She began to writhe, squirming over Robert's lap as he inflicted several more hard smacks in quick succession.

It took a while for Emily to understand what was happening. Amanda's writhing, the soft moans and the slow kicking of her long limbs did not equate to pain. Instead she was lifting herself, raising her punished backside higher to receive the strokes that Robert spanked hard. She moved with the rhythm of her punishment, offering herself, opening her body to the strict chastisement and then sighing ambiguously when the stroke touched its fire to her flesh.

'Stand up now,' Robert commanded, his face flushed a little, though whether it was from excitement or exertion Emily could not tell.

Amanda moved stiffly into place. She stood with her back to her audience and lifted her dress, showing them the punishment marks imprinted on her naked backside. Robert touched her again, letting his fingers play between her swollen pussy lips so that she shuddered visibly with pleasure.

'Emily,' Patrick said, breaking the spell of silence, 'I want you to feel the heat of Amanda's punishment. I want you to put your lips to her behind so that you can sense the smarting pain that Robert has given her.'

Emily was startled. She had been lost in silent contemplation of Amanda's beautifully punished body. Patrick's voice was soft and insinuating; it carried no sense of threat, for which it was all the more effective. She had no option but to obey. This was the test – this was why she had been summoned to Eden.

She walked slowly across the terrace, head held high, trying not to let her nerves get the better of her. When she was closer she knelt down and crawled the last few steps. Her short skirt was moulded over her backside, completely exposing her legs and only just managing to cover the pert roundness of her bottom cheeks. She inched forward, looking up at last at the reddened skin of Amanda's rear. The deepest red was at the centre of each buttock, with the red losing its tone at the upper thighs where it merged with the pale whiteness that was Amanda's natural colouring. From below she could see the swollen pussy lips, almost hairless from behind, the pink tinge of flesh within made visible only by Robert's expert fingers.

Amanda was pulled towards Robert's lap again, but this time her feet remained firmly on the ground so that her bottom was offered completely to view. A surge of excitement pulsed deep in Emily's body; she could feel it in the hardness of her nipples and in the heat of her sex. She touched her lips under Amanda's knee, softly kissing the cool skin, running her tongue across it. She moved higher, running a trail of kisses along the length of Amanda's thigh, enjoying the feel of the taut flesh under her mouth. At last she pressed her lips to the pink flush of punishment, kissing softly with the coolness of her mouth.

Amanda's sigh of pleasure touched Emily's excitement, making her move faster. She kissed harder, moving her lips in silent exploration of the smarting pain that had been inflicted on Amanda's perfect derrière. She stroked the firm flesh and then, finally, she parted Amanda's bottom cheeks to gaze adoringly at the pinkness of her sex and the dark tightness of her rear hole. The pussy lips glistened with moisture and Emily licked them at once, running her tongue along the rear groove and then probing the flesh within.

Emily pressed her tongue deep into Amanda's sex, lapping at the oozing nectar, pushing her tongue into the velvet pocket so that Amanda's body quivered with pleasure. She licked and sucked, used her teeth to excite and then moved to press her tongue against Amanda's pearl of pleasure. Amanda almost fell forward as her body tensed and the spasms of pure bliss rocked through her climax. Her sex was flooded with the liquid essence of pleasure which Emily sucked greedily into her mouth.

Amanda's climax was not enough. Emily felt lost to the world, oblivious to everything but the pleasure to be had in exploring Amanda's body with her mouth. Her own desire was liquid in her body; the wet heat of her sex ached inside her but still she longed to continue to mouth and toy with the other woman's slit. She eased back a little to lick and smooth her mouth across the punished bottom cheeks again and as she did so she became aware of movement behind her.

'There's no need to stop,' Robert told her, distracting attention from the naked figure of Patrick.

Emily looked again at the naked man who stood before her: at the trim waist, the strong muscular thighs and the well-defined chest and arms and, most of all, the thick hardness of his erection. Patrick smiled to her, his face animated by an animal excitement that echoed Emily's own. He brushed a hand through Emily's hair, his fingers flowing through the thick, short locks, before taking hold of Amanda by the waist.

Patrick held Amanda for a moment, letting his fingers grip her by the waist so that she moved into position for him. Emily looked up at him, her face level with the pulsing hardness that thrust out of his body. She smiled and kissed the hardness softly, letting her lips close over the dark plum of his glans. His taste filled her mouth, jewels of fluid easing from the slit and onto her tongue. She sucked for a moment, closing her cheeks over half the length to form a tight, soft pocket for his cock. Then she took it in her fingers, stroking the veined hardness for a second before pressing it to Amanda's soaked pussy.

Emily sat back a little as Patrick pushed himself against Amanda's backside, his stiff rod slipping into the wetness of her cunt. He held the position for a moment: her rounded bottom cheeks pressed flat against the ridged muscles of his stomach, her sex opening to the hardness of his cock, his hands gripping her tightly. When he began to move, thrusting in and out slowly, Amanda let herself breathe a low, murmured sigh of pleasure. Emily crawled round, ducking under Amanda's bent-over body so that she could see Patrick's glistening cock sliding in and out of Amanda's cunt. She used her hands to stroke Amanda's thighs, just as Robert had done earlier.

The movement of bodies grew faster. Patrick's harder strokes caused him to jerk his hips to bury his rod deeper into Amanda's welcoming body. Emily moved in, putting her lips to the join of cock and cunt, lapping at the wetness that eased the fucking motion. She cradled

79

Patrick's heavy ball sac, holding him gently while she tongued his shaft or licked delicately at the apex of Amanda's pussy. They all three moved in unison, their bodies joined in an odd contortion of pure pleasure. Amanda was panting softly, holding on to Robert for dear life as she climaxed repeatedly, driven beyond endurance by Patrick's hard prick and Emily's soft mouth.

At last Patrick jerked forward, a strangled cry of release escaping his lips as his cock pulsed deep inside Amanda's sex. He held her down, pressing his weight on her as the jism spurted into her body. When he drew back his cock was still hard and coated with the juices of male and female, the reddened glans seeping a tear of his seed. Emily was there to tongue it clean, to lap at the blending of his come and the fluid essence from Amanda's pussy.

Patrick stepped away completely and Emily took her place again, crawling round to part Amanda's bottom cheeks with her fingers. Her eyes were wide as she saw the slick come that coated Amanda's labia and the pink walls of her cunt.

'Collect it in your mouth,' Robert said, 'but don't swallow it yet.'

Emily had no time to question, no time to think. She glued her mouth to Amanda's pussy and probed with her tongue, sucking up the mingled tastes and textures of male and female. She licked deep and hard, while stroking Amanda's clit with her fingers.

'Now it's your turn, Alex.'

It was Katerina who spoke, her cold voice causing Alex to move at last. He strode across the terrace and knelt down beside his girlfriend. They kissed instantly, she parting her lips so that his tongue could enter quickly. Together they pressed the juices from her mouth to his, their tongues working together so that the sex tastes were suffused and shared equally.

When Alex turned to Katerina she was smiling. He smiled back and then opened his mouth to show her his tongue, patterned with the white jism that Patrick had emptied into Amanda's pussy.

Patrick looked at Katerina and nodded. 'I think we have to talk,' he told her, his broad smile of satisfaction making Emily remember the ache that pulsed between her thighs.

Robert's long sigh of pleasure forced Emily to look back to Amanda. She was on hands and knees, her face pressed close to Robert's lap. Emily could wait no longer, she squeezed into place beside the other woman. They looked at each other for a second, smiled, and then turned back to Robert's stiff organ, which was already oozing a thin sliver of fluid along its length. They kissed softly, no longer afraid of each other, and then joined their mouths over Robert's hard cock.

Emily climaxed quickly – the very moment that she felt Amanda's fingers press into the red heat of her pussy.

Six

Emily closed her eyes, lay back in the bath, and let the warm water wash gently over her. The days had passed quickly in the summer heat, each one she wished away impatiently, counting down to the time when she and Alex would be able to move to Eden. Her fears and anxieties had all but been dispelled after the eventful afternoon with Patrick and Katerina. It had been a test of course, but one that she and Alex had passed with flying colours.

After their first meeting, Katerina had reported to Patrick Emily's unwillingness to have sex with another woman, but at Eden there had been no such reluctance after the excitement of witnessing Amanda's punishment. At the same time, Katerina had been watching Alex closely, gauging his reaction as he watched Emily with another woman, and then later as he watched Emily greedily sucking the seed from Patrick's cock and Amanda's cunt. Like Emily, Alex's reactions had been perfect, just what Patrick and Katerina had desired.

The final test they had passed together. Emily had responded to Robert's barked order with total obedience: there had not been an ounce of hesitation when she was told to suck Patrick's spunk from Amanda's freshly fucked pussy. Alex had also shown no qualms when ordered to suck the juices Emily had collected in her mouth. He had even sat up to display the thick pool of jism on the end of his tongue.

It had been that simple, that pleasurable. The rest of that afternoon had passed in a daze of sex and sunlight. At one point Katerina and Alex had disappeared for a while, but as Emily was on hands and knees having her pussy mouthed by Amanda, she had hardly noticed.

They had stayed at Eden until the early evening, when a simple meal and a few glasses of wine brought the day to a close. It was then that the final arrangements were made, the details of which were hazy in Emily's memory. Perhaps it had been the excitement, or the wine, but her recollections were vague and disjointed. All that mattered was that she and Alex were asked to spend the summer at Eden.

There had been tears from Amanda when she made her farewells, and promises to keep in touch with all the friends she had made during her brief stay there. Emily had been impressed with the show of emotion; it had all helped to convince her that Patrick, and indeed Katerina, were not the cold, heartless monsters she had feared. By the time they had arrived back at Robert's house, hours later, Amanda and she were curled up in each others arms, fast asleep.

The next few days had been a blur of activity. Both she and Alex had arrangements to make, work to finish, calls to make. Going away for the summer had never been part of their plan, but now that it had been agreed, they had both thrown themselves into it. They had both been so busy, in fact, that they had hardly had time to get to know Amanda better. Now, as she lazed in the warmth of a soapy bath, Emily realised that it was too late to help Amanda settle in at Robert's house.

She sat up and stretched, pushing her chest forward and her arms back so that the warm water poured between her breasts and coursed down over her nipples. It felt deliciously sensual; the feel of the water washing over her body, the way her skin glistened, the sight of her nipples peaked with liquid jewels. Robert had adored watching her in the bath; he liked her to sit on all fours and soap her body slowly, lingering between her thighs and on her breasts. Thinking about it made her feel a soft, hazy excitement in the pit of her belly.

In a way, she envied Amanda, as she still had so much to learn from Robert. He and Patrick seemed so different – the contrast was striking – and not just in terms of appearance. Robert was so attentive. He was a man unafraid to adore women; a man who seemed incapable of causing harm, even unintentionally. Patrick on the other hand seemed more . . . Emily tried to pin a word to him, to describe her impressions in terms that she could relate to someone else, but nothing suggested itself.

She sat back in the bath again, laying back so that the water covered her nakedness, its ebb and flow passing softly over her breasts. Patrick excited her in a way that was different; with Robert she was aroused by his desire and his sensual inventiveness, with Patrick the excitement stemmed from something less certain, less obvious. She had been charmed by him, of course, and his blue eyes seemed filled with a dark promise that set off her excitement.

Thinking about Patrick, imagining the days and weeks ahead of them at Eden, her excitement grew stronger. The heat of the water merged with the suffusing glow in her sex, making her feel hot and restless. Her fingers snaked down slowly, brushing roughly over her wet nipples and then down between her thighs. She lingered for a moment, promising herself that she'd resist the temptation to finger her excitement before easing her pussy lips open. The sensations of pleasure were too strong to resist; she closed her eyes and sighed softly as she stroked her fingers into her sex.

There was a vague feeling of guilt in the back of her head; she was supposed to be getting ready to go out for a last evening with Robert, Alex and Amanda. A farewell dinner had been arranged that was also designed to welcome Amanda – a typical confusion of motives which left scope for anything and everything. She knew it was time to get ready but the feel of her fingers pushing into her sex was divine. With the fingers of her other hand she began to toy at the apex of her pussy, circling the aroused bud as she continued to fuck herself with a slow, dextrous rhythm.

She made herself gasp, the sound bubbling from her throat as she eased her fingers deep into the wet pocket of her cunt and at the same time focused on the nub of her pleasure. She arched her back, pushing her breasts free of the water as her finger movements grew harder, faster. Her thighs were wide and she threw her head back to cry out her climax as her body shuddered suddenly. She dropped back, heart pounding and body tingling with a glow of energy.

Lazily, she sat up in the water, catching sight of herself in a mirror balanced on the wash basin close to the bath. Her short black hair was slicked back; she looked so different, her eyes seemed larger and more expressive, the lines of her mouth more sensual. She smiled to herself, still delighting in the way a change of hair style seemed to have brought about other changes in herself. Her breasts swayed slightly as she went on to her hands and knees, water dripping from her nipples and pouring back into the bath.

Her plastic hairbrush was balanced on the edge of the basin, its shiny black handle contrasting with the pure white of the porcelain. She smiled at the reflection in the small oval mirror as she reached for the brush. Her fingers closed on the hard, cylindrical handle; the phallic shape a pure delight. It was time to get ready to go out, she told herself as she stroked the hard bristles of the brush across her sensitively erect nipples. Her pussy was still aching. She felt the heat of desire burning deep inside her and knew that she had to satisfy it.

She closed her fingers over the hard black bristles and stroked the smooth, cool handle against the wetness of her inner thigh. The plastic floated over her glistening skin, the blackness making her skin seem virginally pale.

The rounded end she used to trace her pussy lips, back and forth, obscenely slow but stoking the heat that burned inside.

'Oh .Jesus . . .' she whispered, plunging the hardness deep into her sex. She held it for a second, rigid inside her soft inner flesh, and then she began to thrust it in and out. Each stroke made her sigh as she pushed down hard, brutally, fucking herself roughly, violating her own body with ruthless abandon. Visions of being fucked hard by faceless men filled her mind; countless cocks took her violently, taking their pleasure in her defiled body. She lost count of the number of imaginary cocks which entered her, fucking her from behind, one after the other.

As she fucked herself harder, the imaginary men merged; changing from anonymous beings endowed with only one attribute, into a single recognisable male. She cried out suddenly, forcing the brush up hard against her clit as the flood of pleasure took her over the edge.

In her mind she cried out as Patrick pressed his hardness deep into her pussy, filling her with the hot waves of his juicy climax.

The evening was turning out to be less straight-forward than Emily had expected. Dinner had turned into a quick meal at a local restaurant; the start of the evening rather than its focus. Robert had been in an excited mood, the sort of mood that was infectious if you knew what it meant. Amanda had seemed flustered by the sudden change of plans, especially when Robert had told them all about the invitation to the party. Then, before there had been too much time to question, he and Amanda had left, leaving Alex and Emily to finish the meal alone.

Sara Casement, a friend of Robert's, was hosting a party at her house, celebrating the publication of her latest book of photographs. Robert had mentioned her before, but neither Alex nor Emily had met her. In any case, Robert had managed to get an extra invitation for them; though in his usual devious way, he had insisted that they turn up to the party later – and once there to pretend not to know either him or Amanda. Emily had wanted to know what game he wanted them to play but he had merely smiled and suggested that they study Sara's photographs before trying to work it out.

The house was pretty full by the time she and Alex had arrived by cab. The gravel drive had been lit well by the lights blazing in every room in the house, although the light had been of little help to the taxi driver trying to manoeuvre between the haphazardly parked cars lining the path. The murmur of voices had been louder than the sounds of the music that drifted from the open door, which meant things were still in hand.

'This is going to be good,' Alex murmured as they walked into the main room. The party was warming up nicely; the buzz of conversation was punctuated by the clink of glass and the sound of laughter. Small groups of people were clustered together in deep conversation but there seemed to be a good deal of movement from group to group.

Emily recognised a few of the faces from the university but there were no real friends and acquaintances present. There was no sign of Robert or Amanda either, but she had seen Robert's car parked outside the house so she knew that he was around.

'I'll see about some drink,' Alex suggested, raising his voice above the din.

There were copies of Sara's book around the room, or at least Emily assumed that it was her book that people were studying intently. She had expected to see some examples of Sara's work up on the walls, but the walls were bare apart from a dense collage that dominated the space above the fireplace.

She finally spotted a copy of the book, resting on the arm of a chair, so she grabbed it quickly before anyone else got to it. There was nothing on the grey jacket of the book: not a logo, not a title, not an author. Emily turned the pages carefully; the heavy art paper and the large format made the book hard to hold. There was a simple profile shot of Sara Casement on the first page; she looked intense, her light-brown hair swept back from her tanned face framed eyes that were unforgiving and a mouth that was set firm. It wasn't an unattractive face; rather, it seemed as if her beauty was deliberately smothered by an excess of attitude.

Alex returned, clutching a couple of glasses of wine.

'I've just seen Robert and Amanda,' he reported breathlessly. 'I think the woman they were with must be Sara Casement,' he added.

'Is that her?' Emily asked, pointing to the portrait in the book.

'Yes, that's her, but she looks in a much better mood than she does there.'

Emily laughed. 'If looks could kill and all that,' she said, turning the page.

The first picture showed a naked man leaning against a plain white wall. He was bathed in strong light that bleached the colour from his body, making him look as clinically white as the wall behind him. His body cast no shadows, and his expressionless face stared blankly back at the camera. The next few pictures were variations on the same theme; naked male bodies stripped of emotion, stripped of colour, stripped of everything but the outlines of form and function.

'Not exactly easy on the eye, is it?' Alex muttered uneasily.

Emily skipped through the rest of that section of the book, finding it cold and depressing. The next section was instantly more to her liking. The first picture was a close-up of a woman's sex; the tanned flesh glowed with colour and texture, from the dense black curls of pubic hair, to the brown furrows of her labia, and the scarlet flesh of her opening. The picture was shockingly alive after the frigid forms Sara had created in the earlier pictures.

'It's a self-portrait,' Alex noted, pointing out the inscription opposite the picture.

'Yes, one of several.'

Emily looked up to find that she and Alex had been joined by Sara, Robert and Amanda.

'Hi,' Emily said, smiling, looking from Sara to the book. 'I ... er ... I don't know what to say really.'

Sara laughed. 'At least you're not going to attempt something profound. Someone tried to tell me that I was being very brave, that I was making an important statement by showing my vagina in public. My vagina, for goodness sake! I told him that I was proud of my cunt and wanted the whole world to admire it. I've never seen a man's smile disappear so quickly.'

They laughed for a moment and then Sara took charge of the introductions. Robert and Amanda feigned total innocence when presented to Emily and Alex, and they in turn pretended to have been invited by Sara's publisher. Robert referred to Amanda as his new research assistant, though it was clear from the possessive way he kept an arm over her shoulders that the relationship was more than purely professional.

'Sara was just trying to persuade Amanda to model for her,' Robert reported, placing his hands on Amanda's shoulders and massaging softly.

Sara smiled. 'I think Robert's a little afraid that I'd do unspeakable things to you,' she told a nervous-looking Amanda.

'And would you?' Emily asked, a wide smile lighting up her face.

'Of course I would,' Sara laughed. 'You obviously haven't been all the way through my book.'

Emily immediately flipped to the last few pages of the book, watched in quiet anticipation by the group around her. She stopped at a page illustrated by a picture of two naked women; their lips were touching in a soft, sensual kiss while their hands stroked each other's sex. Sara was one of the two women. Her eyes were half closed as though the pleasure were too great, her body bathed in jewels of perspiration that suggested the picture had been taken after she and her partner had made love.

'You see what Robert's afraid of?' Sara continued, her eyes searching Emily's meaningfully. 'What about you,' she whispered, 'are you afraid of me too?'

Alex coughed nervously. 'What about Amanda?' he asked. 'What do you think of all this?'

Amanda's face flooded red. 'I – I don't mind modelling so long as I'm not alone.'

'I'm sorry,' Sara responded, 'but I'm not going to have Robert looking over my shoulder.'

'What about if Emily was with you?' Robert suggested helpfully.

Sara nodded instantly. 'That sounds like an excellent idea,' she said enthusiastically. 'Emily?'

'Sure, why not,' she agreed readily.

'Good. My studio's upstairs. I can be ready in a few minutes,' Sara told them excitedly. 'Now, you won't change your minds, will you? I'll only be a few minutes, I promise.'

'I didn't realise you meant now,' Amanda mumbled, reaching up to touch Robert's hand still resting on her shoulder.

'Let's do it now. This could be fun,' Emily urged. 'We'll be up in a minute,' she told Sara confidently.

'Good, the studio's up on the top floor. Oh, one last thing,' she added before turning to go. 'I'd appreciate it if Robert and Alex waited for you downstairs.'

'Of course,' Robert agreed with a relaxed smile.

'Remember,' Emily whispered as she and Amanda waited nervously outside Sara's studio, 'we don't know each other.'

'I know. What do you think's going to happen?' came Amanda's whispered reply.

'I don't know. That's half the fun – not knowing makes things more exciting.'

Amanda looked unconvinced. They were standing at the top of the stairway, waiting outside the closed door of Sara's studio in semi-darkness. From below came the sounds of raucous laughter and the beat of the music as someone turned the volume up. 'What if something goes wrong?' Amanda asked quietly.

'Like what? Just try and relax. You'll enjoy it, I'm sure you will,' Emily replied encouragingly. 'This is how Robert's games always start; everything's got to be spontaneous, nothing's ever planned out very much. Isn't that what it's like with Patrick and Katerina?'

Amanda replied without pause. 'No, it's never like that at Eden,' she said.

'Then how do things happen?'

'Patrick is always in control. Everything is planned out for you.'

'Everything?' Emily asked sceptically. It sounded very melodramatic; it was hard to believe that there was no room for spontaneity or improvisation.

'Yes,' Amanda confirmed. 'Patrick likes things done exactly his way. You never know what's going to happen, but you know that whatever it is it's what he wants.'

'What about Katerina? What's she like?'

'She's a lot nicer than you imagine when you first meet her, unlike . . .'

The sentence was left unfinished as Sara opened the studio door. 'I'm ready,' she announced.

The studio was a wide, spacious area that had once been two separate rooms. The dividing wall had been knocked out, though even a cursory glance showed where the partition had once been. Emily stepped into the room with a feeling of great excitement; she already knew what game she wanted to play, it was just a matter of getting Amanda to play along. One side of the room was stacked with equipment and props, but that still left a raised area in the far corner to pose on. A milky-grey sheet had been strung up high, creating a soft marble effect as a backdrop.

A padded leather bench was positioned in front of the sheet, the polished wood topped with deep red leather that contrasted with the innocuous colour of the grey carpet and the background. Lights had already been trained on the seat, creating a soft, diffuse light that cast few shadows but added an intimate warmth to the scene.

'Why don't you sit together?' Sara suggested, moving towards the camera mounted on a tripod set well back from the bench. She had pulled her hair back, tying it into place with a thick black band, making her look cool and professional again.

Emily sat down first, crossing her legs so that her short dress was stretched tight across her thighs. She sat straight, arms by her sides, pressing her chest forward confidently so that her nipples pressed against the sheer black material of her dress. Amanda sat beside her, leaving a clear gap between them, as though she were afraid to get too close. She was wearing a short, checked skirt which mediated between the pure white of her buttoned blouse and the darkness of her black stockings and patent shoes.

'It's okay,' Sara laughed. 'You can relax, Amanda. I'm not going to eat you up.'

Amanda smiled shyly. 'I'm sorry,' she whispered, the soft lights hiding the nervousness that Emily could see expressed in her deep blue eyes.

Sara took the first few pictures with the camera she had retrieved from a silver case which she had snapped open on the floor. She also took a couple of polaroids, which she carefully placed on a bench to develop.

'Why don't you get a bit closer now,' Sara suggested. 'There's a gap between you that looks odd.' Emily complied immediately, shifting sideways to huddle close to Amanda. 'Good, that looks much better.'

Amanda still seemed very tense, sitting stiffly with an empty smile forced on to her face. 'Look, just try and relax,' Emily told her, taking her by the hand. They looked at each other for a moment, their eyes meeting for a split second before Amanda looked away. Sara continued to snap pictures, moving in close to get a shot of Emily stroking Amanda's long golden hair.

'Turn to each other now,' Sara directed, retreating to the back of the studio to look at the sample polaroids.

Emily turned slightly, leaning in closer, putting her hand to Amanda's knee. She looked into Amanda's eyes and smiled, letting her hand move ever so slightly higher up Amanda's thigh. The click and whirr of the camera was the only reminder that they were not alone. Amanda made no response. She sat with the smile fixed on her face as Emily moved her hand higher and higher.

'Good, that's very good,' Sara whispered encouragingly.

'What should I do now?' Emily asked innocently, not taking her eyes off Amanda.

'Let me see you even closer . . .'

Emily spread her fingers over the silky sheen of Amanda's stockings as she twisted her face round slightly, moving in closer, her lips parted for the kiss. Amanda sat back, her body tensed as their mouths touched softly. She seemed to resist, her immobility implying her rejection of the embrace, and then she melted. She parted her lips to Emily's tongue, accepting the soft, tender kiss with a whispered sigh.

When Emily pushed her hand further, her fingers travelled from the pure silk to pure flesh, the thick black band of the stocking top giving way to the softness of Amanda's inner thigh. They stopped kissing for a moment. Emily sat back and Sara zoomed in to capture the dazed expression that flushed Amanda's face. When they kissed again there was no resistance; Amanda opened her mouth to Emily's probing tongue just as she allowed Emily's fingers to slip under her skirt.

They kissed for a while, separating after each embrace as if to take stock of the situation. Emily enjoyed the feel of Amanda's inner thigh; she could sense the quickening of her breath and the deepening of her excitement.

'No,' Amanda sighed, as Emily's fingers stroked softly against the wetness of her panties.

'Should I stop?' Emily asked, turning to face Sara for the first time.

'No. I want you to do what feels best,' Sara replied, her eyes sparkling with delight at the scene unfolding in front of her.

'I don't know what to do next,' Emily admitted – 'I mean – well, I've never done anything like this before.'

Sara laughed softly. 'You're lying,' she said, 'but I suspect that this is Amanda's first time with a woman. Am I right?'

Amanda hesitated before confirming the fact.

'Do you want me to stop?' Emily asked her, and when Amanda paused she took her by the shoulders and kissed her hotly on the mouth and throat.

'No, don't stop,' Amanda whimpered, returning Emily's hot, sexual kisses.

Emily began to unbutton Amanda's blouse, her fingers working deftly as she continued to kiss Amanda. Soon the blouse was half undone and Emily pulled it aside, exposing the creamy pale flesh of Amanda's chest, the firm breasts laced in a pretty white bra. Sara muttered something under her breath before stepping closer to take more pictures. Emily obliged by slowly undoing the last of the buttons and then pulling the blouse open completely. She moved behind Amanda, sitting up on the bench so that she could smother the other woman's bare shoulders with soft, loving caresses.

When Amanda's bra was unclipped it fell away, exposing the dark coloured nipples that were hard and excited. Emily reached round to cup the bare breasts, covering the nipples with her fingers as she continued to kiss Amanda's neck and shoulders. Amanda had her head back, her mouth was open and her wet lips glistened under the light.

'Lift your skirt now,' Sara ordered, her voice low and indistinct.

Amanda sighed as her nipples were squeezed tightly by Emily, and then she obeyed. Slowly, almost reluctantly, she lifted the front of her skirt up, showing the camera the top of her stockings and the black triangle of her panties pulled tight between her thighs. Sara continued to take pictures, moving back and forth, zooming in and then panning back slowly.

Emily had one arm around her friend's chest, her hand expertly teasing the erect nipples, whilst with her other hand she sought Amanda's pussy. Her own excitement was liquid inside her, a fire that burned in her sex and made her hard nipples spasm with pleasure as she pressed herself against Amanda's back. She reached down to press two fingers into the warm triangle of lace that guarded the entrance to Amanda's pleasure spot. The material was wet and sticky with moisture that seeped from Amanda's pussy, a wetness that seemed to flow even more as Emily's fingers eased the material between Amanda's sex lips.

Amanda parted her thighs completely, pushing her legs apart so that the swelling of her pussy lips bulged deliciously against the tightness of her panties and the sensual pressure of Emily's fingers. Sara knelt down before her, focusing the camera directly on the black wetness and the swollen pussy lips that sought exposure.

'Do you want me to show Sara your cunt?' Emily hissed, bringing her mouth to Amanda's open lips.

'No.' Amanda whispered, but her protest was smothered by Emily's possessive, controlling kiss. Amanda arched her back, she clutched at the side of the bench as the sudden eruption of pleasure spasmed deep in her sex. Her knickers had been pulled roughly to one side, Emily's fingers gripping the material tightly, exposing to full view the beauty of Amanda's aroused pussy. Sara lost no time. She snapped the pictures quickly, the camera eating up the view of the parted pussy lips, the moisture oozing from the red flesh of her opening.

Emily pushed the material aside fully and then stroked a finger into the other woman's welcoming slit. She soaked her finger in the dewy wetness, making it slick and wet for the camera. In and out slowly, never penetrating hard so that Amanda had to push and squirm for her pleasure. When her fingers were soaked, Emily rubbed them against Amanda's hard nipples, passing the sex juices from cunt to breast. Again and again she wet her fingers deep in Amanda's cunt before anointing the hard peaks of her breasts.

Amanda was pushed back on the bench and made to lie flat against the scarlet leather. Her skirt was in disarray around her waist and her black panties had been pulled down below her stocking-clad knees. With her skirt up and her blouse open, she was exposed completely to Emily's gaze and to Sara's camera. Her breasts were dappled with her pussy juices, her nipples glistening seductively under the lights.

Emily looked at her hungrily. Making love with another woman was still a new experience, but one that she was learning to enjoy more and more. She pulled her dress over her head quickly, revealing her own skimpy black underwear, which she then removed. Sara smiled to her before taking a few more pictures. The feeling of excitement was too great to worry about the camera; all that Emily wanted to do was to fuck Amanda, to give and to receive pure unbridled pleasure.

She lay beside Amanda, the two of them squeezing closer so as not to fall off the bench. They kissed again, long and slow, enjoying every second of it, before Emily put her mouth to one of Amanda's nipples. She closed her lips around the fleshy nub, tasting the pussy juices with which it was smeared. She licked delightedly, using her teeth to hold the nipple in place while her tongue lashed back and forth lazily. She repeated the trick on the other nipple, pleased to see that Amanda was cupping her own breasts, offering them to Emily's greedy lips.

When Emily eased her fingers into Amanda's pussy once more she felt the other woman spasm with pleasure, as though she could not stand the bliss that pulsed through her. She began to finger fuck Amanda, driving three fingers into her open wetness, penetrating with rapid, skilful strokes until Amanda cried out as the pleasure came to a sudden, intense peak.

Amanda lay back; her eyes were closed and her breathing was a hard pounding in her chest. She took Emily's hands and began to kiss the soaked fingers, licking away the juices that poured from her own body. She felt desire still, as though her climax was a promise of more rather than the end of the game.

'If you like it so much,' Emily whispered, 'then suck mine too.'

Amanda sat up and watched as Emily began to finger fuck herself, pressing her fingers into her pussy while rubbing sensuously against her clitoral bud. She watched in silence for a moment, fascinated by the ecstatic expression on Emily's face, and then took Emily's hands into her mouth, sucking at the jewels that rained from her sex.

Emily twisted aside and sat up on her knees, her thighs parted and her pussy slick with her own juices. She eased her fingers into her sex again and then tasted herself on her fingers, hardly noticing the steady 'click click' of the camera. Her eyes met Amanda's and something happened; suddenly they knew what to do. Emily swung round easily, sitting astride Amanda's chest so that she could feel the other woman's nipples against her inner thighs. She moved down, laying her body over Amanda so that they were able to mouth each other's slits. Emily sighed hotly, a shiver of excitement moving through her as she felt Amanda's tongue on her pussy. She herself returned the pleasure, pressing her fingers into Amanda's body while seeking the centre of pleasure with her tongue.

In moments, Emily had climaxed, her pussy raining honey into Amanda's mouth as the pleasure shook through her body. She pressed her mouth over Amanda's opening, knowing that the other woman teetered on the edge of orgasm. They sucked and licked deliriously, mouth to cunt, cunt to mouth, sharing pleasure without end. Everything else was a distraction: the blur of the lights, the whispered words from Sara, the whirr of the camera. All that mattered was the pure sexual pleasure of sucking another woman's cunt while having her own sucked in return.

Emily looked around suddenly. Out of the corner of her eye, she noticed a movement. Which caused her to pause. Sara was naked, her clothes piled unceremoniously on the open camera case. 'I don't know what Robert's up to,' she said, smiling, 'but there's no way I just witnessed a seduction here. You do know each other, don't you?'

Emily, still crouched over Amanda, laughed. 'Does it matter?'

Sara walked over and stroked Emily's back, running her fingers firmly over the smooth unblemished flesh. 'No, not all.'

Emily closed her eyes; Amanda began to tongue her again, only this time Sara's fingers were there too, pressing into the wetness. She sighed softly, letting the pleasure flow like a current through her body.

Seven

Patrick watched Emily climb the stairs, struggling with
the heavy black bag she carried in front of her. Her long
legs were perfectly outlined by her tight black leggings;
every curve of calf and thigh, the swell of her backside,
every sinew of her long limbs was delineated and defined
by the skin-tight black lycra. The leggings were matched
by a skin-tight sleeveless black top which followed the
contour of her breasts, the nipples sharp points that
naturally drew the eye. He watched her struggle to the
top of the stairs, enjoying the view of her body from
behind and below.

'To the left,' he directed when she dropped her heavy
bag at the top of the stairs.

She looked at him sharply, her dark blue eyes filled
with annoyance, but said nothing. She inhaled sharply,
grabbed the bag again and heaved it towards her room.
This wasn't the welcome to Eden that she had expected,
especially not after the long journey by car which had
necessitated leaving so early in the morning.

'Where's Alex sleeping?' was her first question on
entering her room. She dumped the heavy bag on the end
of the bed and turned to face Patrick, the look of
vexation still on her face.

He followed her into the room and closed the door. She
crossed her arms over her chest and pursed her lips,
striking a defiant pose that could not hide the sudden
nervousness in her eyes. 'Where Alex sleeps is nothing to

99

do with you,' he told her. 'Although you and he are guests of this household, you are also here to serve the community as a whole. In your case we have work for you to do for us here, which means you'll be staying in this house. In his case it means finding out what the needs are in the other households and then assigning him somewhere to stay according to that.'

'We're not going to be staying in the same house?'

He shook his head. 'No; in fact I'd hazard a guess that you'll not be seeing very much of him for a while. Does that bother you?'

'No,' she said, less than convincingly.

'I don't like lies,' he warned, keeping his voice emotionless. 'You've travelled one road with Robert, but it's a different road to the one we follow at Eden. Ours is a more interesting road but it makes certain demands; demands that you might have trouble meeting easily.'

'Look, I —' she began to say.

'No,' he said sharply. 'You'll speak when I allow you to speak. You're here to learn, which means you look and listen. I'll not allow you to speak out of turn again. Understand?' She glared at him, her eyes wide with barely suppressed anger, but she kept her silence for all the melodrama of her pose. 'Good,' he said, smiling. 'I'm glad you understand.

'I want you to look upon your time here as a time of training, a period of learning, if you like. There are many things in Eden which will strike you as strange — some of them may even seem to be disagreeable to you — but they are things which you'll come to accept. Your perceptions will change over time; we do not expect you to change over-night. However there is one thing that you must understand immediately, and that is that we expect you to be obedient at all times.

'Obedience is perhaps an alien concept to you; I can sense that the very idea of it causes you to grow angry.' He paused to smile at her obvious discomfort. 'Obedience is the first rule; everything else flows from this. And I am

100

sure that you know of the penalty for disobedience – punishment. You are used to the way of pleasure, now is the time for you to learn how that pleasure can be tinged with pain. Do you understand?'

'Am I supposed to speak now?' she responded sarcastically.

He laughed softly, delighting in the insolence of her manner. Her behaviour was the exact opposite of Amanda's – it was a contrast he did not find in Amanda's favour. 'The penalties for repeated disobedience become more and more severe,' he warned calmly.

'And what if I refuse to accept my punishment?' she demanded.

'Then you'll be driven to the nearest train station and allowed to make your own way home. The choice is always yours: remain here and abide by our rules or leave and live according to your own.'

She waited for a moment before speaking again. 'Don't think that I won't do just that if you push me too far,' she warned quietly, finally sitting down on the edge of the bed.

He looked at her and smiled, a warm flush of excitement making his cock harden. 'I suspect that you'll carry out your threat,' he said, 'but only if I don't push you far enough. Quiet now,' he added, stopping any more questions. 'I want you to listen.

'While you are here I want you to learn as much as possible. I want you to understand completely; I want you to know the meaning of every word, every look, every nuance of expression. I want you to be observant at all times, to note anything and everything that you see and hear. I want you to report back to me, to tell me what you've seen and what you think it means and how it all fits in.

'Eden is different. You appreciate that in a very superficial manner at the moment, but in time you'll come to understand just how different it is to the rest of the world. Life here is intense, far more intense than anything you

101

experienced in the playful little games you played with Robert. I may of course be mistaken.' He smiled, showing her that he doubted it. 'But I believe that you are going to learn more about yourself and your capacity for pleasure than you'll ever discover anywhere else.'

She was looking at him strangely, perhaps unable to chose between showing contempt and scepticism, or else excitement at the promises he was making. He relaxed a little, realising that the time for confrontation – real confrontation and resistance – had passed. He walked over to the wardrobe, ignoring his own reflection in the mirrored door so that he could watch her.

'Are you nervous?' he asked her reflection, casually opening the wardrobe door.

'Should I be?' she asked, resting her elbows on her knees and affecting a look of boredom.

'You're not frightened about receiving your first taste of punishment?'

'No.'

He pushed the door of the wardrobe open fully and turned to face her. The rack on the door was lined with glossy black instruments of correction: straps, belts, a riding crop, a leather tawse. Each implement was set off starkly against the matt white surface of the wardrobe.

Her eyes widened, a look of apprehension marring the symmetry of her face. He checked his own smile, suspecting that she would interpret it incorrectly; he did not gloat, rather his smile would have been one of pleasure and excitement. So far he was happy with how things had gone: she showed signs of insolence, but it was tempered by her good judgement in not pushing too far. It was a delicate balance between resistance and submission; too much in either direction and the relationship would not work.

'You've not been punished before?' he asked, making her focus on him and not the implements on display.

'No,' she answered flatly.

'When you watched Amanda being punished, did it excite you?'

She looked away from him quickly, the colour rising to her face and he guessed that embarrassment was not an emotion she was used to. 'Sort of,' she admitted hesitantly.

'Take your top off,' he told her.

For a moment he half-expected her to refuse, but she obeyed, albeit with obvious reluctance. She stood and pulled her tight black top over her head before dropping it on to the bed behind her. Her slender frame accentuated the prominence of her breasts, making them appear rounder and more voluptuous. The way she stood – legs slightly parted, head slightly tilted to one side, hands held in front of her so that her arms funnelled her breasts forward – suggested a certain arrogance; she was posing even as she affected artlessness.

'Come here,' he ordered, gesturing to her to stand beside him.

She walked slowly towards him, her eyes darting from him to the row of black instruments of punishment. He stepped behind her, put his arms on her shoulders and turned her to face the display of implements. Her skin was warm and inviting, her bare back unmarked, the smooth, unblemished skin a sensual temptation. He massaged her shoulders softly, kneading his fingers into her flesh so that she sighed unexpectedly.

'You're very beautiful,' he whispered, breathing the words into her ear as he pressed his thumbs across the tense muscles of her shoulder. He was hard and he pushed himself against her, pressing his erect cock against the roundness of her behind. 'You're so beautiful,' he continued, 'that punishing you is going to be sheer joy.'

She leant her head back as he continued to massage her tense muscles and, at the same time, she pushed her backside against his erect hardness, rubbing herself against the shaft that pressed between her bottom cheeks. Her eyes were closed and her mouth was glossy and enticing; its full red lips parted slightly, her breath whispering in and out slowly.

He took her hands and put them to her breasts, moulding her fingers to cup the full roundness, pressing them together to emphasise the deep, natural cleavage of her chest. When he kissed her on the neck and throat she sighed softly, a half-smile flickering nervously about her lips. Her skin was warm to the coolness of his lips; he tasted her flesh, breathing the clean fragrance of her hair and body.

'It's time now,' he whispered, running his hands down her sides slowly, tracing the curves of her body.

'Will you hurt me?' she asked softly, her eyes still half closed with sensual delight.

He held her by the waist and kissed her softly on the shoulder again. 'Yes,' he told her tenderly. 'I'm going to hurt you.'

She accepted the fact without complaint, her eyes fixed on the array of straps and other implements that lay in front of her. Gingerly, she put her hand to one of the belts, a thick, wide strip of stiff leather that was doubled over the rack.

'Does this frighten you?' he asked, carefully unfurling it from its place so that its tongue reached to the floor.

'Yes,' she admitted, letting her fingers linger on the glossy marbled surface of the belt. It was as though she were fascinated and frightened at the same time; afraid of the pain that it could no doubt inflict, and yet fascinated by the austere simplicity of the object.

'Go and sit by the bed, on the floor,' he ordered.

She hesitated for a moment, her eyes locked on to his, then turned away nervously. There was no need to repeat the order, however; she walked back to the bed and then sat on the floor with her legs tucked under her bottom. He kept his back to her while he selected the instrument with which he would chastise her, ensuring that she could not see what it was.

He sat on the edge of the bed and motioned for her to come to him. She started to stand up but then caught herself and stayed down on hands and knees. He leaned over and kissed her once, on the mouth, pushing his tongue between her lips before drawing away again.

'I want you to stay in this position,' he said, moving her into place in front of him. She was still on all fours, her tight leggings moulded like a second skin across her backside, her breasts hanging down, the nipples pointing directly to the floor. He stroked his hand across her backside, following the contours of her thigh right around and up over her bottom cheeks. It was clear that she was wearing nothing under the leggings; the moist warmth touched his fingers as they brushed against her pussy.

He showed her the object he had chosen for her: a stiff rubber paddle, the matt surface of heavy latex joined to a thick, padded handle. She swallowed hard, and her eyes clouded with real fear and apprehension.

'Kiss it,' he urged, offering it to her lips. She looked at him, her eyes full of questions but she obeyed, touching her full, swollen lips to the black rubber. When she pulled back there was an imprint of her lips on the black latex.

He raised the paddle high and then, while she watched anxiously, over her shoulder, he swung it down swiftly. The sharp snap of sound echoed through the room, a percussive blast that seemed to still the words he knew must be rushing to her lips. He spanked her again, smacking the heavy rubber surface directly against the fullness of her lycra-clad bottom cheeks. Strokes three and four fell in quick succession, the slap of rubber against her backside filling the room. Her face was turned away, her expression shielded from his gaze, her only reaction a sharp intake of breath with each stroke of her punishment.

It took several more strokes, delivered with cool precision, before she sighed audibly, the gasp escaping from her lips as though against her will. He paused to caress her backside, to feel the heat that radiated from her flesh through the thin covering of her leggings. She turned to him finally, a look of pleading in her eyes. He kissed her on the mouth again, sucking away her resolve before raising his arm to recommence the punishment.

He did not count the number of strokes; there was no need to. Soon she was moving with his rhythm, lifting herself, raising her backside for each stroke, accepting it with a quiet sigh. He guessed that the heat of the correction had suffused her rear, that the red heat was livid under the black covering on her skin. When he paused to touch her again she pressed her backside against his hand, and sighed with undisguised relief.

'Turn now,' he said, pulling her to her knees in front of him.

She did as she was told, sitting up on her knees, instinctively cupping her breasts in her hands. He stroked her nipples with his thumbs, delighted to find that they were already erect and aroused. A faint flush marked her chest and neck; a pink tinge of pleasure that made him smile inwardly.

He brought the paddle down hard between her breasts, snapping it down with a sharp, jagged motion so that it smacked loudly against the softer flesh of her globes. She cried out, shocked by the unexpected focus of punishment. He ignored her complaints and the anger suddenly expressed in her eyes and continued to spank her breasts. He varied the strokes, making sure that every inch of her chest was patterned with the same redness. Her nipples grew harder as he smacked them, making her cry out repeatedly as the strokes grew stronger.

At last, he let the paddle drop to one side. He was sure that the fires inside her were burning well; that the red heat on her backside and on her breasts burned with the same intensity. He pulled her roughly towards him, keeping her on her knees but bending her across his lap. Her leggings were tight but he easily pushed a hand under the soft material, his fingers sliding between the warmth of her skin and the warmth of the lycra.

'Oh, no,' she whispered, as if alarmed by the way she was being handled. His fingers smoothed across the punished flesh of her bottom cheeks and then down along the anal cleft to find the wetness soaking her pussy. She gasped and moved, struggling momentarily as he roughed his fingers across her pussy lips before entering her body. She gasped again, only this time there was nothing but pleasure in her exclamation. She pushed her backside upward, opening herself so that his hard fingers could penetrate deep into her sex.

She was wet, her moist desire sliding over his fingers as he thrust them in and out of her sex. She struggled in his arms until he understood what she wanted; he gave way and she tugged at her leggings until they were down at her knees. He smiled openly at the sight of her chastised backside, her bottom cheeks glowing with an even, delicious pink. He held her again, using his fingers expertly to bring her closer and closer to orgasm until she was panting deliriously and gyrating wildly.

'Are you going to be a good girl?' he whispered.

'Yes . . . yes . . .' she replied, using her own fingers to play with her clit while his fingers slipped in and out of her pussy.

She cried out suddenly, her body tensing as the pleasure became too great to hold back. She shuddered and fell across his lap as his fingers brought her to the peak of ecstasy.

Alex stood in the doorway and watched Katerina crossing the room, walking with a long, elegant stride that snapped her heels down hard on the polished marble flooring. The room seemed to extend right across the whole house; an open space that functioned as her studio, library and play area. If the house as a whole was shared with Patrick, then this part of it was obviously her own private domain. She stopped next to a sofa which was positioned under one of the large, rectangular windows which allowed the hazy sunshine to fill the room with light and warmth.

'Will Emily be alright with Patrick?' he asked nervously

when she turned to face him. He was still standing in the doorway, torn between his desire to follow Katerina and his feelings of concern for Emily.

'Probably,' Katerina replied casually, waiting for him to join her.

'Probably?' he repeated, glancing over his shoulder towards the stairs.

'Yes, probably. Why are you afraid for her?'

The question was disconcertingly direct. He looked at Katerina for a moment, silhouetted by the light that poured through the window behind her. She was dressed in white; a simple dress cinched at the waist so that it flared slightly around her thighs and emphasised the fullness of her breasts. There was no easy answer to her question, he realised. He was nervous, not just for Emily, but for himself as well.

He walked fully into the room, crossing the pattern of light that coloured the floor. He was aware of her eyes fixed on him; she made him feel nervous, as though she could tell what was going on in his head all the time. Women generally didn't make him feel like that; he had always felt relaxed in female company, but somehow Katerina was different.

'Sit here for me,' she suggested, pointing to a spot on the floor to one side of the sofa.

'On the floor?' he asked stupidly and then regretted it.

'Yes, by my feet,' she explained quietly, her dark eyes glittering with something that might have been amusement.

He sat down on the floor, his face turning red and his ears burning. She waited for him to sit before she sat on the sofa. 'Do I make you nervous?' she asked, running her hands through his hair, tenderly. He looked up at her and met her dark, brooding eyes which seemed to see right through to the very heart of him. Her lips were glossed, deep crimson against the dark tan of her face. She was beautiful, so dark and mysterious; she could easily see into him but her eyes carried expressions he could not hope to fathom.

'Yes, very nervous,' he admitted, unable to turn away from her eyes. He felt a stab of fear deep in the pit of his stomach, a sudden flurry of sensation caused by the look in her eyes and the feel of her fingers on his face.

'That's good,' she said, a faint smile animating her face. 'If you are nervous it means that you instinctively recognise the power relationship between us. Do you understand why you are on your knees in front of me?'

'Because that's what you want,' he replied. 'It shows that I've been obedient.'

She smiled again. 'More than that, Alex, it shows that I am above you. Your true position is at my feet, down at heel. I am going to teach you the ways of being a slave. I am going to show you the many ways to worship your Mistress.'

'Like kissing your heels?' he asked, thinking back to his first meeting with her, when he had lapped at her heels like an obedient puppy. The memory filled him with intense shame, yet, at the same time, it stirred an excitement that made his penis harden.

'That's one of the ways,' she agreed, 'but there are more, many more. You are here to be trained – and, as your Mistress, I will ensure that your training is as thorough as it is arduous. For now, there is only one thing you must remember, and that is that you are here to serve your Mistress first and foremost. Your guiding light, the rule which should never be forgotten, is that my pleasure is everything. Do not forget this. My pleasure is everything.'

'I understand,' Alex promised, inhaling sharply as he spoke.

'No, you do not understand,' she told him firmly. 'You say that because you imagine that it pleases me, but it does not. I have been indulgent in letting you speak to me directly. The lessons begin now, as will the penalties for disobedience or insolence. You will speak when spoken to and not before; that is one rule. In future, you will address me as Mistress; that is another rule.'

Alex looked at her open mouthed, confusion in his eyes and a thrill of fear linking strangely to the excitement in the pit of his stomach. Her voice was cold and hard, her dark features more austerely beautiful because of the ice in her soul. He was trembling, and the strength of his reaction surprised him all the more because it was so unexpected.

'You and Emily have been invited to Eden as our guests, but you are here to help the community as a whole. There are other helpers already here; you are not the first, nor will you be the last. The labour of all helpers is placed in a pool and all tasks are assigned to workers according to the amount of labour available. Emily has already been assigned a job in this house, which is why she will be staying in the room upstairs. Your name has been put forward for the next job on the list, which means that it is probable you will be given a room in another household.'

'But – but I want to stay here,' Alex responded, the panic cutting through everything.

'Silence! Have you not been listening?' Katerina demanded angrily.

'But I want to stay with you!'

Katerina ran her fingers through his hair again, bringing him to silence. He looked up at her sadly, unable to believe that he was going to be moved out almost before he'd arrived. It was so unfair; there was only one reason for him to be at Eden and that was to be with Katerina, to be at her feet, just the way she wanted. Her fingers tightened in his hair, grabbing handfuls so that her knuckles pressed hard against his skull. She pulled his head towards her – making him sit up on hands and knees – and his face twisted into a scowl of pain.

'Do you really wish to be punished so soon?' she whispered, bringing her face down to his level.

'No,' he replied, breathing hard as he looked into her deep brown eyes.

She moved forwards and kissed him softly on the

mouth, while gripping his hair even harder. He cried out in pain as he accepted her kiss, the pleasure of her mouth mingling with the sharp daggers in his head.

'You'll be punished for speaking out of turn,' she whispered, kissing him again, tenderly. She pulled his head back and he tried to resist, wanting to feel her lips on his for as long as possible. She jerked his head back suddenly, making him cry out loudly. There was the faint trace of a smile on her lips, a suggestion of cruelty or pleasure or something he could not read.

He stopped resisting; she pushed him down, pressing his face down to her black heels. She held him in place as he began to kiss her feet, touching his lips to her heels, sucking the hard, shiny dagger into his mouth. His heart was pounding, throbbing violently in his chest as he pictured himself on hands and knees before his Mistress. The idea filled him with wonder, a secret delight beating with the pounding in his chest.

She pulled him away, making him sit up on his knees in front of her. Her heels were wet with his saliva, the smear of his lips on the shiny black leather. She swung her legs round and parted her thighs, lifting her dress back so that he could see the white triangle of her panties pulled tightly between her thighs.

'Undo your top,' she told him, keeping her thighs wide so that he could feast his eyes on the bulge of her sex. The thin strip of white did nothing to hide the dark, dense bush that shielded the opening of her pussy. He fumbled for the buttons to his denim shirt, unable to look away from Katerina's pussy.

She stroked his bare chest as he let his shirt slide to the floor. The sun, too, stroked his body with a warm, orange glow that was nothing compared to the heat that burned in his chest. His cock was rock hard, pressing painfully against the constricting tightness of his jeans. Her long, elegant fingers traced patterns across his chest, moving through the dark curls of hair again and again.

He uttered a sharp cry of pain when she caught one of

his nipples between her finger and thumb. He moved forward to lessen the pain but she tensed harder, pulling the nub of flesh so that it stood painfully erect. She let go for a second and then grabbed the other nipple and pulled hard, making him cry out again. When she released him, his chest was marked with dark red around the nipples, which ached with an unfamiliar but intense pain.

'You'll train well,' she remarked, flicking her fingers across his nipples casually. She grabbed him by the hair again and directed him backwards, making him lie flat on the ground at her feet. The sun was in his eyes, blinding him, until she stood up and blocked its path. She reached under her skirt and pulled her panties down slowly, letting him watch in silence. Then, when she was naked under her dress, she stepped over him, planting her heels on either side of his head.

'Pleasure me well,' she warned, 'or you'll suffer a worse punishment than the one I have in mind.'

She squatted down over him, heels on either side of his head, knees pointing outwards, and her backside hovering above his mouth. He breathed in deeply, inhaling the musky, cloying scent of her body. Her pussy lips were slightly parted, offering a glimpse of heaven within. Gently, almost reverently, he touched his lips to her sex. He kissed her softly, hardly daring to press his tongue into the folds of her pussy.

He wanted to hold her – to run his hands across the smooth expanse of her thighs, to stroke her clitty with his fingers as he penetrated with his tongue – but he held back, afraid to touch her with anything but his mouth. He traced the groove between thigh and labia with his tongue, back and forth slowly, and then again on the other side. He brushed his mouth against the dark petals of her pussy lips and flicked his tongue back and forth slowly, working deeper and deeper with each stroke until she murmured softly.

He used his teeth to gently nip at her labia before

112

spearing her sex with his tongue again, pressing in deep to brush against the moisture laden walls of her cunt. In and out, pushing his face right against her backside, eating from her pussy directly, deliriously. Her juices soaked him, wetting his mouth, lips and face. He sucked harder, wanting to eat her, to devour the beauty of her cunt, to suck away at the centre of her pleasure.

She sighed and squatted down harder, trapping his head under her body. He did not falter; her cunt, her sex, her pleasure were all that mattered. She began to use her fingers on her clit, rubbing concentric circles around the bud as he mouthed her open pussy. He could sense the urgency of her pleasure; she was moving faster and faster, grinding down on his feverish mouth. Her juices rained into his mouth, every jewel sucked and savoured until she cried out her climax.

He kissed her softly, the tip of his tongue working the outer lips of her sex with slow, even strokes. She sighed, lifting herself slightly. Her fingers were soaked with her nectar and she pressed them into his mouth so that he could lick them clean.

'Suck me here now,' she told him, running a wet finger from her pussy up between her bottom cheeks.

He traced the moist trail left by her fingers, from the opening of her slit back to the dark button of her anus. He hesitated for a moment, his eyes fixed on the forbidden orifice from which she demanded pleasure. He pushed his mouth against her open pussy, licking up the moisture within and then he smeared it along her rear crack. He lapped softly at the tight ring of muscle, circling it slowly in the way she had circled her clit with her fingers.

He cried out suddenly as her heels dug hard into his shoulder. Her fingers alighted on his nipples again, squeezing tightly, sending sharp jags of pain through his body. He pressed his tongue against the tight anal ring, his mouth pressed tight against her bottom cheeks. She sighed loudly and pressed herself down, grinding herself slowly against his mouth as his tongue penetrated into her rear passage.

He waited for a moment before withdrawing, and then went in again, his tongue slipping in and out of the sheath of muscle as he tongued her anus. Her pleasure was real, her nails digging into his chest as she sighed and gasped. He licked harder, pressing his mouth deeper into her behind, ignoring the pain that spasmed from his nipples. It didn't matter; all that counted was the pleasure Mistress was receiving as he sucked deeply at her anal hole.

He lost track of time. He mouthed and kissed and caressed her backside, exploring every inch of her pussy and anal hole. He moved with her pleasure as her thighs and heels and body held him in place, her whispered sighs growing louder as he tongued at her rear opening. Arching her back, she pushed herself flat on to his face, so that his tongue sank even deeper into her body. As she gripped his head tightly between her thighs and stroked her sharp nails across his chest, he uttered a strangled cry of pleasure and then his cock pumped thick waves of come into his jeans – just as her climax rained pussy juices over his face.

114

Eight

Alex waited silently outside the door, listening intently for Katerina to call him back into the room. He still felt stunned by what had happened. He glanced at his bare chest and saw the red marks that she had inflicted on his nipples, marks which still smarted terribly. But it was a strange sort of pain; for every twinge of it he felt a corresponding echo of pleasure. The faintest trace of her musk still suffused his mouth, and with every breath he could taste the pussy juices with which he had slaked himself.

His cock twitched responsively, hardening again as he thought of sitting under her – under Mistress – and pleasuring her pussy with his mouth, of pleasuring also her tight anal hole until she shuddered to a second climax. He touched himself, easing the pressure of his hardness in his tight denim trousers. He had soiled himself shamelessly, spurting his climax like an inexperienced schoolboy, while she rode his mouth blissfully. Now he had cleaned himself up as commanded and he waited anxiously to be allowed back into her sanctuary.

Should he knock once more? Ordinarily there would have been no hesitation; he would have barged straight into the room, but now things were different. She was Mistress and he was her slave. *Slave*. It sounded so dramatic, so unreal, and yet he liked the implication of it; he liked the idea of being her slave, of being at the beck and call of his Mistress, of existing only for her pleasure.

There were voices from the room. He listened more closely but the pulsing of his heart seemed the loudest sound of all. Was Emily in the room too? He had recognised Patrick's voice instantly and now he wondered about Emily. Had she too been forced to serve? Had she been told that she was nothing but a slave? That she was at Eden to serve her Master before all others?

The door opened suddenly. Emily was there, holding the door open. Their eyes met for an instant but then they both looked away, unable to face the truth they saw in each other's face.

'It's okay, you can come in now,' Katerina called from the far side of the room. She was sitting at her desk, peering at a computer monitor, with Patrick beside her, also hunched over the screen.

Alex walked into the room self-consciously. He was clad only in a pair of faded black denims and he was aware that his chest was still marked with red. Emily closed the door before turning to walk back to Patrick, deliberately avoiding Alex's gaze. He watched her go. She too had changed out of her clothes into something more comfortable. The short skirt she was wearing barely covered her backside and it, along with black knee-length socks, drew attention to her long bare legs.

He followed a second later, wondering just what she and Patrick had done together. Had she been punished? He tried to imagine her going willingly over his lap to receive a spanking but it was an idea he could not quite accept. Emily didn't go for that sort of thing; she was too proud to let someone punish her, far too proud, in fact.

'Did you enjoy your first lesson?' Patrick asked him, looking up from the computer.

'It was – it was very intense,' Alex replied softly. He could feel his skin prickling, making him feel even more uncomfortable.

'It was very intense, *sir*,' Patrick corrected.

Alex looked away sharply. He could not reply; he could not repeat the words, not with Emily standing so close. His face was burning and he felt the beads of sweat forming on his skin.

'Say it,' Katerina warned, her voice as cold and emotionless as her eyes.

Alex was trembling. Why did he have to say it? Had he been alone with Mistress it would have been nothing, but there, in front of Emily, it suddenly seemed too much to ask.

'Your Mistress has spoken,' Patrick warned him, his voice rising higher.

If only Emily had remained with Robert, if only she had decided against Eden then everything would have been alright. He turned to her, looked at her standing quietly, beautifully, beside him and then he turned back. Her presence was disturbing whereas it had always previously been reassuring; he could not stand the idea that she would be witness to his submission.

Katerina stood up angrily. 'You disappoint so quickly,' she told him, walking round to stand by the side of her desk. 'Perhaps I have not made myself clear enough. Or else you really do hunger for harsher treatment.'

'I'm sorry,' Alex whispered miserably.

'Say it properly,' Patrick ordered.

'I'm sorry ... Mistress,' he complied, trying not to think of Emily standing so close.

'When you address Patrick, you'll address him as "sir" at all times,' Katerina explained. 'That is another of the rules you must abide by. You are here to obey both of us: your Mistress and your Master. Step forward now,' she added, her voice assuming the strictest tone of command instantly. Alex stepped forward as ordered, facing the edge of the desk, hands limply at his sides and head bowed. A sick feeling of dread swept through him. Punishment was inevitable; there was no way he could stop it now.

'Put your hands on the table,' Katerina continued. 'Keep your feet where they are. That's it; good. Lean right across.'

117

Alex was bent at the waist, his feet apart, the weight on his hands as he leaned across to support himself on the edge of the desk. His breathing was laboured, the excitement and the fear making his head swim and his heart race.

Katerina walked round casually, putting her fingers to his back, letting her long nails slide across his skin. She reached round and unbelted his jeans and then tugged them down slowly. When she passed her hand down between his thighs she found that he was erect, his penis a stiff rod of flesh in the soft cotton of his boxer shorts. She squeezed his hardness for a second, her fingers curling around the base, and then she slipped his shorts down too.

He closed his eyes, the shame of being exposed made worse by the knowledge that his hard cock was evidence of the arousal his intended punishment had caused. Despite the fear, the confusion and the sense of embarrassment, he was still excited by Katerina's touch. Emily was watching; she would be able to see that the threat of punishment did nothing to diminish his ardour.

'Patrick?' Katerina asked softly, cupping the coolness of Alex's balls in her fingers. Alex looked up and saw that Patrick was smiling, his eyes alight with unconcealed excitement.

'I think it only fair,' Patrick agreed.

'Be good,' Katerina warned Alex, tightening her fingers around his scrotal sac.

'Yes, Mistress,' Alex whispered, too afraid of his Mistress to resist. Katerina looked into his eyes and then stepped back, making way for her partner.

'In future, you will show me the respect due to your Master,' Patrick warned.

Alex readied himself, tensing his body and gritting his teeth. The sharp pain burned like a flame to his flesh as Patrick's heavy hand came crashing down. He barely had time to catch his breath before Patrick's second stroke landed. Again the pain swept through him, Patrick's hand swinging through the air in a tight arc that landed fully on Alex's behind. He could feel the heat burning on his bottom cheeks, the skin raised and imprinted with the finger patterns of Patrick's hand.

Alex closed his eyes again, unable to endure the steady rhythm of his punishment, the steady slap of flesh on flesh as Patrick's hand spanked him so vigorously that he felt the breath knocked out of him with each stroke. His backside ached, the smarting pain of each impact merging into a background glow that seeped through his body. He tried not to think of anything; not to see himself being physically chastised by another man, not to imagine Emily's eyes focused on his backside quivering with every stroke, not to think of the excitement that made his own cock flex harder and harder.

'Emily,' Patrick directed, suddenly, 'I want you under him, now!'

There was a momentary respite; the rhythm of hard-handed strokes was interrupted for a moment that felt too good to last. Alex looked down, past his cock with its silvery jewels of fluid seeping from the slit, and into Emily's wide, blue eyes. She looked up at him, her face as red as his own. He felt his shame redouble, and the humiliation amplify a thousandfold as she saw his pleasure measured by the hardness of his erection. He closed his eyes, unable to endure the degradation that merged with the dark and intense feelings of arousal that burned with the heat on his backside.

Emily's lips closed around his glans, her cool mouth working to suck away the droplets of pre-come that beaded its tip. He sighed softly as her mouth worked up and down his shaft, closing on his hardness with gentle firmness and the rhythm that she knew caused him maximum pleasure. He gasped as the sensations she awakened with her lips merged with the burning of the marks that covered his buttocks and the top of his thighs.

Patrick began to spank him again, beating down hard with the flat of his hand. Each time his palm landed, the intense pain caused Alex to jerk forward, to push his cock deeper into Emily's accommodating mouth. The pain grew stronger and stronger, as the pure pleasure that Emily worked with her agile mouth increased.

Alex uttered a strangled cry and fell forward, his legs no longer able to support him. It felt as though his body were alight, the sharp daggers of sensation on his naked bottom cheeks reaching a peak. He could hold back no longer; the seed exploded from his cock into Emily's mouth, flooding thick waves of come on to her tongue and down her throat.

He stood back shakily, gasping for breath and balance. Emily was on her knees in front of him, her eyes wide with pleasure, a strand of semen trailing from her lips. Patrick and Katerina were standing to one side, smiling. Alex looked down at his cock, smeared with spit and spunk but still rock hard despite the pain from his punished backside.

'We think we may have found a good home for you,' Patrick remarked casually, settling down comfortably in the sumptuous leather armchair that dominated the main living room. The sun had set an hour earlier and yet its light still streaked the blue sky pink, the patterns of light and dark hanging high over the horizon visible from the window.

The unfairness of it all still rankled. Alex felt as though he were being cast out for some unknown crime committed in all innocence. He said nothing but looked up at Katerina, who was sitting on the sofa while he knelt quietly at her feet. Idly, she patted him on the shoulder. 'I have explained the situation to you already,' she told him.

'You'll like Helen and Joanna,' Patrick continued. 'They're an interesting couple. It'll be a whole new experience, being in their house.'

'You don't want to go?' Katerina asked.

'No, I'd rather stay here, Mistress,' Alex complained

softly, relieved that he had finally been given permission to speak. Emily was upstairs, having a shower, giving him the chance to speak without having to worry about what he was saying in front of her.

Patrick smiled indulgently. 'I understand that you want to stay with your Mistress; that's commendable, but you can prove your devotion in other ways.'

'Why can't I prove my devotion here, sir? Why do I have to live elsewhere?'

'Because you're here to work for the wider community, not just your Mistress,' Patrick explained. 'All that was explained to you the first time you came here.'

Alex sighed. Patrick had, indeed, explained the rules when they'd met, but it had been a day full of such sexual highs that everything else had paled into insignificance. 'Let me stay a little longer – please?' he begged, looking to his Mistress for her support.

'These are the rules of our community,' Katerina told him, her voice soft and tender. 'Do you not think that I am aware that you need more time? Your training has barely begun, of that I am well aware, but there simply is no other way to do this.'

'You'll have time to see us every day,' Patrick chimed in. 'Your Mistress and I do not plan to neglect you.'

Was Patrick joking? Alex didn't know him well enough to judge whether his tone was sincere or not. He looked to Katerina but it was no clearer with her; were they playing some elaborate joke on him? The idea made him feel wretched. The only thing he was sure of was that there was to be no reprieve. He was going to have to stay with Helen and Joanna, whether he liked it or not.

'Do well, and you'll please me,' Katerina promised, letting her hand rest on his shoulder. He longed to kiss her fingers, to show her that he wanted to please her more than anything else in the world. Hadn't he done everything she'd asked?

'Yes, Mistress, I'll do my best,' he heard himself saying, still sitting obediently at her feet. He could not explain to himself what was happening, it did not make sense to him. There was something in him that Katerina had touched; she had awakened a part of him that had lain hidden for so long. For her, he had accepted a punishment from Patrick. For her, he had allowed his girlfriend to witness the abject humiliation of his being spanked by another man.

'Good boy,' Katerina whispered and Alex felt his heart beat faster. It was true; he was going to show her what a good boy he could be.

'Tomorrow afternoon, your Mistress will take you over to meet Helen and Joanna,' Patrick told him. 'While you are with them you must do everything that they ask. No matter how menial or how great the tasks they set you, you must comply. When we last spoke they said they needed somebody for at least a week, so don't imagine you're exiled there for the whole of the summer.'

'And, at least once every day, you will be allowed to come to this house,' Katerina added.

'There is one last thing,' Patrick said, leaning forward in his seat. 'We will expect you to observe and understand everything that you see here in Eden, and that includes what you see in the other houses that you visit. During your time with Helen and Joanna, we will expect you to learn about them, to gain insight into their lifestyle and their relationship. Do you understand? Part of your training will depend on how much you learn from those around you.'

Alex realised that Patrick was waiting for something; he was sitting forward and his voice was low and conspiratorial. 'Yes, I'll do my best, sir,' Alex promised.

Patrick smiled. 'Good boy,' he said, sounding a little relieved. 'Your Mistress has high hopes for you, and I'm sure you'll not want to displease her.'

'No, Mistress, I won't disappoint,' Alex promised. Each time he called her 'Mistress' he felt a thrill of pleasure, as if in calling her that he was proving to himself and to her just how much the bond between them meant.

122

'Good,' she replied. 'I'd like some coffee. You'll find everything you need in the kitchen.'

Alex stood up slowly, letting her stroke his bare back with her fingertips. It felt good to be touched by her, it excited him immensely; each whisper of a caress felt like a reward. He waited for a moment to see if there was anything else, but her attention had already shifted to Patrick.

The kitchen flooded with pale fluorescent light as soon as he entered it, the sensors on the wall detecting his presence as soon as he walked through the door. It took a while for him to find everything but he soon had the percolater on, the roasted aroma of freshly ground coffee weaving its pleasant spell.

'Smells good.'

Alex turned suddenly. He had been so preoccupied that he had not heard Emily padding in to join him. Her hair was wet and slicked back close to her scalp so that she looked cute and loveable, an effect that was enhanced by the long loose T-shirt which reached down to her knees. She was a picture of girlish innocence. He looked at her and felt his face redden with shame.

'Hello,' he whispered, looking away from her eyes.

'Hi,' she replied, walking over to lean on the counter beside him.

'I was just making some coffee,' he told her, desperate for something to say, to keep at bay the awkward silence that threatened to fall between them.

'Yes, I can see,' she replied. 'Did Katerina ask you to make it?'

He looked down at her bare feet, flat on the icy tiled floor. The loose white cotton shirt covered her to her knees, but he knew that she was probably naked underneath it. 'Did Patrick punish you earlier?' he asked hesitatingly.

'Yes,' she replied simply, without any obvious trace of embarrassment. 'He spanked me with a kind of rubber thing.'

123

He looked at her sharply. 'Did you enjoy it?' he asked.

Emily smiled. 'Sort of,' she admitted. 'I hated it at the beginning, but towards the end I was getting more and more turned on by it. I suppose it's the same when Katerina punishes you.'

'I suppose so,' he agreed, doubtfully. The idea of Emily being punished by Patrick in turn excited him and yet caused him pangs of jealousy. In all their time together, he and Emily had never really explored the idea of erotic punishment. It was something that had never even been a possibility.

'What's wrong?' Emily asked, turning to face him properly.

'Nothing.'

She took his arms and put them around her waist. 'Come on, Alex, what's wrong?'

She felt soft and warm and sensual in his arms, the thin cotton sliding over her perfumed skin. He held her close and inhaled the scent of her hair and the subtle aroma of her skin. He linked his hands behind her back and pulled her closer, letting her face brush his so that her lips touched him by accident.

'This is all so weird,' he whispered, nibbling softly at her earlobe. He reached down and cupped his hands around her bottom cheeks, gently squeezing the flesh that had been punished earlier.

'But this is what you wanted,' she whispered, leaning back so that they were face to face, her eyes gazing into his.

'I'm not sure what I wanted,' he admitted.

'You wanted Katerina,' she told him.

'Are you jealous?'

'No,' she stated, and he knew that she was telling the truth.

They kissed softly, their lips barely touching and their breath mingling. She felt so good to hold, so soft and sensual and loving. He pulled her closer again and massaged her backside, stroking her body, lifting the T-shirt higher and higher with each movement.

124

'You know – you know when Patrick punished me earlier . . .'

'It's okay,' she whispered. 'It turned me on. I loved watching you being spanked by him.'

The questions were there, bubbling in the back of his mind and filling him with doubt and shame. He had submitted to a man; it somehow seemed even worse than submitting to a woman. Emily's fingers traced a path from his chest – still bearing the faintest marks left by Katerina – down to the bulge in his jeans.

'You turn me on so much,' he whispered, 'I don't want you to forget that.'

'As if I would,' she giggled.

He cupped her breasts in the soft folds of her shirt, flicking her erect nipples with his thumbs so that they pressed against the material. She exhaled softly and then reached down to pull her shirt up at the front, exposing the full length of her legs and the strip of black hair above her sex. He touched a finger between her pussy lips and was rewarded with a sweet sigh of pleasure.

'Lean back,' he whispered, getting down on his knees in front of her.

She parted her thighs wide and leant back against the white topped counter, still holding the front of her baggy shirt up at waist level. He kissed her softly, starting at her feet and then, working upwards slowly, showering every inch of her flesh with hot, hungry caresses. Higher and higher, with lips and tongue and teeth, he explored her body eagerly, as though for the first time.

He began to kiss her between the thighs, his mouth pressing softly against her labia, his tongue flicking in and out of his lips as he teased her. Her pussy was sweetness itself, her sexual scent filling his lungs as he breathed deeply. She closed her eyes as he licked long and slow along her slit, skilfully opening her sex with his mouth. Her sighs of pleasure were all he needed to hear; he slipped a finger into her wetness as he lapped at the half-hidden pearl of her desire.

125

'Is this how you serve your Mistress?' Katerina demanded, her angry voice snapping Alex and Emily back to the moment. She was standing in the doorway with Patrick behind her, both of them looking angrily at the couple in front of them.

Alex stood up quickly, torn between the urge to laugh about being caught and the feeling of confusion that gripped him. Emily also looked flustered as she brushed her baggy T-shirt down, covering herself up guiltily.

'Perhaps it's better that you two are not going to be staying under the same roof for a while,' Patrick said, marching into the kitchen. His face was set hard and his eyes seemed cold and emotionless.

'I'm sorry Mistress,' Alex whispered, 'we just got carried away –'

'Silence!' Katerina snapped angrily. 'I'm not interested in your feeble excuses.'

'On your knees, both of you,' Patrick ordered.

Alex and Emily obeyed without question, dropping down to the cold tiled floor as though felled. Katerina looked at them harshly, her dark eyes sparkling with a cruelty that made Alex fear the worst. He knew that Emily, no matter how much he loved her, could never inspire the complexity of emotions that Katerina had turned on in him. She glared at them both for a moment and then strode to the other end of the kitchen, wearing a look of haughty disdain that seemed entirely fitting.

Patrick stepped forward, planting his feet wide and pointing to the space in front of him. 'Emily,' he hissed, 'come here.'

Emily turned to Alex. Her eyes were wide and full of excitement but he could also see the fear that surged through her. She crawled along the floor to Patrick, keeping her face to the floor so that she could avoid meeting his ice-cold stare. He stood over her and grabbed the hem of her white T-shirt and pulled it high over her waist, exposing her long limbs and the tight roundness of her backside.

'Haven't you been fucked enough, slut?' he hissed. 'Haven't you been beaten enough?'

'I'm sorry, sir,' she whimpered, as he glared at her exposed body.

He bent over and smacked her hard, landing a heavy slap on the side of her thigh. She yelped and cowered as he laid several more blows at the top of her thighs, marking her skin red with his fingers. He reached down and parted her buttocks, revealing the opening of her pussy and the tight rear orifice of her anus. He gazed at her for a moment, feasting his eyes on her cruelly exposed body, before thrusting his fingers into her pussy. She cried out and lurched forward to escape the rough movements of them in her sex.

'Isn't this what you want? Isn't this what you need?' he taunted, fucking her with his fingers.

Alex watched, horrified and fascinated by Patrick's violent penetration of Emily's compliant body. He felt the excitement in the air, the tension rising as Emily's cries of pain became unbridled cries of pleasure and she began to open herself to him. She rocked back, moving with the hard rhythm of Patrick's fingers as they plunged in and out of her wetness.

At last, Emily gave a strangled cry of pleasure, a scream that tore through the air, before she slumped forward convulsively. Her climax had been as violent and as powerful as Patrick's finger-fucking and, as she lay on her belly, her thighs were smeared with the slick juices he had drawn out with every stroke into her cunt. She stirred a few seconds later, pushing herself shakily on to her hands and knees again. Alex watched her as she knelt forward and pressed her lips to Patrick's shoes, kissing his feet softly; gratefully.

Katerina's heels were a staccato blast on the tiles, a click-clack rhythm that made Alex shiver with anticipation. He turned to see her advancing towards him, a heavy wooden spatula in her hand. He scooted forward quickly, kissing at her heels feverishly in a bid to win her favour and to make amends before the punishment commenced.

'It's too late for that,' she told him, slapping the flat side of the wooden implement against his bare shoulder.

He sat up, realising that it was his turn now to be the centre of attention. Emily seemed dazed by her experience. She was sitting at Patrick's feet, resting her head against his thigh, her eyes half closed as she watched the scene unfolding. 'I'm so sorry, Mistress,' he whispered. 'So very sorry.'

'Be quiet; I have no interest in stale apologies. It seems that you are in need of another lesson,' she said. 'Take off your clothes and bend over across the counter.'

He stood up and struggled with the buttons on his trousers, his fingers fumbling shakily. He managed to get half of the buttons undone, before he wriggling free of his jeans and undershorts. The counter was cool against his nakedness, the sharp lines digging into his skin when he bent across it. He turned to one side, keeping his face flat against the smooth surface, so that he could see his Mistress prepare.

She touched him with the flat surface of the wood, stroking it along the inner thigh and then across the curves of his backside. He was hard again, his cock pressed tight against the side of the counter, the head slippery with silvery fluid that leaked copiously in his excitement.

'Every stroke will hurt,' Katerina promised.

Alex moved his legs apart and closed his eyes, ready for the punishment to begin. He heard the whistle as the spatula moved through the air and then the world exploded in a white light of pure pain that touched his left side. The strength of the impact made his skin burn, and the snap of sound echoed through the cavernous room. He had no time to recover as Katerina brought the hard wooden implement down on the other side of Alex's backside. He tensed and jerked forward as it smacked down on his naked rear.

The smarting sensation spread quickly, moving across his punished flesh and then deeper into his being. Another stroke landed, slicing through the air to land flat on his right bottom cheek, the sharp stab of pain followed by a gasp that he could not hold back. The next blow landed at the top of his thigh, forcing him hard against the counter so that his cock rubbed wetly against the smooth surface.

Alex lost count of the number of strokes. He no longer thought of Emily watching; he no longer cared that his humiliation was being witnessed. Everything fell away until his attention was focused purely on the steady and unrelenting physical correction that his Mistress was so beautifully inflicting. The hot pain became blurred with pleasure, the heat of punishment seeping through to touch his cock and under his thighs.

The last few strokes were heaven and hell combined. They fell like fire on his reddened arse cheeks, adding to the heat that blazed through his body. His erect prick rubbed deliciously against the wet patch he had smeared on the flat surface of the side of the counter.

'No!' Alex cried suddenly. He moved back, pushing his buttocks against Katerina's hand as she pressed a finger against his anal hole. The pain on his backside was intensified by the feeling of being invaded and it peaked suddenly in a fountain of pleasure. His body quivered and jerked as he jetted thick arcs of semen on to his stomach and against the counter.

He moved back, standing hesitantly on his feet, and looked at the slippery pools of come that lay dripping from the edge of the counter. The tight curls of hair around his semi-erect cock were matted with thick drop-lets of sticky spunk. He turned slowly to face the others, his face burning with shame as he began to understand the full extent of what had happened.

Emily looked at him, her dark blue eyes unreadable. Was she disgusted by him? Did she think him weak for finding so much pleasure in the dark ritual of his punishment.

'What about the mess?' Katerina asked, using the wooden implement with which she had punished Alex to point to the pool of sperm that was dripping slowly to the floor. Emily crawled forward quickly, keeping on her hands and knees as she headed towards the droplets of come.

'No,' Patrick told her. 'Not this time.'

Katerina smiled. 'What about the mess?' she repeated, fixing her dark eyes on Alex.

He looked at her and then at the fluid that had squirted from his cock. He lowered his eyes, unable to resist Katerina's unspoken command. He knelt down quickly and pressed his lips to the edge of the counter. He lapped at the thick jewels of liquid with his tongue, tasting his own spunk, letting it fill his mouth. There was more on the floor; he bowed his head and kissed it all up, collecting it on his tongue.

He turned to Katerina and the others and opened his mouth. He let them see the creamy pool in his mouth and then he swallowed. Katerina's smile made him sigh with pleasure, his cock twitching to hardness once more. He had pleased his Mistress.

130

Nine

Helen and Joanna lived in one of the houses at the bottom of the hill, close to the main entrance to the estate. Katerina, dressed casually in black jeans and a loose burgundy sweatshirt, drove Alex down to their house a little after lunchtime the next day. The morning had started on a high, as far as he was concerned. He had bathed Mistress first thing, soaping and cleansing her body before patting her dry. It had been a delight to attend to her; to be allowed to touch her was pure bliss. His cock had been rock hard but she had ignored his obvious arousal, hardly deigning to notice his discomfort as he had clothed her.

At breakfast, which had been served by Emily, Katerina and Patrick had discussed the day's plans while Alex had knelt at her feet. He had been tempted to touch his lips to her feet, to kiss her softly as she spoke, but he was wary of being punished again. His being down on the floor had meant that he had been tantalised by glimpses of Emily's long legs as she had scurried back and forth serving Patrick. She had been wearing a tiny skirt that had moulded itself to the contours of her backside, and from where he sat he could see that she had nothing on underneath it.

Patrick had touched her several times as she'd served him, running his hands along the smoothness of her thigh or brushing his fingers against her pussy. Alex had watched in silence, tormented by the view and yet unable to act on what he saw. He longed to crawl towards Emily and to push his mouth on to her sweet pussy, to lick at the wetness he knew had to be there. Or else he had longed to slip under the table to pleasure his Mistress, and then to suck on her juices as she climaxed over his tongue.

After breakfast, he had been summoned into Patrick's office to talk about his allotted tasks. He had resigned himself to leaving the house. He could see there was no way he could get out of doing so. Only the thought that he would still be able to see Mistress sweetened the bitter pill.

Patrick had talked vaguely of the difficulties of recruiting suitable people for Eden, and Alex had listened inattentively. The main thing that Alex remembered had been Patrick's insistence that he report back on what he saw at Helen and Joanna's house. It was something that Patrick had made a big deal of and which Alex had accepted without comment. If reporting back was what Mistress and Patrick wanted then he saw no reason to argue, especially if he thought that doing a good job was going to please Mistress.

'Just try and relax,' Katerina murmured, steering the car off the track and towards the front of the house.

'Yes, Mistress,' Alex replied softly.

After lunch, he had gone to her part of the house to pack some clothes to take with him. She had joined him a little while later, walking in on him as he was getting undressed. Her presence had changed everything; the atmosphere seemed to have been altered, and he felt the charge in the air around him. Everything about her was sexual, every touch, every word, every gesture. He had undressed slowly while she had watched and then, when he was nude, she had smiled and motioned for him to come to her.

Her hands had travelled smoothly over his back and chest, her nails scraping softly against his skin. He had been afraid to make any moves; he was there for her

132

pleasure and he could not presume to take the initiative. She had touched him playfully, as though delighting in the freedom that his submissiveness gave her.

She had turned and walked back to her desk, leaving him naked in the middle of the room. He had watched, excitedly, as she had hitched up her loose skirt to reveal her long dark thighs and the sliver of satin between them. She had bent across her desk and parted her legs, thrusting out her behind so that her sex bulged against her panties.

In moments he was under her, kissing her intensely, pulling her panties aside so that he could tongue the wet slit of her sex. He sucked and kissed, lapping at the opening of her body, seeking the pulsing of her clit with his tongue. Her pleasure had turned to honey and he sucked at it, eager to taste his Mistress, to slake his thirst for her essence. She had moaned softly when the pleasure grew stronger, and had pushed her hips back, balancing on the points of her heels as he had buried his face between her thighs.

She had wet a finger in her pussy and then had pressed it deep into her rear hole, making herself cry out blissfully. He had then taken her finger and licked it clean, before pressing his mouth to her behind, wanting to caress every pleasure centre with his tongue. Her climax had made him stiffen even more, until he had teetered on the edge of ecstasy, his mouth paying homage to her body.

She had swivelled round quickly and pushed his face to her pussy, before curling her right leg over his shoulder. Her heel had snaked down his body, pressing painfully into his flesh as he had brought her closer to another climax. She had pushed herself higher, sitting on the edge of the desk as she fingered her pussy bud to the rhythm of his tongue deep in her cunt.

His climax had come a moment later, when she had dug her heel against the stiff rod of his cock. He had fallen back as the sharp pain had combined with the pleasure of orgasm, shooting his climax across her heels. There had been no need to wait for the command; he had lain flat on the floor and taken the hard point of her heel in his mouth, sucking off his spunk for her pleasure.

And now they had arrived in front of the house. Katerina had switched off the engine and was looking at Alex, her dark eyes full of questions.

'I was thinking back to what we did earlier,' he explained quietly.

'Good,' she remarked, smiling. 'A good slave always thinks of his Mistress first. Now, do not think of your time here as a punishment – it is not.'

'Yes, Mistress,' he replied, without enthusiasm.

They got out of the car and walked up the steps to the front door, which had been left slightly ajar. Katerina pushed the door open and stepped into the relative coolness of the house. 'Come on,' she urged Alex, 'they're expecting us.'

There were rooms on either side of the long hallway and, at its far end, stairs that led up to the first floor. The layout was similar to that of Katerina's house, but Alex noted that there were to be fewer doors leading off the hallway. Katerina led the way, walking through the house confidently, as though it were her own.

'They must be working,' she said, not finding them in the main living room next to the kitchen.

'What do they do?' Alex asked, glancing into the empty room. The place looked a mess – clothes and books were strewn all over the floor, magazines that had been piled high in a corner had toppled over and been left.

'They develop software together,' Katerina replied, showing him the way back towards the terrace.

The canopy was drawn down in the corner of the terrace, creating an oasis of cool shade in the otherwise blinding whiteness. A couple of chairs had been positioned under the shade, and there were desks, too, stacked with computer monitors, cables, printers and a pile of magazines and manuals. The tapping of the

134

computer keyboards was accompanied by a background hum of dance music from a CD player positioned between the desks.

The woman behind the desk on the left was young and spiky haired. She was peering at one of the computer manuals through little round glasses and chewing on the end of the pencil. Her attention seemed to be completely focused on her task, her eyes fixed on the book which was balanced precariously on the corner of her desk.

Her partner was sitting at the other desk, jabbing at the keyboard with sharp, jerky motions while she hummed softly to the music. She had long frizzy hair and light coffee coloured skin, full red lips and sultry dark brown eyes fringed with long lashes. She was wearing faded blue dungarees over a black top that was shaped by her generously proportioned bust, and her bare feet were visible under the desk.

'We'll be with you in a minute,' the first woman said, looking up suddenly from her computer manual. Her voice was cold and unfriendly, which matched the lack of welcome in her eyes.

The second woman looked up at Katerina and Alex and smiled, her dark eyes scanning Alex quickly. He smiled back, sensing that, of the two women, she was the one who wanted him there. 'Get yourselves something to drink,' she suggested, waving her hand in the direction of the kitchen.

'Thanks, Joanna,' Katerina said, taking Alex by the arm and leading him back into the house.

'What's wrong with the other one?' he asked quietly.

'Helen? She can be a bit difficult at times,' Katerina explained casually. 'Don't worry if she appears a little hostile at first.'

'You mean I'm not going to be welcome in their house?'

Katerina ignored the remark and pointed to the fridge in the corner of the kitchen. 'Drinks are a good idea,' she said.

135

Alex grabbed a couple of glasses from the dishwasher near the door and then walked to the fridge. 'Is there something going on that I should know about?' he asked over his shoulder.

'No. They need help around the house and you're available. That's all there is to it.'

He poured two measures of ice-cool orange juice and then turned back to face Katerina. She was looking at him with a half-smile on her face, her eyes filled with the look of amusement that he had noticed before. Was she laughing at him in some way? 'Then why did Helen look at me like that?' he asked.

'Because you're male,' Katerina told him simply. 'She doesn't like men in general, so don't take things personally.'

'Then I take it the relationship between Helen and Joanna extends –'

'We're lovers,' Helen said, walking into the room with Joanna by her side. They were holding hands, as if to make the point, though Helen's hostile gaze contrasted with Joanna's more relaxed smile.

'I think introductions are superfluous at this point,' Katerina said, leaning back against the kitchen table. 'Alex is here for as long as you need him.'

'I'll make this plain straight off,' Helen said. 'I don't like having men in my house. It fucks up the vibes, it causes an atmosphere, okay?'

'If you don't want me here . . .' Alex said, turning to face Katerina.

'It's your choice, Helen,' was Katerina's response. 'If you want the work done now, then Alex will do it. Otherwise, you wait.'

'No,' Joanna replied quickly. 'We're late as it is. I'm sure that Alex won't get in our way.'

Helen looked at Joanna sharply. 'I just want him to know, that's all,' she snapped. 'As far as we're concerned, the quicker you finish the better it is all round,' she added, looking at Alex coldly.

'I'll show you where to put your stuff,' Joanna suggested, detaching herself from Helen and indicating that Alex should follow her.

He looked at Katerina with a feeling of hopelessness. He was going to hate his time away from her even more than he had thought he would. She had told him not to regard his stay with Helen and Joanna as punishment, but already it felt like purgatory. Helen watched him go, her eyes without warmth or welcome.

He followed Joanna into the room at the top of the stairs, while trying to listen to the murmur of voices coming from the kitchen below. There was an argument going on, though he could not clearly make out what was being said. All he could hear was Helen's angry stage whisper, and Katerina's conciliatory and calming tones in reply.

The room was larger than had expected – a double rather than a single – but like the other rooms it looked a mess.

'Don't worry about Helen,' Joanna told him, sitting on the unmade bed and crossing her legs under her. She was smiling, the fullness of her lips parted over pearl-white teeth, and her smile seemed to light up her eyes.

'She doesn't exactly make me feel welcome,' Alex muttered, stepping over a box full of clothes and shoes to get to the large square window which faced the bed. He struggled with the catch, but it gave eventually and he pulled the window open to let the air into the room.

'We're late on a contract,' Joanna explained, 'so she's in ultra bitch mode.'

'That's not my fault, is it?' he complained, turning to face her. The faded dungarees were old and shapeless, but there was enough cling in the material to reveal her firm bust, encased by the tight black T-shirt she wore underneath.

'You'll get used to her,' she consoled him. 'She talks a mean fight but she's okay. No, really,' she assured him, when he looked unconvinced. 'She's okay.'

137

'Well,' he sighed, 'it sounds like she's giving Katerina a hard time down there.'

They listened to the murmur of voices from below; Katerina's voice was louder, the discussion more heated. 'Just leave them to it,' Joanna suggested. 'Have they told you what wants doing around the house?'

'I think I can guess,' Alex replied, surveying the untidy mess that littered the room.

Joanna laughed softly. 'Sorry. This was my room. We're not nearly as slobby as we look, it's just that with the amount of work we've taken on . . . Well, you know how it is.'

'So,' he concluded. 'I've got to tidy up the entire house and make sure it stays clean for a while.'

She nodded and then got up to walk to the window. 'And there's that,' she said, pointing down behind the terrace. Alex looked down at the garden area; it was growing wild. Grasses were fighting it out with weeds and thick undergrowth was invading the area beyond it. A mound of dark compost had been dumped in one corner and was beginning to sprout a wispy layer of yet more grasses, weeds and wild flowers.

'Let me guess,' he sighed. 'You've had so much work on that you've not been able to start the garden the way you'd planned to.'

'Yep,' Joanna agreed. 'That's it exactly. We don't want much, really. The compost's not for the garden; we wanted some stuff planted in pots for the terrace. Once you've done that, all that's left is for the garden to be weeded and the grass trimmed back to a manageable state.'

'I'll do my best,' he promised, without enthusiasm. 'I mean, I'm sorry I'm not a woman; Helen's obviously got a thing about having men in the house.'

'She's just pissed off because she was expecting to have Amanda to do all the work,' Joanna explained, whispering. 'She really fancied having a pretty little blonde around the house.'

'I can't help that; do you really think I wanted to be here? I wanted to stay up at the house with Katerina, Patrick and Emily.'

'Emily?' Joanna asked, turning back from the window to face him.

'Yes, she's my girlfriend. We're both here for the summer. To be honest,' he added, dropping to a whisper as she had done, 'I had expected to stay with them all through the summer. I didn't really expect to be dumped on other people the moment I arrived.'

'Listen,' Joanna said, dropping her voice to a whisper. 'Don't you dare mention your girlfriend in front of Helen – she'll hit the roof. She's only accepted you because she thinks she's got no choice. If she hears that there's a woman staying up at the top house then she'll demand her instead.'

'This is a fucking disaster,' Alex moaned unhappily. 'She'll blame me, won't she? I didn't make the bloody decision; it was Patrick. He's the one who decided that Emily had to stay with him and that I was the one who was going to come here.'

'It doesn't matter who made the decision,' Joanna warned him. 'Just keep it quiet. Okay?'

The sound of the front door slamming was followed moments later by the sound of the car accelerating away. Joanna looked at Alex and shrugged as they heard Helen running up the stairs.

'I was just telling Alex what needs to be done,' Joanna explained as Helen marched into the room.

'And I was just telling Katerina what needs to be done about this place,' Helen replied, looking pleased with herself. 'There have got to be changes and soon,' she added. 'Enough is enough. We built Eden to do more than serve as an arena for Patrick's ego or an advert for her bloody architectural practice.'

'None of this has got anything to do with me,' Alex informed her, defensively. He could see that Helen was fired up; she was breathing hard and her voice had a hard

139

aggressive edge to it. Things were becoming clearer now; he understood what Patrick had meant about an enclosed community potentially being a breeding ground for dissension. It felt as though he had walked into the middle of a battlefield; he made the perfect target for Helen – not only was he male, but he had also been sent to her house by Patrick and Katerina.

'Then you'll keep out of it,' Helen warned him. She walked over to Joanna and cuddled up to her. 'The quicker you get your work done,' she told him, 'the quicker you'll be out of here – which is what we all want.'

He watched as Helen put her arms around Joanna's waist and held her close. Joanna turned to her and they kissed each other softly on the mouth, faces pressed together, tongues entwined. Alex watched for a second and then turned away, embarrassed because he felt as though he were intruding.

'Can you cook?' Joanna asked him, turning suddenly towards him.

'A bit.'

'We're sick to death of microwave meals; make us something nice for tonight,' she suggested, good-naturedly.

'That's a good idea,' Helen agreed. 'It'll be good to eat something real for a change.'

'Okay, I'll do my best.'

'Thanks,' Joanna said, looking slightly relieved as Helen pulled her closer.

Helen looked at her watch. 'Do you want to call Scott or shall I?'

Joanna sighed audibly, her smile dissolving instantly. 'You phone him,' she decided. 'I'd better check if there's any news on the compiler bug. She turned to Alex. 'Start in the kitchen first, you can leave this stuff till later.'

'Anything you say.'

'We'd better get back to it, then,' Helen said, holding Joanna's hand tightly.

* * *

140

The two women worked through the rest of the afternoon, sitting under the canopy while the sun tracked slowly towards the horizon. Alex could see and hear them from the open kitchen window, sitting at their desks and working diligently at their keyboards. They hardly spoke, and when they did it was to discuss their work or to comment about the music that was playing in the background. They even took their phone calls sitting at their desks, and Helen would often cradle the phone under her neck so that she could type and talk at the same time.

At one point Joanna had come into the kitchen for a drink, padding barefoot across the tiled floor to the fridge. Her toe-nails were painted a vivid red that contrasted with the drab blue and black of her shapeless clothes – Alex had wondered at the contrast, suggesting as it did that there was more to her than the dreary clothes and a dull addiction to work. She had chatted for a few minutes, making small talk about the mess in the kitchen and about how behind they were with their project.

Her apology for the state of the kitchen was not unwarranted. Although on the surface it looked clean enough, it was only because everything had been shoved into the cabinets, drawers and units that lined the walls. Things had been dumped haphazardly all over the place, from cooking utensils to packets of rice to old newspapers; everything was disordered behind the gleaming counters and shiny white surfaces.

Alex had started with the intention of preparing an extravagant evening meal but had soon realised that it was a task doomed to failure. Apart from a freezer full of manufactured meals ready for the microwave, there was little else to eat. A thorough search uncovered a multitude of tins, rice, dried pasta and pulses, but nothing in the way of fresh ingredients. Many of the cans were battered and dented and had no labels so there was no way of telling what they contained. It would not have been so bad had all the food been in one place, but, instead, he kept finding packets of rice under piles of newspapers or tins of tomatoes hidden behind industrial-sized cartons of soap powder.

As the evening drew closer, he surveyed the bombsite that had once been a kitchen; drawers and cupboards were open and their contents sprawled across the floor in an effort to sort things out. The kitchen table was piled high with items of food that he had salvaged. The sink was stacked with unwashed plates and utensils that were furred over with interesting growths.

'What the fuck?' Helen gasped, stepping into the kitchen late in the afternoon. Alex looked at her, saw the horror in her eyes. She looked at him and then at the mess and then, much to his relief, she began to laugh. 'You've uncovered our guilty secret,' she confessed. 'We just kept stuffing things into the cupboards in the hope they'd go away.'

'About dinner tonight . . .' he began.

'We're starving, both of us,' she told him.

He smiled politely. 'Good. I'm sure you're really going to enjoy what I'm cooking up,' he promised.

'Great, what is it?'

'It's going to be a surprise,' he replied, looking quickly at the disastrous jumble of food piled on the table.

'Look,' Helen sighed, 'I'm sorry about being so nasty earlier. It's just that – well, there are lots of problems here that you don't know about. And, well, things are really hectic at the moment.'

'Sure. I understand,' he said, grateful for the conciliatory tone.

'Good. Well,' she said, backing out of the kitchen slowly, 'I'll just tell Joanna to expect a feast tonight then.'

Alex smiled grimly, wondering what the hell he was going to cook up out of the hotchpotch of stuff that he'd found. He walked to the window and saw Helen standing behind Joanna, leaning over to look at something on the computer screen. They were both laughing softly, looking relaxed despite the hard work they'd been putting in.

Helen seemed transformed; her face had seemed hard and angular, but without the anger she looked impishly attractive, her eyes sparkling behind her glasses.

Helen massaged Joanna's shoulders, her fingers easing away the tension so that Joanna closed her eyes and leaned back. They kissed again, softly, tenderly pressing their lips together, dark and pale skin contrasting beautifully. Joanna took Helen's hands and pulled them round, over her shoulders and down to her breasts. Helen kissed her again, pressing her mouth harder and more passionately.

Soon, Helen's hands were sliding under the loose cover of Joanna's dungarees to stroke and tease her breasts. She began to slowly gather up the T-shirt, pulling it higher and higher until she had uncovered Joanna's breasts under the rough denim of the dungarees. Joanna sighed softly as Helen began to play with her nipples, pulling gently at them or else smothering them with her fingers.

Alex watched, his excitement growing as he spied on the two women through the kitchen window. He was becoming increasingly fascinated by the contrast of their skin tones, and by the way Helen's fingers smoothed and stroked Joanna's flawless skin. He could not actually see Joanna's nipples under her dungarees, but he could imagine the globes of her breasts cupped lovingly in Helen's slim hands. His cock was hard, a pole of rigid flesh that pressed painfully into his jeans as he watched the two women together.

Joanna said something and Helen laughed before returning to her seat. They sat and faced each other for a while, Joanna smoothing her T-shirt back into place as they talked. They made notes and consulted thick scrolls of paper that had been churned out of the printer. Alex felt disappointed; he had hoped to see more of Joanna's body. He longed to see Helen suckle from Joanna's dark nipples, to see the two women naked in the sunlight, bodies entwined sensuously as they made love.

He turned back to the pile of food and grabbed a

packet of rice which he put on to boil. It wasn't going to be a feast but he felt bound to make the effort; anything had to be better than another microwave lasagne or tasteless curry. He worked diligently, sorting things out while the rice cooked; chopped tomatoes, tinned vegetables, a can of tuna and a packet of unidentified spices were the best he could do.

'How's it going?' Joanna asked, walking up to the hob while he put the vegetables into a bowl with the tuna.

'This is the best I could do, I'm afraid,' he apologised.

'It smells good.'

'How's it going with your project?' he asked, changing the subject quickly.

'We're three weeks late on delivery and our client's beginning to get jumpy,' she replied. She walked over to the window and pointed to Helen, speaking animatedly into the phone. 'She's just giving him a progress report and he's not happy about it.'

'Well, I'll keep out of your way,' he promised, 'and I'll make sure the house is sorted out for you. It's not much, but at least you'll not have that to worry about.'

'Thanks.'

He returned to the food and she wandered out of the kitchen and upstairs. The music had been turned off outside and he was vaguely aware of Helen arguing on the phone, the aggression in her voice loud and clear again. She was going to be in a foul mood again and he hoped that he wasn't going to be on the receiving end of it.

He felt sweaty and uncomfortable by the time the food was finished, and decided to go up for a quick shower before serving dinner. He walked into his room to get some clothes and then turned to walk towards the bathroom but stopped. For a second, he was transfixed by the sight of Joanna under the cascading water, but then he closed his door gently, careful not to disturb her or to let her know that he could see her.

His heart was pounding when he opened the door a

crack and looked again. Joanna had her back to him, completely oblivious to anything but the flow of water over her naked body. Her skin was smooth and glossy, the water glistening on her soft brown flesh. She was beautiful; there was no other word to describe her – legs that were long and lithe, a full, pert backside and a smooth flawless back. Her hair was tied back loosely with a ribbon, and hung down in long black tresses, drenched by the flow of water.

He watched, totally transfixed by the vision, his cock rock hard once more. She turned to one side and he thrilled at the sight of her bare breasts, glistening curves peaked with nipples that were large dark discs. She soaped herself lazily, running her hands over her breasts, massaging her body so that the white lather covered her nipples before washing it all away. The water ran down the slight bulge of her belly towards the dark bush between her thighs. She turned again, offering him another view of her backside, her fleshy buttocks perfectly shaped.

He wanted to look away. He felt slightly ashamed to be peeping secretly from behind the door, but at the same time he could not take his eyes away from her. Every curve of her body seemed to link directly to his desire, and when she moved he felt his cock grow harder. She was so innocent, washing away the tension of the day, her hands moving tantalisingly over her body while he watched and enjoyed the silent, distant pleasure of the voyeur.

The sound of footsteps on the stairs made him move back into the room. Helen had finished her call and had come up to report to Joanna. He listened carefully before taking another peek. Joanna had stepped out of the water and was standing in front of Helen listening. She was still wet, the water dripping from her body as she stood attentively, and then Helen began to undress, stripping off slowly while Joanna smiled.

Alex watched them kissing for a moment, their naked

145

bodies pressed close. It was too much; the excitement was becoming unbearable. Helen's breasts were small and pointed compared to Joanna's fuller roundness, with pink nipples that grew hard as they brushed against Joanna's chest. Soon Joanna's dark fingers trailed down Helen's back to rest on her backside, squeezing the bottom cheeks tightly as they kissed.

Helen's soft purr of pleasure seemed to float in the air as Joanna's fingers pressed even lower. Alex unzipped his trousers, unable to resist the temptation as he watched the two women making love. Helen moaned again, stepping forward on tiptoes as Joanna's fingers slid into her pussy from behind. Joanna held her with one hand and fingered her with the other, moving in and out with a slow, lazy rhythm.

Alex worked his hand up and down his cock, matching the rhythm of Joanna's fingers. He felt his face burning and his heart racing, but the guilty pleasure was too good to resist. He watched Helen's fingers moulding to Joanna's breasts and pictured himself touching the dark woman's gorgeous body. Then, as he focused on Joanna finger-fucking her friend, he fantasised that it was Joanna who was working her fingers up and down his hardness. When the two women kissed, he imagined Joanna's tongue entering his mouth, their breath mingling as the pleasure mounted.

When Helen cried out her climax, her body collapsing into Joanna's arms, Alex jetted thick spurts of come into his hand. He stepped away from the door quickly, suddenly afraid that he had been seen. He leant back against the wall, his cock still twitching and covered in a smear of thick semen, unable to tell whether Joanna's dark eyes had fallen on him at the moment of release.

146

Ten

Emily waited for an hour after Katerina's return before she knocked on the door of her study. She had watched Katerina from the window of her room, driving back from Helen's house in a pure fury, the car screeching to a halt outside. Patrick had been awaiting Katerina's return impatiently, pacing backwards and forwards in her study. The tense atmosphere did not bode well, and Emily had preferred to keep out of the way until she was sure that things were a little more relaxed.

Something was going on, probably something to do with Alex having been sent away, but she had no idea as to exactly what. She wanted to ask Patrick, but he seemed unapproachable. There was anger behind the charming expression he invariably wore. His pleasant smile was not matched by the cold steel of his voice or the fire in his eyes. She sensed that it was safer to keep out of his way; she knew instinctively that the burning anger inside him threatened to be expressed in ways that were cruel and painful, and yet exquisitely sexual. It was that edge of danger that made him attractive, drawing her close to the naked flame that threatened to devour her.

'Come in,' Katerina answered, eventually, waiting until Emily was ready to knock again. She opened the door gingerly and peered into the long, dark room. 'Yes?' Katerina asked, standing by one of the large, rectangular windows over which silver grey blinds had been drawn.

Emily entered the room properly, closing the door

quietly behind her. Katerina's part of the house was still off-limits, and she felt that she was entering alien territory. The large, open space functioned as Katerina's working area, but, with the blinds down, it seemed mysterious and forbidding; a dark domain, rather than a studio or an office.

'I just wanted to ask about Alex,' she said softly, walking across to where Katerina stood.

'What about him?' Katerina asked suspiciously, turning to face Emily.

'I just wanted to find out if he – if he liked Helen and Joanna,' Emily replied quietly. Was she making a big mistake? It struck her that, in some way, Alex was now Katerina's, that she owned him in an ill-defined but nevertheless real way – just as she herself belonged to Patrick.

'Alex is fine,' Katerina said, in a tone of voice that effectively finished the discussion. 'And what about you? How are you finding life with us?'

'I'm still getting used to it,' Emily told her.

'Have you got used to the idea of obedience yet?'

'I think so.'

'Show me,' Katerina challenged. 'Prove to me that you are an obedient little girl.'

Emily stared at her blankly. 'How?' she asked, annoyed by the way her own question had been brushed aside.

Katerina looked at her and then turned to walk back to her desk. Her eyes were unreadable; was she angry, sad, jealous? It was impossible to tell which dark emotion ran through her; whatever it was there was no doubt that it was black and brooding, Emily was certain of that.

'What do you want me to do?' Emily asked, trailing after her.

'I want you to show me how well you are taking to your training,' Katerina said. 'I want you to show me that you are ready to serve us properly.'

'How?' Emily sighed.

Katerina pulled one of the drawers of her desk open

148

and carefully extracted a coiled strip of glossy black leather. She looked at Emily without smiling and placed the strap on the desk in front of her.

'You want to strap me?' Emily asked, looking at the strap nervously.

'That would not be a test of obedience,' Katerina told her. 'Why, would you like me to strap you?'

'No.'

'You would prefer to be punished by Patrick?'

Emily hesitated before shaking her head. 'No, I don't think so.'

Katerina smiled. 'I think perhaps you're not being completely honest with me, perhaps not with yourself also. However, I want you to show me how obedient you are, and how willing to please. I want you to undress and then to use the strap on yourself.'

Emily smiled. 'You want me to punish myself?' she asked, relaxing a little. The idea of spanking herself seemed far less daunting than being spanked by either Patrick or Katerina.

'Yes, I want you to give yourself six strokes.'

'Six strokes?' Emily repeated, smiling broadly.

'Yes, six strokes. I want you to count them out for me. However, there is one proviso.'

'Which is?'

Katerina smiled. 'I want you to count out only those strokes which you think are worthy of being counted out; the rest you'll ignore.'

'You mean I only count a stroke if it feels like the sort I would have got from you or Patrick?'

'Correct.'

'But how would you know? I mean, I could just tickle myself with this strap six times and then I'm finished.'

'That's right,' Katerina agreed, her lips forming into a smile at last.

Emily undressed quickly, slipping off her skirt and her top but keeping on her lacy black panties. She looked sceptically at Katerina, who was regarding her with a sly smile. The leather strap was stiff and heavy; it uncurled as she picked it up.

'Lean across the armchair over there,' Katerina said, her tone of voice hovering between command and helpful suggestion.

Emily walked across to the chair and then bent herself across the padded arm, making sure that her backside was jutting high and that her feet were firmly on the ground. She gripped the strap and tried to bring it down hard, but there was no play, no room to swing or take aim. It was no good, and neither was the next position – on her knees with her upper body resting on the seat. Finally, she stood up and walked to the back of the chair where she stood, legs parted wide, with one hand on the chair and one hand free to swing properly. She was bent over very slightly, her legs straight and her breasts hanging free as she moved.

This time there was more room to manoeuvre and when she swung the strap round it hissed through the air before making contact with the side of her thigh. It stung slightly and when she looked she could see the faintest of pink marks on her leg. She tried again with the same result, a slight blush at the top of her thigh. She knew that she could have counted out two strokes, but the slight sting that had touched her was nothing.

She moved away from the armchair completely and stood defiantly in front of Katerina's desk. She kept her long legs straight and widely parted while she bent very slightly at the waist. Holding the strap tightly she moved her right arm across her body so that the leather whistled round and landed heavily on her left side, its tip stinging her right buttock hard. The pain was stronger, more intense, but still she did not count out the stroke.

'Like this?' she asked, swiping down hard again, putting greater energy into the movement of her arm. She gritted her teeth as the strap landed on her left side and the tip whistled right around again to slap hardest on her right bottom cheek.

Again – much harder this time – putting her weight into the agile movement so that the strap smacked down with a harsh slap of sound that echoed through the room. The sharp contact on her behind made Emily inhale quickly, sucking in air as the pain pulsed through her.

'One,' she whispered as her backside began to register the pain.

She tried again, varying the position so that the strap came down lower, marking the inside of her thigh with its wicked leather tongue. It stung painfully; when she glanced down she saw the imprint of the tip marked red on her pale skin. It had hurt, but she held her breath, not counting the hard stroke because it had not touched her backside.

The next few strokes were wasted; she could not find her target no matter how hard she tried. Her thighs were marked, and the painful sensations were pulsing through her body, but still she did not utter a single count. There was the knowledge that she could end it all by counting every stroke, but this was tempered by her pride – there was no way she wanted to appear weak in front of Katerina.

'Two,' she cried, as the lash finally made contact with her backside, falling squarely, and painfully, between her bottom cheeks.

'Three,' she gasped, when the fiery touch of the strap landed again on her right side.

The next few strokes were wide of the target; her thighs were marked and so was her lower back, but she did not count the strokes. It was so difficult to hit her own buttocks hard and accurately. No matter how hard she tried, she knew that she could not mark herself in the way Patrick would have marked her.

'Four,' she whispered. 'No – No, don't count that.'

Katerina was watching silently, showing neither approval nor disapproval.

When the next few strokes landed painfully but uselessly, Emily stopped. Her thighs and her bottom were marked haphazardly, little licks of red blurring painfully on her flesh. She held the strap tightly, but the frustration was building inside her, making her hit hard but aim wild. It had sounded so easy – she had smiled at the simplicity of the challenge – but she had not understood herself as well as she had imagined. Katerina had known; the bitch had understood precisely how Emily would think.

'Please,' she whispered, looking at Katerina pleadingly, 'you beat me.'

Katerina smiled. 'Why?'

'Because I can't hurt myself the way I need to be hurt. You knew that, didn't you? That's why you asked me to do it.'

Katerina took the strap and held it in front of her. 'You've counted out three strokes from more than a dozen,' she said, 'which is to your favour. However, if I take over I will start again – are you prepared to receive six hard strokes on top of the ones that have marked you already?'

Emily looked away, ashamed of the colour that marked her face. Desire was already burning inside her, triggered by the sensations that touched her reddened skin and by the vision she had of herself being beaten. 'Yes,' she said softly. 'I'll take my punishment in just the way you say.'

Katerina walked round slowly and passed her fingers up over Emily's punished bottom and then down the inner thigh that had been marked red. Her fingers trailed gently up and down, easing closer and closer to Emily's pussy but never quite brushing against the warmth and the wetness of the girl's panties.

Emily cried out when the silky touch of Katerina's fingers was suddenly replaced by the hard impact of the strap across her behind. The pain wrapped around, touching both her bottom cheeks with a cruel intensity that washed back to leave a smarting glow. It was the first of six, each delivered with a perfect aim and a power that made Emily cry out every time.

152

The sixth stroke still burned like lava, when Emily's panties were pulled down roughly. She opened herself instinctively, whispering wordlessly as Katerina's fingers plunged into the velvet pocket of her sex. The pleasure washed through her with all the intensity that the strap had kissed to her behind. She climaxed quickly, shuddering as she fell into Katerina's welcoming hands, the sting of her behind connecting to the pleasure in her sex.

Alex woke up early, with sunlight bright in his eyes. It had been a difficult and tormented night that had finally given way to a deep sleep early in the morning. His dreams were gone but his cock was still hard, evidence of the images that had taunted him throughout the night. He lay back in bed, lazily stroking his erection with the tips of his fingers, as the sun warmed his naked body.

The door to his room was closed but he was aware of the soft whisper of voices that carried from across the landing. Helen and Joanna were awake; he could hear their stifled giggling and their soft moans of pleasure as they made love in the morning light. He tried to block out the sounds but instead his mind was filled with images of what they would be doing. He was haunted by the memories of watching Joanna shower; her wet, glistening body filled him with a desire so strong that he felt close to orgasm just thinking of it.

The women had made love noisily during the night, ignoring his presence in the room across the hall. No matter how hard he tried to sleep, the soft murmuring of their voices, punctuated by their cries of pleasure, had forced him awake, his erect cock aching for release. It was only when they had drifted off to sleep and silence had reigned that he was able to sleep too – and even then his dreams had been deeply erotic and strangely disturbing.

Nevertheless, he resisted the urge to stroke himself to orgasm. Strewn around the room was a reminder of the work that lay ahead: boxes packed with clothes were stacked all over the place, books and magazines were lying around, Joanna's things were stuffed into wardrobes and drawers almost at random. He grabbed a towel and some clothes from his bag and then listened at the door – he was grateful for the silence.

He opened the door a crack and checked that the bathroom was empty. He felt vaguely disappointed that Joanna was not there under the water, or making love with Helen, as though for his benefit, but also a sense of relief that he could get on with things. It was still early so he had plenty of time to have a shower before going down to prepare breakfast. As he walked to the bathroom he glanced across the hallway to the other bedroom, the door of which was ajar. At first he could see nothing, but gradually, as he drew closer to the bathroom, the bed the two women shared came into view.

Joanna lay flat on it, on her back, with one leg cocked and her arms by her sides. She was naked but for a pair of high-cut white panties which barely covered her backside or the dark mound of her sex. Her breasts were bare, her dark nipples erect and ringed with glistening circles where Helen had been sucking them. Helen was beside Joanna, completely naked, her skin tanned by the sunshine that covered them both.

Alex stopped still, unable to take his eyes from the two women, enticed by the image of their differing bodies side by side. Helen was lying on her stomach, talking softly to Joanna, whose hand rested on the small of her lover's back. He realised that just as he could see them, they would be able to see him. He crept quickly into the bathroom and carefully closed the door, hoping that they had not noticed him. He inhaled sharply, vowing not to spy on the two women having sex, knowing that it was the wrong thing to do; that it was a sleazy, sick, unfair thing to do. But, when he breathed out, he exhaled all of his resolve – he needed to watch them, even if he was tormented by guilt and shame afterwards.

Joanna was cupping her own breasts, her fingers clasped tightly around the large round globes of flesh, her nipples pressed together. Helen was on her side, moving in closer so that she could flick her pink tongue against the hard coffee-coloured nipples. Her hand was sliding slowly down between Joanna's thighs, her fingers passing over the bulging mons and then down to stroke the pussy lips concealed by the lacy white covering of Joanna's panties.

Alex watched as Helen's fingers pressed harder and harder against the white panties, pushing the material in against the dark pussy lips as though using it to scoop up Joanna's sex juices. He was fascinated by the sheen of Joanna's dark skin, her dark flesh radiant in the sunlight. She moaned softly and parted her thighs, bending her knees and drawing her feet closer so that her pussy bulged deliciously against the thin white lace that Helen was stroking.

She squeezed her breasts again, exhorting Helen to feast on her nipples and, as Helen did so, Joanna closed her eyes and shivered with pleasure. Helen's mouth was teasing each fleshy nub in turn while her fingers eased back and forth between Joanna's thighs. Joanna sat up for a moment and her eyes suddenly locked with Alex's. His face coloured instantly, the shame burning his flesh like a hard slap across the cheek but he could not turn away. Joanna closed her eyes as Helen's fingers finally slipped under the tight white briefs and into her pussy.

Joanna half opened her eyes and smiled at Alex, looking over Helen's shoulder and directly towards him. He could not smile back; instead his face burned redder still as his heart pounded in his chest. Joanna turned over suddenly, rolling on to her stomach before pulling herself up on to her hands and knees. Helen began to nuzzle Joanna's backside, smothering her firm bottom cheeks with loving kisses as she eased the tight panties down slowly.

Alex felt his cock harden even more, his prick becoming impossibly rigid as his eyes fixed on Joanna's beautiful backside. Her panties were down, and the thin white strip of material was now stretched between her long thighs. The deep, inviting cleavage of her rear opened at the join of her thighs, her dark pussy lips like petals that opened on a pure pink heart within. Helen was spreading her kisses over Joanna's bottom cheeks, her lips pressing between them and then moving down to sup long and slow between the pussy lips.

Joanna was moaning softly, her voice growing louder and louder as Helen's fingers and mouth worked faster and faster. She cried out her orgasm suddenly, pulling her bottom cheeks apart so that she was open, exposed, invaded by Helen's skilful fingers and tongue.

Alex stepped back and closed the door, unable to take any more. His cock ached and he felt the fire in the pit of his belly but he dared not touch himself. He was breathing hard as he rested against the back of the door, his eyes closed so that he could revel in the images in his mind.

Helen was in excellent spirits at breakfast; all signs of her bad mood of the previous day had vanished. She chatted to Alex about the work that needed doing around the house and garden, though Joanna did not say a word as she drank the coffee he had prepared for them. If Helen had noticed the slight flush of red on Alex's face she was saying nothing about it. Nor did she seem to register Joanna's silence, or the fact that she and Alex did not exchange a single word of greeting.

He felt relieved that Joanna had not told Helen about his spying on them; were she to find out, he was certain that her anger would have been explosive. Helen not knowing was the only light in the situation – he felt ashamed of what he had done, and yet excited by it and by Joanna's silent complicity. Why had she kept quiet? When she had seen him watching she had half smiled and then carried on, exciting him even more as she climaxed in front of him. Had she been turned on by his presence?

'Where will you start today?'

'Sorry?' Alex suddenly realised that he'd lost track of the conversation.

'I said,' Helen sighed, 'where will you start? In the garden or in the house?'

The thought of working in the garden, under Joanna's direct gaze, was not something that instantly appealed. 'In the house, I think,' he replied, not daring to glance at Joanna despite the feeling that she was looking directly at him.

'As you like,' Helen told him brightly. 'There is one thing, though,' she added. 'Make a shopping list for some food and I'll send the order by modem – we might as well eat properly while you're here.'

'Right, I'll do it later this morning,' he promised.

'I'll get started,' Helen sighed, turning to Joanna. 'I'd better log on to see if there's any more news on that bloody compiler.'

'Yes,' Joanna agreed mechanically, 'you'd better do that.'

'I'd better get started too,' Alex said. 'I want to clear my room up first.'

'As you like,' Helen said, downing the last of the coffee. 'And don't forget that shopping list.'

He bounded up the stairs quickly, making his getaway before there was any chance of his being left alone with Joanna. How could he face her? How could he explain away his guilty voyeurism? He closed the door to his room and sat on the bed, his heart beating hard as he listened for footsteps on the stairs. There was nothing; Joanna had not followed him up as he had feared she might.

His window overlooked the front of the house, so he had no view of the terrace. He waited for a long while, standing at the window and staring across the green, open space of Eden, until he was certain that Joanna was not coming upstairs. It was only a temporary reprieve; he knew that there would be a confrontation finally. In a household of only three people he could not avoid being alone with her forever.

157

When he felt it was safe, he opened the door and listened carefully – the silence sounded perfect. He walked to the bathroom and looked out from the window, but it was difficult to see anything under the canopy on one side of the terrace. He realised that the best view had to be from the other bedroom. He walked across the hall quietly, feeling all the more nervous that he was going to enter the room Joanna and Helen shared.

He stopped at the door and peered in. There was far less mess in the room than in his; things were neatly arranged and, apart from the discarded clothes and the unmade bed, everything else seemed well ordered. The window was open and he thought he could hear the steady tapping of the keyboards from outside. He had good reason to be there, he told himself. The bed needed to be made and the discarded clothes put in the laundry basket in the bathroom and it wouldn't take more than a second or so to see if Joanna had joined Helen out on the terrace.

He took two steps towards the window and then stopped, his attention caught by the white lace panties that lay on the bed, half hidden by one of the pillows. Joanna's white panties; the ones that she had been wearing that morning, the ones that Helen had eased down before pressing her lips to the black woman's pussy. He was physically excited by the memory, his cock twitching to erection as he stared at the flimsy garment casually cast aside after the two women had made love.

He sat on the edge of the bed, his erection bulging painfully in his tight jeans. He reached out slowly and touched the panties; they were still moist with the juices that had run from Joanna's pussy as Helen had fingered her. He closed his fingers around the garment and then brought it to his face to breathe in the scent of her pussy, to feel the wetness that had poured from her body. The heady aroma of her sex made him shiver with pleasure, her aphrodisiac scent filling his lungs as he pressed the soiled panties to his face. The crotch was still so very wet,

158

soaked through by Joanna's pleasure and, when he licked softly, he was rewarded with a taste of her body.

His erection was painful and the feeling of tension deep inside him was growing stronger, coiling tightly and aching for release. He unzipped himself without thinking, freeing his hardness as he tugged his trousers down. He lay back on the bed, breathing hard through the moist panties so that he could imagine himself closer to Joanna's naked body. The pleasure pulsed through him, leaving him on the edge of orgasm and robbing him of all reason and self-control. He took the pussy-moistened panties and wrapped them around the base of his cock, the silky sensation making him shudder and sigh.

'Let me do that.'

He looked up suddenly, the shock pounding through everything to bring him back to his senses. Joanna was standing in the doorway, watching him wrapping her panties around the stiff, fleshy pole of his cock. She was wearing a loose wraparound skirt and a tight white top that was moulded to the contours of her body.

'I'm sorry . . .' he whispered, lying back and closing his eyes as the shame burned like a fire inside.

She came and sat beside him on the bed, her body so close to his, her loose skirt sliding open to reveal an expanse of smooth dark thigh. He dared not look at her, afraid to meet the anger or the scornful disdain that had to be in her sultry eyes. When her fingers entwined with his around the base of his cock he shivered with pleasure. He withdrew his hand to leave her fingers entangled in the soft lace of her panties around the stiff pole of his hardness. Her fingers tightened and he felt the pleasure redouble.

'Were you watching me last night?' she asked softly, sliding her hand up and down his cock.

Her voice was low, breathy and without the harsh edge of anger that he had feared. 'Yes,' he admitted finally, 'but I didn't mean to . . . Not in the beginning.'

She worked her fingers magically, bringing him ever

closer to the peak of pleasure without pushing him over the abyss. The feel of her fingers wrapped in the moistness of her panties and rubbing against the skin of his hardness was a bliss that he wanted to endure for always.

'And this morning?' she asked.

'I didn't know that I'd be able to see you like that. I'm sorry . . .'

She smiled, looking at him lopsidedly as he closed his eyes to the pleasure. 'And now?'

'I just wanted to be close to you,' he whispered, his voice trailing to a sigh of pleasure as she teased him with her fingers.

'Close to me?' she repeated.

'You're – you're so beautiful. I just wanted to be close to you, to suck the taste of your pussy into my mouth . . .'

Joanna leaned over and kissed him softly on the mouth, taking the breath that escaped from his lips in a long, ecstatic sigh of pleasure. 'You mean you wanted to be close to me in the same way that Helen is close to me?'

'Yes . . . yes. I want to put my mouth to your pussy.'

'Do you know that Helen likes to wear my things? Is this why you're using my knicks?'

'Yes . . . yes, I'd wear your things. I'd do anything you want me to.'

Joanna stood up and unclipped her skirt, letting it float to the floor behind her. She was wearing tiny black panties under it, which she removed to expose her sweet pussy to his eyes. He moaned softly as she sat astride his face, pressing her backside over his mouth as she continued to play her hand up and down his cock. He pressed his face between her thighs, flicking his tongue over the full, puffy lips of her sex. She sat lower and he tasted her nectar, his tongue sliding between her dark sex lips to suck at the jewels of her essence.

He climaxed a moment later, his cry of pleasure uttered directly to her sex as he sucked long and deep. Thick waves of spunk spurted into the tight white bundle that she held around his glans, catching his wetness just as hers had been caught earlier.

'I've got to go now,' she told him, pressing the soaked undergarment to his face. He lapped at it wetly, tasting himself as he licked, searching for the mingling of their sex juices. 'Helen will be wondering where I am,' she explained hurriedly. 'I wish I could stay longer; I like the way you use your tongue.'

'Make up a story,' he suggested, sitting up to watch her wrapping her skirt around her waist.

'No, she'll go mad if she finds out about this.'

'Look, I'm sorry about spying on you.'

She looked at him and smiled. 'I enjoyed fucking with Helen and knowing that you were watching. I want you to watch us again, this evening, when we shower together.'

'If that's what you want.'

'There's one other thing,' she said, bending over to kiss him quickly on the lips. 'I want you to wear something of mine. I want you to wear these,' she breathed, pointing to the black panties that she had dropped to the floor.

'You want me to wear your knickers?'

Joanna smiled. 'Yes, just my knickers for now.'

He lay back after she went and closed his eyes. Her taste still lingered in his mouth, tantalising him because he hungered for it even more. If only there had been more time . . . He longed to make her climax over his mouth, to tease her to orgasm with his tongue the way he did with Mistress. The warmth and the sunlight conspired with the afterglow of his pleasure to make him feel dreamy. After a while, he shook the feeling from his head and sat up. He had work to do – he picked up Joanna's black panties and touched them to his face before putting them on slowly.

Eleven

Katerina was already downstairs working when Emily went down for some coffee. Emily had spent the night in Patrick's bed, serving him with her mouth and body to give him the pleasure he demanded. Her own pleasure had been denied; each time she tried to touch herself he had punished her until, in the end, the punishment itself had become the focus of her desire. Even the spanking of her breasts had been a pleasure filled with pain, the hard smacks on her nipples feeding back to the desire that flooded her pussy with wetness.

No matter how much she had begged, he did not fuck her. Instead he had come in her mouth, his hardness pulsing wads of salty juice deep in the back of her throat. She had pleaded with him to let her sit astride his cock, to feel his hardness pressed deep into her cunt, but that, too, had been denied. When it was over – when her mouth was filled with the taste of his seed and her body tingled all over with the red marks of her punishment – she was given a choice; curl up beside him and go to sleep, or go back to her own room.

She had chosen to stay with him, preferring the warmth of his body and the steady rhythm of his breath to the cold, empty bed in her room. He woke her up just after dawn, the feel of his fingers rubbing insistently on her nipples awaking the desire inside her again. This time he rubbed his penis between her bottom cheeks, stroking it against her pussy lips until she moaned with an angry, needy complaint. She wanted him desperately, urgently. She wanted to feel his cock rubbing deliciously against her clit; to feel him open her pussy with his hardness; to feel *him* inside *her*.

He had teased her for a while, and then, when she could take no more, he had pushed her face down towards his cock. Her fingers moved to her pussy instantly, assuaging the yearning ache inside her as she mouthed his stiff shaft. This time he was merciful, allowing her to play with her pussy as she sucked deliriously on his cock. She climaxed several times before he let go and filled her with another mouthful of his seed, causing her to climax once more in turn.

He was gone when she woke up the second time, when the sun was higher in the sky and the heat of the morning was starting to make itself felt. She padded across the landing to her room to put on a baggy T-shirt to cover her nakedness. There was no sign of Patrick upstairs or downstairs, though she could hear Katerina working behind the closed door of her studio.

She made herself some coffee and sat down at the table. What was Alex doing, she wondered? He hadn't been happy about going to stay with the other women, that was for sure. He had wanted to stay with Katerina; she was the real reason for his being at Eden. He wanted to be with her.

Emily recalled how she had begged for Patrick's cock, pleaded to be allowed to ride him or to have him fuck her. Was that what she wanted? She tried not to think about it but the memory of begging to be fucked disturbed her. The more she had begged, the more desperate her pleas, the more excited she had become. And the more excited her entreaties, the greater the vehemence of Patrick's refusal had been. She didn't need to beg, she had never begged . . .

'Tomorrow, you'll be up early to make breakfast,' Patrick told her, walking into the kitchen from the door

163

to the terrace. His voice sounded relaxed and indulgent, as though he felt completely in control and everything was as it should it be.

She had been startled by his arrival but she tried not to show it. 'Do you want me to make something now?' she asked, getting up from the table.

He laughed. 'You're an hour too late.' Then, with a smile still on his face he added, 'Tomorrow you'll receive a stroke of the cane for every minute that you're late.'

She looked at him, at the charming smile and the clear blue eyes, and knew that he was serious. 'I won't be late,' she assured him quietly, turning away from his piercing gaze.

'Come with me,' he said, turning on his heel and heading out of the kitchen. She followed quickly, up the stairs and into the bathroom.

'Another little test of obedience,' he explained.

'Another one?' she asked, and then regretted saying anything when he looked at her angrily.

'Learn to hold your tongue, young lady,' he warned. 'Your mouth can get you into trouble far easier than it can get you out of it.'

'I'm sorry. It's just that – how many times do I have to be tested? Does it always have to be like this?'

'Don't you dare presume to question,' he told her coldly. 'You're here to be obedient and to learn, and if we choose to test that obedience, then that is our right. Do you understand? Well?' he snapped, 'Do you?'

She nodded her answer, afraid that if she opened her mouth one more time she'd say something that she would regret.

'Get down on your knees,' he hissed. She obeyed instantly, dropping to the floor and crawling towards the corner that he pointed to. He stood in front of the toilet and unzipped himself, glancing down by his side to make sure that she was watching everything. His penis was half erect when the stream of pale golden fluid jetted out, splashing down into the white porcelain toilet bowl.

164

She watched with total fascination as the stream of liquid hissed from the slit in his cock, the translucent urine forced out powerfully from his body. It felt odd to be watching him relieve himself; it was such a private, intimate act that to watch him was more shocking than anything she had seen or experienced at Eden. Her eyes were fixed on the end of his penis, on the fountain that poured from his glans.

As she watched, the flow began to lessen, the jet losing its strength as he passed his fingertips through it. She gasped, shocked by his action, and was then horrified when he offered his soaked fingers to her mouth. Her eyes widened as she stared at the droplets of fluid that innocuously dappled his fingertips.

'I can't,' she whispered, appalled by the act she was being asked to perform.

'Do it!'

'Patrick,' she whispered, 'I can't.'

He looked at her scornfully and then wiped his fingers on a piece of tissue by the toilet. His penis was growing harder as he held it in the fingers of his other hand; a large, heavy droplet of piss balanced precariously on the slit at the top. He was waiting, his erection growing as she watched, the sparkling droplets of fluid oozing from his glans.

'Show me that you're an obedient little slut,' he whispered.

She moved forward, unable to resist, her heart pounding as the excitement made her breath run faster. An obedient little slut. She inched forward, opening her mouth as the excitement in the pit of her belly grew stronger. Her pussy was already wet and she could feel herself melting with pleasure. An obedient little slut.

She closed her lips around the top of his hardness, her mouth trapping the fluid that oozed from his body. She tasted him on her tongue, the watery liquid diffusing through her mouth as he became harder. He jerked his cock deeper into her mouth, releasing more of the salty fluid so that she could suck it down.

An obedient little slut. The thought of what she had done, what she was doing and what she was going to do made her feel dizzy. The wet heat swept through her as he began to fuck her mouth, stroking his hand through the dark hair of his obedient little bitch.

The feel of Joanna's panties against his skin was a constant distraction as Alex worked. Each time he moved he felt the silkiness against his hard cock, reminding him not only of what they had done together that morning, but also that she was wearing nothing under the loose skirt that flapped in the pleasant breeze that wafted across the terrace. He tried to work diligently, wanting to clear the kitchen up completely before starting on the rest of the house. That he could look out of the window at Joanna, and that she frequently wandered in for a drink, was purely coincidental – or so he told himself.

The first time she came in she leant against the counter and let her skirt fall open, revealing the full extent of her lithe thighs and giving him a glimpse of the jet black curls of hair around her sex. She was playing a game, pretending that the exposure was accidental, and he in turn pretended that he had not noticed. She laughed and came over to him and slowly unzipped his trousers.

'Just checking,' she whispered, closing her fingers around the silky satin of her panties that clothed his crotch.

'That feels so good,' he whispered hotly.

'I like the idea of your hard prick inside silky lingerie,' she told him, sliding her hand inside the panties. 'I'll have to find more things for you to wear.'

A scream of frustration from Helen, out on the terrace brought them back to reality. She came storming into the room a few seconds later, by which time Alex was back at his chores, sorting out the accumulated junk that had been stashed in the cupboard units.

'That bloody bastard!' she hissed venomously. 'You'll never bloody guess what he's done.'

'You're talking about Patrick,' Joanna guessed, putting some coffee on.

'Who the fuck else?' Helen responded angrily. ' Do you know what his latest plan is? He only wants to buy the plot of land next to this one so that he can expand the community. Did you know about this?' she demanded, glaring at Alex.

'No, I don't know anything about his plans,' he told her quickly.

'Well, what he wants to do is build up the place next to this,' she explained furiously. 'Except that he wants to pack more buildings in a smaller area, and he's not going to bother with any of the equal shares crap either. This time he's going to make it clear that he's the boss.'

'Who told you all of this?' Joanna asked calmly.

'Does it matter?'

'It matters if it's true or not,' Joanna said patiently. 'Was it Oliver again?'

'He's got a contact in the planning department of the local council,' Helen told her.

'But how would he know about the equal say business?' Alex asked softly.

'You keep out of this!' Helen cried violently. 'You're here to work for us, nothing more! You keep out of our business!'

Alex felt his own anger rising but he kept quiet, afraid that if he said anything it would cause even more trouble. Helen was glaring at him, almost as if she wanted him to answer back, relishing the chance to fight and argue.

'Have you spoken to Katerina about this?' Joanna asked, her voice cool and calm despite her partner's rage.

'Why the fuck should I talk to her about it? You know the bitch does as he tells her to.'

'Because he might be doing this behind her back,' Joanna suggested reasonably. 'You know how paranoid he gets. What makes you think he trusts her any more than he trusts anyone else?'

Helen shook her head, unwilling to listen. 'They're in this together Jo. You know that,' she insisted. 'We've got to stop them; you know we have.'

Alex wanted to join in; he wanted to tell Helen to listen to Joanna, to listen to reason, rather than to rage and scream defiantly without knowing the facts. Helen looked at him coldly, as though he were to blame for what was going on. He looked away, frustrated by having to keep his mouth shut but unable to do anything else. Things were complicated enough without his becoming involved in their internal community arguments.

'We've got work to do,' Helen reminded Joanna, sullenly.

'I'll be out in a minute,' Joanna promised. 'I'm just waiting for the coffee to brew. I'll bring you a cup.'

'Be quick,' Helen said, before returning to her desk on the terrace.

'You'd better keep out of her way for a while,' Joanna suggested quietly.

'I'm going to, don't worry,' Alex replied, relaxing a little now that Helen was outside. 'She's got a real attitude problem when it comes to Patrick and Katerina, hasn't she?'

'You don't know enough about this,' Joanna cautioned, 'so Helen's right – keep out of the argument.'

'I'm sorry,' Alex whispered, chastened.

'That wasn't meant as a reprimand, just a bit of friendly advice.'

'Is life always this complicated here?'

Joanna sighed wistfully. 'Yep, always. Now, go upstairs for me, into my old room, and wait.'

'Should I undress?' he asked hopefully.

'Yes, go on. I'll be up in a minute.'

He walked through the kitchen trying to appear casual, just in case Helen should happen to glance in through the window. He bounded up to his room quickly, and undressed down to the silkily feminine underwear that pressed tightly against his thick erection. The feel of the soft material was tantalisingly sensual against his hardness, rubbing delightfully whenever he moved.

Joanna came in a second later. She smiled and went straight for one of the boxes piled up in the corner of the room. Despite the apparent disorder, she seemed to know exactly where to find the things she was looking for.

'Here,' she said, handing him the pretty bundle that she had retrieved. 'Put these on.'

He looked at her and then at the pink lace suspender belt with matching stockings and a garter. 'You want me to wear these?' he asked, looking embarrassed.

'Yes, all of them. I want you to wear my things. It turns me on thinking about a man wearing my lingerie close to his skin. I've got to get back to work, now,' she added, 'but I want you to wear them for me.'

'It – it doesn't feel right,' he said, trying to explain away his reluctance to do as she asked. Wearing her panties was one thing; it seemed like a romantic, sexy thing to do, but wearing her stockings and suspenders was something more serious.

Joanna shrugged. 'If you don't want to play this game . . .,' she let the statement hang in the air as she left.

He looked at the things she had given him and imagined the pretty pink things close to her skin; the contrast of dark flesh and pale silk worked its way into his imagination. His cock bulged and flexed in the silky trap of her panties, arousing his excitement even more. He took the suspender belt and put it on, doing up the catch in front of him then passing it round to the back. The stockings were a soft, diaphanous delight as he pulled them on slowly. The garter he put on last, rolling it up to the darker top of the stockings.

He looked at himself in the mirror on the wardrobe, where only the bottom half of his body was reflected. His cock jutted out from the constricting tightness of Joanna's lingerie, emphasising the contrast between his masculinity and her femininity. When he moved it felt like heaven; sensations he had never imagined touched him between the thighs. He turned and looked over his shoulder; his long stockinged legs led up to the black strip of the panties which were pulled tight between his bottom cheeks.

Putting on his trousers on top of the stockings suddenly seemed like sacrilege, a denial of the sensuality that her things engendered in him. When he walked, however, he felt as though she were there, caressing his body with feather touches and soft, whispered kisses.

Having walked downstairs, he looked at Joanna from the kitchen window and smiled; she understood and smiled back approvingly.

Emily lay on her back, naked, her wrists bound to her ankles with thick leather cuffs that meant her heels were pulled tight against her bottom cheeks. Her knees were parted, opening her sex to view, exposing her vulnerability as she lay quietly on the bed. Katerina took a step into the room and stopped; Emily was staring up at the ceiling and had not seen her enter. The girl's eyes were half closed, and puffy, as if she had been crying, though, if she had been, the gag tied tightly around her mouth would have muffled her sobs.

Patrick had been more than efficient; Katerina could see that he had taken great care in the way he had trussed Emily and she knew that it would have given him immense pleasure. She did not know which rule Emily had transgressed to be treated so harshly, not that it mattered. What counted was that she had been punished and then bound securely. Now, as she lay helpless on the bed, she was open and available, unable to move, struggle or speak. Patrick was evidently determined to take Emily to the absolute limits.

Emily stirred suddenly, opening her eyes wide as she noticed Katerina standing before her. She tried to speak, but the gag took her words and turned them into pitiful moans that teetered on the edge of hysteria. She tried to move, pulling at her restraints, tugging sharply with her arms but unable to move her securely tied limbs.

'Don't struggle,' Katerina told her. 'It will do you no good.'

Emily's eyes were full of pleading, expressing what she wanted to say but was unable to.

'I won't release you,' Katerina told her. 'You are being punished by Patrick, not me. It is not my place to end this.'

Emily fell back, finally accepting the fact that her struggling was useless, that it caused more pain than it did good. Her eyes were full of tears again; tears of anger and frustration, tears that had to take the place of words now that she had been robbed of the power of speech.

Katerina looked at her without smiling, wondering what it was that had provoked the open defiance which was now being punished. She sat beside her on Patrick's bed and put her hand to Emily's belly, feeling at once the fear that made the girl squirm away from her touch. Emily's breasts were pushed forward by the downward pull of her arms, her nipples hard and erect and jutting upwards enticingly. Katerina leaned over and flicked her tongue over each in turn, lapping over the erectile flesh slowly, enjoying the way the hard points flexed and moved with her tongue. Emily moaned softly, lifting herself forward as Katerina sucked harder, taking a nipple into her mouth and biting it softly between her lips and teeth.

Emily moved her knees further apart as Katerina's hand trailed down over the pubis, her fingers brushing through the triangle of hair to rest over Emily's pussy lips. Katerina curled her middle finger, sliding in softly between Emily's cunt lips to feel the heat that oozed within. She felt as though she had dipped her finger in warm, sticky honey. She probed deeper; curling and uncurling her finger in the younger woman's sex, drawing out the hidden moisture so that it was smeared deliciously over her finger.

Emily's sighs and moans were growing more insistent, her mouth opening and closing around the tight leather gag. Katerina kissed her softly on the lips for a moment and then she smeared her pussy-soaked finger over Emily's mouth, wetting Emily's lips with the dew that poured from her own sex. When they kissed again Katerina licked the sex-honey from Emily's lips and then pushed her tongue against the wet leather of the gag. She put her hand down between Emily's thighs once more, pushing two and then three fingers in to her cunt, forcing them in and out and making Emily move her hips up and down with the same steady rhythm.

Katerina began to suck and kiss the younger girl's nipples again as she worked her fingers harder, making Emily pant and moan as she was moved closer and closer to orgasm. Emily moved her head from side to side, her eyes closed and her breath working furiously against the gag that turned her cries of pleasure into muffled sighs. Katerina began to work her thumb directly against the hard nub at the apex of Emily's sex while continuing to pump the three fingers in and out, penetrating deeply and pressing them against the slick walls of her cunt. Emily's gasps grew higher and she arched her back suddenly, pushing down with her feet to lift her backside off the bed as Katerina's fingers dug in deeply and pushed her to climax.

Katerina sat back and watched Emily's limp body, patterned with a pink flush across the chest and neck that marked her orgasm. Her legs were still widely parted and her pussy lips were open, the pink flesh glistening visibly where jewels of her essence leaked from her body. Her breath steadied and she opened her eyes to look at Katerina with a dazed expression that seemed unfocused.

'We have not finished yet,' Katerina told her, smiling. She walked to the other side of the bed, to the chest of drawers that flanked it. Still smiling she reached down into the bottom drawer and carefully made her choice from the selection of toys that Patrick kept there. She chose a thick black dildo first, and then a couple of the other items.

Emily's eyes widened with alarm when Katerina showed her the black phallus; the gleaming plastic looked dangerously large in the bright sunlight. Katerina held it by the base, marvelling at the heaviness of the object and enjoying Emily's look of apprehension and the muffled complaints that issued from behind her gag. The sight of the phallic object seemed to give Emily the energy to struggle once more and she tried to push her way up the bed, as far away from Katerina as possible.

'Do I have to spank you?' Katerina asked, her voice cold and emotionless but her eyes filled with unmistakable anticipation. Emily seemed to understand, she shook her head vigorously and then lay still.

Katerina pulled Emily forward so that she knelt with her arms pulled back to her ankles and her breasts thrust forward. Sliding her hand under her, Katerina stroked Emily's pussy lips softly and felt the girl tense nervously. The look of apprehension in Emily's eyes softened as Katerina's fingers probed further, pushing deep into the wet slit of her pussy. Emily's first sighs of pleasure were soft, as she pressed herself down on the fingers that invaded her sex. Katerina moved her fingers in and out slowly, building up the tension and the pleasure so that Emily's cunt was slippery with juices.

Emily moved suddenly, trying to lift her bottom away from the hardness of the black plastic that Katerina inserted into her. She squirmed and writhed, but the beast was pushed in relentlessly, penetrating her until it filled her cunt. Katerina looked into Emily's eyes and smiled as she forced the dildo all the way in so that the thick, round base pushed against her bulging pussy lips.

'Is that good?' Katerina whispered, flicking her tongue over Emily's hard nipples, which were thrust forward by her stance. There was no reply from Emily; not a murmur or a sign, nor even a nod of the head. Katerina pulled the dildo out slowly and thrust it back hard, making Emily inhale sharply as a rush of pure pleasure pierced her core.

Katerina continued to fuck Emily with the dildo, alternating hard, sharp stabs with long, fluid strokes that had the girl mewing softly with pleasure. She continued to suck on Emily's nipples, closing her lips around them so that she could brush the very tips of them with the edge of her tongue. With her free hand, she began to explore Emily's backside, tracing the curve of her buttocks, slipping her finger along the crack between them to stroke against Emily's tight anal hole. She smeared some of the wetness from Emily's pussy on to her fingers and then used them to spread the slick juices across the cleft of her bottom.

Each time Katerina's finger pressed against Emily's rear opening, the girl seemed to shudder, lifting herself away from the threatening fingers. By now, Emily was dancing up and down on the hard dildo, screwing herself down on it as it pushed into her sex. She thrust against it, impaling herself on the hardness as she sucked excitedly for breath through the gag. Her body seemed to radiate energy; she was flushed pink and her brow was beaded with perspiration.

Katerina slid her finger deep into Emily's backside, penetrating smoothly into the anal passage that had been lubricated with the nectar from the girl's cunt. Emily stalled for a moment and then continued, riding up and down on the hardness in her cunt and on to Katerina's finger as it pushed up into her behind. She moved faster and faster, her eyes closed as she thrashed wildly and then she fell forwards, crying out as the pleasure stormed through her body.

The dildo protruded from Emily's pussy, the black plastic smeared with a glistening layer of pussy honey. Emily had fallen forward so that her face and breasts were pressed flat on the bed and her bottom poked up, exposing the dildo lodged inside her. The vivid red stripes that lined her backside were a surprise for Katerina;

Patrick had not told her that Emily had been beaten with a crop before being bound so tightly.

Emily moaned softly as Katerina's finger travelled the red stripes that had been left by the riding crop. Each line lay straight across her buttocks, the result of a hard cropping that had been delivered by a skilled and cruel hand – Katerina recognised Patrick's work instantly. It meant that Emily's training was moving forward at a rapid pace, that she had already gone beyond anything that Amanda had experienced. She kissed Emily gently on the backside, pressing her cool lips to the angry red stripes in a gesture that was at once an apology and yet deeply sensual.

'Did you climax after he beat you?' she asked softly.

'Yes,' Emily admitted, as soon as Katerina had loosened the gag by undoing the strap that held it in place.

'Did he beat you before or after binding you with the cuffs?'

'Both,' Emily whispered.

'Why are you being punished?'

Emily paused. Her face was already flushed pink but Katerina thought she saw shame in her big blue eyes. 'Because – because I refused him and argued and . . .'

'What did you refuse?' Katerina asked, passing her hand over the punished globes of Emily's bottom.

'It's so – so horrible.'

'What did you refuse?' Katerina repeated, her voice harder than before.

'I refused to suck the piss from his fingers,' Emily whispered shamefully. 'I sucked it from his cock later,' she added, as though fearing another punishment for her crime. 'But he said it was too late.'

Katerina took the dildo in her fingers and pulled it out slowly from Emily's vagina. It was smeared with sex juices, a thick layer of glistening fluid that flowed with each of Emily's orgasms. Katerina knew that if she put it to the young girl's lips she would suck every trace of herself from it, delighting in tasting her cunt on the stiff tool that had worked her to countless climaxes. Instead, she touched it against Emily's distended anal hole, pressing the smooth rounded tip against the rear opening that she had earlier frigged with her finger.

'No, don't,' Emily cried. 'You'll hurt me.'

Katerina ignored her. She pushed the dildo harder, easing it in slowly. She was fascinated as she watched it going in, the thick black girth invading the tight orifice and taking possession. Emily was whimpering, her mouth open and her face twisting into an ugly grimace which softened when the pain she had expected failed to materialise. When the dildo was halfway in, Katerina began moving it out again, and then back in with a little more speed and force.

'Does that hurt?' she asked, as she began to find a smooth, fluid rhythm with which to sodomise Emily with the dildo.

Emily sighed breathlessly. 'No – oh, it feels so good,' she whispered as Katerina's fingers began to tease her pussy again. She sighed even more when she felt Katerina's tongue lapping softly at the juices which poured from her cunt, smearing her thighs.

Katerina stood up, leaving the dildo pushed deep into Emily's anal hole. She undressed quickly, letting her clothes fall untidily to the floor. The excitement was like fire inside her; the pretence of cool disinterest was becoming harder and harder to keep up. She reached for the other objects she had pulled from the drawer, watched hungrily by Emily.

She stepped into the harness quickly and pushed the ribbed latex dildo into her pussy, pressing it hard so that it nudged exquisitely against her clit. The other end extended from her pubis, a thick, erect phallus that mirrored the one she had inserted into herself. She tightened the straps quickly, testing the penis that jutted out from her body and delighting in the feeling that it caused as it pushed back against the one inside her.

She stepped on to the edge of the bed and took hold of Emily by the waist pulling her into place. She gazed down adoringly at Emily's backside, at the perfect roundness of her bottom which was still marked by the crop, at the tight dark anal muscle that was forced open by the black dildo and then down at the splayed lips and pink flesh of Emily's cunt.

Without a word, she leaned forward and pressed the tip of her false penis against Emily's pussy. She inhaled sharply and then pressed forward, sliding the cock into her compliant partner's body, enjoying the reciprocal feel of penetration as Emily's pleasure was echoed in her own sex. Jerking forward, she pushed herself as deep as she could go, her belly rubbing against the tight curves of Emily's bottom cheeks.

The rhythm was slow at first, as she enjoyed the look of wonder and excitement on Emily's face, reflected in the mirror opposite them. Then it became gradually faster as that wonder was replaced with a look of pure pleasure. Katerina held Emily tightly and thrust back and forth, moving with a curving, fluid motion that rubbed tendrils of pure ecstasy against her clit. As her body moved with a hard fucking motion over Emily's posterior, she cried out suddenly, gritting her teeth and forcing herself down harder on Emily until the girl cried out with pleasure and pain. Katerina collapsed forward, falling bodily across Emily's back as the orgasm shook through her.

When she got her breath back, Katerina moved off, sliding the cock that was still impossibly hard out of Emily's soaked pussy. She lay back for a moment, letting the pleasure suffuse her body with its radiance. The hardness that she had strapped on jutted from her belly, slightly curved and slick with sex juices.

'Now suck me,' she ordered, but the harsh tone she wanted was not there.

Emily slipped over on to her side and moved round as best she could. Her eyes were fixed on the solid object that had fucked her so well. 'What about the thing that's still inside me?' she whispered, turning over to display the other phallus, still lodged in her anal hole.

Katerina smiled. 'I'll fuck you there also,' she promised. 'But first I want your mouth on this,' she added, lewdly gripping the strap-on cock with her long elegant fingers.

'Yes ... Mistress,' Emily sighed softly.

Twelve

Helen's foul mood did not dissipate during the rest of the day, not even during dinner. Alex had prepared a shopping list earlier, which Joanna had sent to one of the local suppliers who had been rigged up with a computer and a modem. It meant that supplies could be ordered and delivered without the need for anyone to leave the walled sanctuary of Eden. It was supposed to be another example of the way in which the community minimised its contact with the outside world but Alex couldn't help seeing it as a bad idea. Self-sufficiency was one thing, self-imposed isolation another.

All day he had watched Joanna and Helen from the window, excited by one and wary of the other. The feminine underwear that he wore under his dull, functional clothes was a constant source of excitement. The tactile sensation of soft, silky lingerie against his skin caused nothing but arousal, keeping his cock erect throughout the day so that it poured silvery trails of fluid against his stomach and into Joanna's black panties.

'This is really good,' Joanna complimented him, spooning more of the food on to her plate. Her glass was empty and, without being asked, he leant across the table to refill it with a blood-red wine that had been his best find when he'd sorted out the mess in the kitchen.

He looked towards Helen, half hoping that she'd say something appreciative too, but she glared at him coldly. To compliment him on the food would have been tantamount to surrender and it was obvious that for the moment she had gone back to regarding him with nothing but anger and contempt.

'Where shall I start tomorrow?' he asked Joanna, pouring himself more of the wine. 'I'm finished in here. Do you want me to start outside or shall I do the rooms upstairs first?'

'Helen?' Joanna asked, looking to her for an answer.

'Outside,' Helen muttered, looking deliberately at Joanna and not at Alex. 'He can sort that out before he goes near our room.'

'Okay, I'll make an early start tomorrow,' he said, keeping his voice calm and even. Helen was spoiling for a fight and he knew that it would give her immense pleasure for him to argue back. At the very least it would prove to her that she had been right to object to his presence in the first place.

'I think we ought to go over to talk to Oliver,' Helen said, ignoring Alex completely. 'I'm sure that between us we can sort something out.'

Joanna looked pained. 'Do we have to?'

'Look,' Helen insisted, 'we have to sort this out. Patrick's intent on turning Eden into his private little dictatorship – is that what you want?'

'No, of course not,' Joanna sighed. 'It's just that I'm tired and spending the night arguing about Patrick and Katerina is not my idea of fun.'

'It's not my idea of fun either, but then neither is the idea of having Patrick running our lives. The whole point of Eden is that we're free to live as we please. That's not the same as living the way that bloody bastard pleases.'

'But you've spoken to Oliver already,' Joanna countered. 'What more can you possibly say on the subject? The annual general meeting of the company is where this thing is going to be sorted out, not in Oliver's front room.'

Helen glared at her angrily. 'If you don't care, then just say so,' she snapped. 'But don't give me that bloody

180

reasonable shit. You know that if we don't do something Patrick's going to run the AGM the way he always does. He'll get his way again, as per bloody usual.'

'Helen, I'm tired,' Joanna said, quietly. 'Please, let's not fight about this. You know that I don't like the way Patrick does things, and you know that I don't want him to build another place next to this one, but I'm tired. Very tired.'

'I'm tired as well,' Helen responded, her voice losing its strident edge, 'but this is important to me. You have an early night, or something. Let me go over and sort things out with Oliver. Besides, he knows that we're together on this; what I say goes for the two of us.'

Alex remained silent, certain that the wrong gesture or the wrong word would provoke Helen all over again. Previously, he had imagined Eden to be an idyllic retreat from the outside world; a real alternative, a sanctuary from the rat race and a place to build a new world. From the inside, things looked a good deal less idealistic; Patrick had been right about the tensions within the community, only it looked as if Patrick himself was the primary cause of dissension.

'I'll see you later,' Helen said, walking over to kiss Joanna on the mouth before leaving.

'Yes, see you later,' Joanna responded, returning Helen's kiss and squeezing her partner's fingers reassuringly.

Alex waited for her to go before relaxing enough to breathe again. 'Are things always so heavy around here?' he asked.

'Sometimes it's like this, sometimes it's worse, occasionally it gets better, much better,' Joanna sighed. 'But like I said earlier, keep out of it. Things are never are clear and as simple as they seem.'

'Okay, but let me ask one question.'

'Yes?'

'Is Patrick really the dictator that Helen makes him out to be?'

181

'I said you could ask the question,' Joanna replied, with a sly smile. 'I didn't say I'd answer it.'

'Hey, that's not fair! I bet you got that trick from Helen,' Alex said laughing.

'Wrong, it's a trick I picked up from Patrick.'

Alex fell silent, realising that conversation risked going in the wrong direction; he didn't want a long heavy discussion, even though he was curious to find out what Joanna's real view of Patrick – and of Eden itself – was. He shifted uncomfortably in his chair, the stockings pulling softly against his skin.

'Are you too tired to help me out of your underwear?' he asked softly.

She looked at him for a moment, tilting her head quizzically before smiling. 'I'm too tired to play with a man,' she told him. She laughed when she saw the disappointment on his face. 'I'm not too tired to play with a girl.'

'What do you mean?'

'I mean I want you to go to the bathroom, take my razor and shave your legs for me – there's cream and lotions in the bathroom cabinet. Then I want you to put the stockings back on; you'll feel like you're in heaven when they brush against your smooth skin. When you get out of the bathroom, you'll find some more things to wear; I'll lay them out on the bed. Finally, when you're ready, when you're a nice little girl for me, then we can play.'

Alex looked at her. She was smiling serenely, her dark eyes filled with an infectious excitement that made him ache with desire. 'You really want all that?' he asked softly.

'Yes, I want you to be a nice, sweet, innocent young girl for me.'

He averted his eyes, afraid to look at her directly in case she could see the shame and the confusion that surged through him. 'I'll go up and start,' he whispered, trembling as he stood up, his hard cock bulging against

182

the constricting panties that were pure rapture on his skin.

Alex looked at the clothes that Joanna had chosen for him, spread neatly on the bed. The sharp stinging on his legs had begun to subside, soothed by one of the lotions that had been arrayed in the bathroom cabinet. Looking at himself in the mirror he was surprised at how much of a difference it had made: his long legs looked altogether less masculine and his skin had a silky sheen that had always been hidden by the curls of hair. His chest, too, was free of hair, his nipples two dark dots on otherwise smooth, satiny skin.

He rubbed his hand against his thigh once more, trying to get used to the new feeling of skin that was so much more sensitive without the rough covering of hair.

The stockings lay on the bed next to the clothes; his legs had been too sore to put them back on immediately. Joanna had selected a short, pleated skirt and a simple blouse for him, as well as a pair of white panties and a matching pair of lacy suspenders.

He wondered what Katerina would make of his shaved legs. And Emily? The thought of their reaction had been uppermost in his mind as he had carefully applied the razor to his legs. He had a few days' work ahead of him, and he was counting on the hair growing back quickly before he had to return to Katerina's house. In the meantime he hoped that any visits to see his Mistress would not involve him stripping off – the thought of it made him feel very nervous.

The white blouse was loose around his chest, hanging in gentle folds that hid the fact that he was male. The skirt fitted much better, clinging to his body as he pulled the waist tightly, making the pleats flare around his hips. He stood in front of the mirror and looked at his reflection critically: the skirt was tight, but it didn't seem to be the wrong shape for his body. His legs were parted awkwardly; he knew he didn't stand like a woman. And yet he felt a surge of excitement at the idea of being dressed as a girl, an excitement that made his cock stand hard against the front of the skirt.

Carefully, he slipped the white panties on, stepping into the soft, flimsy garment and pulling it up tightly. His hardness was pressed in, so that the bulge in the front of the skirt all but disappeared. He lifted the skirt slowly and looked in the mirror, turning round to look at the reflection of his backside. The panties were pulled tight, the white strip of material edging sexily into the parting of his bottom cheeks.

'What are you doing?' Joanna asked, standing in the doorway and looking at him, sombrely. Alex dropped the skirt instantly, embarrassed by her sudden appearance. She walked into the room, to the bed where the stockings were carefully laid out in readiness.

'Where you being a bad girl?' she asked, her expression still unclear. Her sultry eyes were fixed on him, questioningly.

'I – I was just getting ready,' he said softly. She had changed, too; the long wraparound skirt had been replaced with one that was short and tight, and she was now wearing a white blouse that had been unbuttoned to reveal an enticing glimpse of her cleavage.

'You're not ready yet,' she replied, ignoring the stockings and walking over to the dressing table. 'You need to put this on,' she said, picking up one of the vividly-coloured lipsticks that were scattered around. She popped the top off and slowly extended a bright glossy finger of red.

She was still straight-faced; her lips, already glossed red, did not part in the inviting and conspirational smile that he waited for. He went over to her, nervously, his bare feet padding on the soft carpet.

'Purse your lips,' she instructed, turning him towards the mirror. She took his cleanly shaven chin in her fingers and carefully applied a thick layer of sweet-tasting colour to his mouth. He watched her add blusher to his cheeks and then mascara to thicken and tint his eye lashes until they looked long and feminine. When she released him, he smacked his lips softly, the way Emily always did after she had glossed hers, and then he stood back.

'Well?' Joanna asked, standing behind him and looking at his reflection in the mirror.

'I look so different,' he whispered, hardly able to recognise himself. The transformation that Joanna had effected with a few dabs of colour to his face was astounding; the lines of his face had been subtly changed and, along with the clothes, he no longer felt so – so male.

'I like playing with girls more than I like playing with boys,' Joanna whispered softly, her hot breath touching his neck as she spoke. 'Now that you're ready . . .'

He turned to her and managed a nervous smile. 'Am I a good girl or a bad girl?' he asked. The idea of being a girl was intensely arousing, more arousing than he had imagined possible. When he turned to walk the skirt swished gently about him, rubbing softly against his bottom cheeks and against his hardness through its covering of soft lace.

'A good girl about to be turned into a bad girl,' Joanna told him, making him sit on the edge of the bed and then sitting down beside him.

'What if we get caught?' he asked, dreading the idea of Helen walking in on them unexpectedly.

'Don't worry,' Joanna whispered, taking his hands in her own, 'the other girls haven't even noticed we're missing. They'll never think of looking for us here.'

The game had started and it made Alex shiver with excitement. 'Shouldn't we be getting back?' he asked, looking innocently into Joanna's big brown eyes.

'It's okay,' she promised, 'we're safe here. You've got such lovely smooth legs,' she added, glancing down at the short skirt which had risen high above Alex's knee. She moved her hand to it, letting her fingers rest on his leg while she smiled innocently and gazed adoringly into Alex's eyes.

'I think we'd better be going back,' Alex said, his voice filled with feigned nervousness.

'Relax,' Joanna urged, moving her hand higher.

Alex put his hand on hers to stop it going higher. 'I think I can hear someone,' he lied.

'I can't hear anything,' Joanna replied, pushing her hand under the hem of the skirt and squeezing the smooth flesh at the top of his thigh.

'Don't – You mustn't do that.'

'Do what?' Joanna asked innocently, smoothing her hand up and down softly, insinuating her fingers higher and higher up his leg.

'It's – it's not right . . .'

Joanna looked hurt. 'But I'm only playing,' she told him, pouting her full, glossed lips seductively. 'It's just that you've got such lovely pale skin compared to mine and . . .'

Alex trembled as her fingers began to circle over his thighs again, smoothing back and forth across the satiny flesh. Her face was close to his, her eyes staring into his own, her lips so very close. She moved forward an inch, touched her lips to his and then drew back again. 'You're lovely,' she whispered.

'Please. We mustn't do this,' Alex complained softly, his words barely audible. He felt as though his heart beat were the loudest thing in the world, pounding in his chest as his excitement rose higher and higher.

Joanna took his hand and pressed it to her bosom, spreading his fingers before putting them to her erect nipples. 'There's nothing wrong with playing,' she told him, pressing his hand down until he began to ease his fingers tentatively over her breast.

'But we're girls –'

'Then there's nothing to be afraid of,' Joanna countered, kissing him on the lips once more. This time, her kiss lasted a little longer, her lips lingering on his so that he inhaled her breath and tasted her lipstick.

When he made no complaint, she sat back and smiled.

186

'You're going to get us both into trouble,' she whispered, beginning to unbutton her blouse. The game was becoming real; with the feelings of desire he felt something else, the fear of being caught, the fear of letting another woman explore his – her – body.

Joanna sat up on the bed and opened her blouse to the waist, exposing her large round breasts completely. She cupped her bosom, squeezing her breasts together so that her dark brown nipples protruded even further. Her face was a picture of excitement, her glossy lips wet where she had licked them, her dark eyes shining wickedly.

'It's okay, you can touch me,' she urged, pushing her chest forward, the pure white of her blouse contrasting with the dark sheen of sugar brown skin.

Alex looked into her eyes and melted; even if he – she – were a good girl then Joanna's expression, the fullness of her lips and the light in her eyes, were enough to seduce him – her – completely. Shakily he reached out to stroke the valley between Joanna's breasts, delighting in the smoothness of her skin and excited by the idea of touching another woman for the first time. Everything was in disarray – 'he' and 'she' were now meaningless concepts, irrelevant labels, and in the confusion he felt nothing but pure physical excitement.

'Let me call you Alexandra,' Joanna suggested. 'Let that be your girlie name.'

'Alexandra,' he repeated softly, excited still further by the idea. Alexandra. Alexandra. Alexandra. The name echoed in his head and he was, secretly thrilled by it.

'That feels good,' Joanna murmured as Alexandra continued to caress her, her fingers playing across the dark nipples making them stand prouder. 'Now kiss them, kiss my nipples,' Joanna sighed.

Alexandra sat up and moved closer, her cock smearing wetness into her pretty white panties as she moved. Her glossed lips touched Joanna's breasts, leaving a smudge of sweet scarlet just above the nipple. She kissed softly, sucking in a nipple to stroke with her tongue and then doing the same to the other one. Joanna's sighs of pleasure were her guide, making her suck harder, closing her lips tightly over the rubbery points of flesh.

'Lie back now,' Joanna whispered, after kissing Alexandra passionately on the mouth. Alexandra looked up at her friend; bountiful breasts exposed, nipples ringed with saliva and smeared with smudges of red lipstick. As she watched, Joanna lifted the front of her skirt to reveal that she wore nothing underneath.

'Do you want to touch me here?' Joanna asked, pressing her fingers against the dark outer lips of her pussy.

'But we shouldn't,' Alexandra whispered, unable to take her eyes from the other woman's sex.

Joanna pushed a finger into her pussy, rubbing it slowly and then pulling it out to show Alexandra the glistening feminine honey of her body. Alexandra's eyes widened; she felt excited by what she was seeing, but was still afraid to go any further.

'We mustn't,' she whispered, but her resistance was gone, she realised she was simply going through the motions like the good girl that she was.

Joanna licked her fingers clean, grinning mischievously as Alexandra's face registered shock and fascination in equal measure, and then she lay beside her. They kissed again, Alexandra's reluctance diminishing, and then Joanna pushed a hand under her new friend's skirt. Joanna's fingers travelled over the smooth flesh, sending ripples of sensation through Alexandra's body so that she trembled with pleasure. She was breathing fast, matching the beat of her heart as her excitement mounted.

'Oh,' Joanna whispered seductively, 'you're so wet . . .'

The feel of the woman's fingers on her hard cock made Alexandra moan softly, her whole being quivered and she felt close to orgasm. Her hardness was smeared with the thick sticky juices that poured from its slit, wetting her panties as Joanna stroked the stiff organ tenderly with her fingertips.

'You're such a bad girl,' Joanna murmured softly,

rubbing her thumb slowly over the engorged glans, sliding it over the slippery wetness so that Alexandra stiffened with pleasure. Carefully she eased the skirt higher, bringing it up over Alexandra's waist so that the little white panties and her hard cock were fully exposed.

Joanna smoothed the wetness on to her fingers and then put them to her lips, her pink tongue lapping quickly to scoop up the jewels of moisture that she had milked from Alexandra's stiffness. She smiled and then eased Alexandra's panties down, releasing the stiff organ from the damp white lace. Her dark fingers closed around the base of the stiff rod, pulling back gently on the soft skin to increase the hardness of the erection. Very slowly she moved down, kissing Alexandra on the thigh before licking at the purple bulb of her cock. Alexandra moaned deliriously, and gripped the side of the bed as she struggled to contain the ecstasy that threatened to explode from her body.

'You're really a very bad girl,' Joanna told her. 'You're making me do all these nasty things to you.' She lay back and parted her thighs, giving Alexandra the best possible view of her cunt, and then began to frig herself, pushing her fingers deep into her pussy with hard, rapid strokes. In moments she was panting loudly, her head thrown back and her eyes closed as she pleasured herself. Her dark breasts were forced upward between her arms, the erect nipples pushed almost together, and then she uttered a single brief exclamation as she climaxed violently.

Alexandra watched for a moment and then leant over to kiss Joanna softly on the mouth. At the same time she took each of the woman's nipples between a finger and thumb and squeezed gently. 'You're so beautiful,' she told her. 'I don't care what you do to me.'

'Do you really mean that?' Joanna asked, opening her eyes slowly, as though coming out of a dream.

Alexandra bowed her head and kissed Joanna on the chest, running her tongue from nipple to nipple. 'Anything . . .' she murmured, almost afraid to say it because she knew that Joanna was capable of anything.

189

Joanna sat up and pushed Alexandra flat on her back, then leant across her to kiss her on the mouth. Her breasts were squashed flat across Alexandra's chest, the nipples tantalisingly hard through Alexandra's blouse. Joanna stroked Alexandra's cock lovingly, and then passed her hand lower, her juice-soaked fingers sliding under the coolness of the ball sac to press against the hidden opening. Alexandra tensed, sucking in her breath as she felt Joanna's slippery fingers exploring her rear cleft, tracing a line from the base of the penis to the tight dark anal hole.

'I want to finger-fuck your tight little pussy,' Joanna sighed. 'I want to see what a bad girl you can be.'

Alexandra nodded tensely, afraid to speak. Her eyelids fluttered as Joanna's wet finger pressed harder, pushing against the tight ring of muscle to penetrate it slowly. She felt as though her body were being prised open, as Joanna's finger entered her with a hot, burning sensation. She gasped painfully as the digit slipped in finally, and was pushed as far into her rectum as it could go. It was in her, deep in her back passage, Joanna's knuckle gripped by Alexandra's sphincter.

Joanna began to suckle on Alexandra's painfully stiff cock, taking the glans between her lips to suck away the fluid that leaked copiously from the tiny slit. At the same time, she began to move her finger in and out of Alexandra's anus, slowly at first but then faster as she felt Alexandra relax enough to begin to enjoy the sensation. She worked her mouth and hand in unison, creating a rhythmic, driving motion that had Alexandra gasping with pleasure and moving in time with each thrust into her backside.

Alexandra was whimpering, unable to cope with the simultaneous pleasure of being sucked and fingered. She moved urgently, opening herself so that Joanna's finger could go deeper, faster. She could feel nothing but pleasure, nothing but the pure bliss of Joanna's mouth on her cock and the finger penetrating deep into her rectum.

She ached for release and yet she wanted the pleasure to go on forever, afraid that when the moment ended she would revert to being Alex.

Joanna shifted suddenly, moving over Alexandra and squatting down over her face. She continued to finger Alexandra's enticing anal hole, fucking her harder and harder as she mouthed her stiff cock, but now she also had the pleasure of being sucked in turn. Her pussy was pressed down over Alexandra's open mouth, giving Alexandra the chance to suck and lick and drink deep from her cunt.

Alexandra cried out and her body tensed, arching into spasm as the pleasure burst like liquid fire. The white flash of pure energy seemed to take her outside her body, wiping out everything but the feeling of blissful ecstasy. She rocked back as the orgasm spurted from her cock into Joanna's waiting mouth, her cock pulsing and her rear hole closing tight around Joanna's finger buried deep inside her. Her mouth was filled with Joanna's taste, with the liquid essence that had been the prize of Joanna's climax.

Emily felt as though her life had taken on the intense and unreal aspects of dream. And, as in a dream, every action was imbued with a bizarre erotic significance; there were layers upon layers of meaning attached to words, looks, gestures. Time had become a fluid, mysterious force and she felt that during her few days in Eden she had learnt more about herself than in any other period of her life.

Patrick had called it training and now, as she studied the uniform that had been selected for her, she sensed that there was a reason for the training, a purpose that was beyond what she knew at the moment. She was being trained for a specific task; every experience had been directed and nothing had been left to chance, even if it had seemed at the time as though every scene had been a spontaneous sexual exploration.

The shiny black rubber dress which had been hung up

191

behind her door was edged with frilly white lace at the hem and around the plunging neckline. There was also a matching cap and a pretty white apron, which had been put on a separate hanger. A pair of latex stockings were carefully folded over for her, along with a suspender belt and rubber panties. The final touch was the pair of shiny patent shoes that towered by her feet, the high stiletto heels gleaming like the rest of the uniform.

It was a maid's uniform, perfect in every detail and executed in shiny black latex, which caught the light and reflected it back vividly. Every fold in the material, every detail shimmered seductively. Katerina had been the one to tell her, informing her casually that she and Patrick had decided that she was ready to serve and that her uniform was ready for her.

The uniform had the characteristically acrid smell of rubber, and when Emily touched it for the first time, it felt very strange: smooth and clingy at the same time, cool to the touch and yet very sensual. She had been told to bathe and to dust her naked skin with a layer of fragrant talc before trying on the dress for the first time. She was ready, perfumed and powdered as instructed and yet she felt nervous. Wearing the maid's uniform seemed a big step to take. She knew that it signified a great deal; that it meant she had been trained to a certain level and that she accepted without question her allotted *rôle*.

She sat on the bed and decided to begin with the stockings. The insides of them had been powdered, the innocent scent of sweet-smelling talc combining with the vaguely sulphurous smell of rubber. She rolled the first stocking carefully up to her knee and pressed her foot in slowly. The fit was nice and tight. She then rolled the stocking upwards, aware of how cool and tight the rubber was against her skin. She put on first one then the other stocking, pulling them up carefully, smoothing them down and wiping off the stray blotches of powder that blemished the shiny purity of the black latex.

Looking down, she could see that the tops of the

stockings were tight around her thighs, making her flesh bulge slightly where the black rubber gave way to her creamy skin. She stood and looked in the mirror, a smile forming slowly as she studied herself critically. Her long legs were outlined elegantly by the gleaming black rubber and the contrast between the unreal fantasy surface and her pale flesh added to the beauty of the picture.

The panties and the suspender belt, too, contributed to the cool beauty of the look and, when she stepped into the high heels, she felt as if she had been transformed into some perfect, fetishistic creature. There was a sensation of constriction as she moved, the tight rubber clinging possessively to her skin, and the towering heels made her feel incredibly elegant while heightening her awareness of her own vulnerability. She looked at herself in the mirror, admiring her reflection from all angles, delighting in the way the tight panties pressed sensuously against her pussy and the shiny thong between her bottom cheeks seemed to splay the curves of her backside enticingly.

The dress itself had only been lightly dusted with powder and it took a while for her to wriggle into it. When it was finally on, however, she was delighted by the tightness of it against her skin; every curve of her body was highlighted, from the slenderness of her waist to the swell of her breasts. Her nipples protruded, seeming to attract haloes of light against the jet black rubber, and the lace frill around the hem drew attention to how short the dress was. Even while standing still she could glimpse a flash of white thigh between the tops of the stockings and the start of the dress.

The frilly apron and the cap went on last, the finishing touches to complete her uniform of subservience. She looked at herself and realised that the uniform was designed to make her look submissive, that it moulded not just to her body, but to her personality. Dressed as a maid she could sense the vibes that she gave out: sexual, obedient, servile. She was everything that Patrick and Katerina had set out to create.

'I'm glad you're ready,' Patrick said, entering her room unannounced.

She looked at him sharply, surprised at how well he had judged the timing – a few minutes earlier and she would have been struggling into the uniform, a few minutes later and she might have been struggling out of it.

He looked at her and smiled disarmingly, the expression in his clear blue eyes washing away any questions and any doubts. She lowered her eyes respectfully, aware that the effect of the uniform and his charm had combined suddenly to make her feel very excited. It was a feeling that was electric and it was there in his eyes as well – a look of pure desire.

'This is how you'll feel when you serve,' he told her, walking slowly around her as she stood in the middle of the room. 'You'll feel aroused; you'll feel nervous; you'll be obedient and you'll be available to all you serve.'

'Yes, sir,' she whispered, shivering slightly, alarmed by the accuracy with which he had described her feelings.

He trailed his hand under the skirt of the dress to feel her backside through the smooth rubber. She inhaled sharply as his fingers pressed hard against her sex from below and behind, slowly easing the material between her pussy lips. 'Katerina and I are expecting a visitor soon, someone very important to us. When he arrives, you'll treat him as your Master, understand? You'll serve him in any way that he desires, no matter what that might be.'

'Yes, sir,' she whispered, the feel of his fingers rubbing the rubber material of her panties into her sex exciting her more and more. She felt herself teetering on the high heels, balanced delicately on the sharp spikes.

He pulled away sharply, leaving a wet tingling of desire deep in her pussy. She saw him reflected in the mirror, standing behind her, a devious smile fixed on his face.

'You look very desirable,' he assured her. 'I am sure our guest will be more than delighted with you.'

She watched him undo the heavy belt around his waist,

194

the shiny black leather gleaming like the surface of her uniform. He doubled the belt over and, gripping the weighty gold buckle in his hand, he sat down on the end of her bed, his knees angled widely apart.

'Approach your Master respectfully,' he told her, his voice losing its complimentary tone. It was an order, delivered cold and in the knowledge that, despite the fire of defiance that burned inside her, she would not disobey.

She turned slowly, keeping her eyes averted and her hands in front of her. She walked towards him slowly, still not quite used to the towering heels, and then she knelt down on her hands and knees. He motioned for her to crawl towards him, to move between his thighs. The skirt of the dress had lifted high at the back; she could feel her bottom exposed to the air, the rubber suspenders and the panties conspiring to part her buttocks slightly.

He pulled her forwards and then stroked a hand across her thighs, moving it slowly from the smoothness of the stockings to the creamy white flesh of her thigh and then to the firm roundness of her cheeks. He explored her intimately, pushing a finger against her pussy so that he could feel the rubber take on the wet heat of her excitement.

'I'm sure our guest is going to adore having a maid like you to look after his needs,' he whispered, hotly. She looked up at him nervously; the more that she heard of their mysterious guest the more apprehensive she became. She had been trained for *him*, not for Patrick or Katerina, nor anyone else, it had all been done with their guest in mind.

Patrick unzipped his trousers to free his hardness, holding his cock in his fingers for a second. He looked at her and she knew what he wanted. She closed her lips around the stiff organ instantly, pressing softly against his glans with her tongue so that she could suckle the first drops of his fluid. He sighed softly, jerking forward so that more of his length was pushed into the slick welcome of her mouth.

The first stroke of the belt smacked down hard on her backside, whistling through the air to impact, with a loud report, on her flesh. She winced, moving forward as the fire touched her flesh. She sucked harder, closing her cheeks around the stiff shaft of his cock so that he could fuck her mouth. Her pussy was wetness and heat, and when the belt came down again she felt the echo of the sensation deep in her sex – the pleasure was a reflection of the pain.

He gripped her hair tightly and forced her down on to his hardness with one hand, while, with the other, he wielded the leather belt again, strapping it across her backside with a sharp snap of his wrist. She could not cry out her pain, nor could she murmur her pleasure; instead she sucked on his cock and looked forward to the explosion of his seed into her hungry mouth.

Thirteen

Alex waited for Katerina to call to him before walking nervously out on to the sun-drenched terrace. Patrick stood behind Mistress, both of them waiting for him sombrely, their stern expressions cast in shadow by the heavy canopy overhead. Looking at them he felt the tension rise, and with it the fear that he would be punished and that the secret he shared with Joanna would be exposed.

'Well, Alex, how have you settled in?' Katerina asked as he approached her.

'Okay, I think,' he replied, standing awkwardly in front of her. Patrick's presence was disturbing; it suggested that there was more to their meeting than polite interest.

'And how has Helen been?'

'Difficult,' he admitted, avoiding Katerina's sharp gaze.

'In what way difficult?' she persisted.

'She doesn't like me. You saw what she was like when I arrived.'

'And she hasn't changed her attitude towards you?' Patrick asked pointedly, an unexpected edge of anger in his voice.

Alex looked at him for a moment before answering. 'She did start to relax a bit – but then she went back to hating my guts.'

'Why was that?' Katerina asked, her voice softer than Patrick's but her questions no less direct.

Alex shrugged. 'She's under a lot of pressure, I suppose,' he suggested, making it sound like a guess.

'It's nothing to do with the meetings she's been having with Oliver, then?' Patrick said, looking at him coldly.

Alex felt the colour drain from his face. He had assumed that Patrick and Katerina did not know about what was going on with Helen and Oliver, and he had planned on keeping it from them completely. 'Yes,' he admitted, 'her attitude changed after she spoke with Oliver. That's when she went back to treating me like a piece of dirt.'

'What else do you know about Helen's contact with Oliver?' Katerina asked.

'And we want the whole truth,' Patrick warned, coldly.

'Helen and he are convinced that you want to build an annexe of some kind,' Alex explained, realising that he had to tell the truth if he was not to fall foul of Mistress and Patrick together. 'An addition to Eden, but one where you are in complete control, without any kind of democratic decision making.'

Patrick nodded with grim satisfaction. 'What else?' he demanded.

'That's it. They know you've been talking about buying up some land.'

'What do they intend doing about it?' Patrick snapped.

'They want to stop you,' Alex answered, simply. 'But I don't know more than that. Helen thinks that I'm there on your behalf and so she doesn't trust me at all.'

'What about Joanna?' Katerina asked.

Alex lowered his eyes quickly. 'She's not involved in this,' he replied. 'She just wants to keep out of the arguments.'

It was Patrick's turn to question him. 'She's not had any meetings with Oliver?' he asked, sounding as though he found the fact hard to believe.

'Not while I've been there,' Alex replied, honestly.

'And what of your relationship with Joanna?' Katerina asked, allowing herself a smile.

Alex could feel the embarrassment colour his face. 'She's a lot – she doesn't hate me.'

198

'Is Helen aware that you and Joanna are having sex?' Patrick demanded.

'I didn't say we . . .' Alex started, but the argument was pointless; they could tell he was lying. 'No,' he admitted, softly, 'Helen doesn't suspect a thing.'

'Then you'll make sure she does suspect,' Patrick instructed. 'You'll make sure she knows precisely what's going on between you and Joanna. Is that understood?'

'But why?' Alex responded, shocked by the callousness of the order. It was obvious that Patrick did not care what happened, so long as he got his own way. As far as he was concerned if Helen was too busy handling the emotional fall-out of Joanna's infidelity with Alex then she would not have the time or the energy to fight his and Katerina's plans.

'You'll do it because you're told,' Patrick told him, speaking slowly, enunciating every word with icy finality.

'But that's not fair,' Alex retorted.

'How many strokes of the cane will it take before it seems fair?' Patrick asked, turning to Katerina with a sly smile on his face.

Alex felt sick, the fear pulsing in the pit of his belly. Under his trousers he wore a pair Joanna's frilly white panties, and his legs were smoothly shaved the way she liked them. If he were caned then his secret – his new identity as Alexandra – would be exposed, and he knew that Patrick would have no compunction about letting everyone else know about it. The thought of Emily finding out made Alex shudder.

'I'm sure that Alex is sensible enough to obey his Mistress,' Katerina assured Patrick calmly. 'Isn't that right?'

Alex looked at her and nodded. Her eyes looked into his and seemed to suck away all his resolve. Did she suspect? The idea made his heart race with excitement. 'Yes, Mistress,' he whispered.

'Instruct him on what to do,' Patrick ordered sharply, addressing Katerina with the same cold and imperious tone that he used on Alex and Emily. He glared at Alex for a moment longer and then marched back into the house.

'Do I really have to do as he asks, Mistress?' Alex asked her, looking at her beseechingly. He already hated the idea that Helen had been right – he had been sent to spy on them – but the idea of deliberately destroying the relationship between Helen and Joanna was infinitely worse.

'You address me as Mistress,' Katerina replied quietly, 'but do you mean it? Do you really accept that I am your Mistress?'

'Yes,' he answered hesitantly. He knew that if he had remained with her for a few more days his answer would have been more certain; his loyalty and love for Mistress would have grown into something that was strong and sure. But now he felt another pull; Joanna commanded a degree of affection and desire that interfered with his feelings towards Katerina.

'Do you accept that you are my slave?'

'Yes,' he replied, still uncertain as to what he felt.

'Prove it to me,' she commanded. 'A good slave has a duty to obey without question. A slave who is worthy of his Mistress must swear undying and unconditional devotion. These are not merely verbal formulae, these are rules that we must abide by. I repeat, are you worthy of your Mistress?'

'I want to be,' Alex whispered, almost trembling with emotion. He felt confusion more than anything else, torn by his desire for Mistress and his desire for Joanna.

'Then you'll obey,' she told him. 'When I order you to kiss my heels you obey without question. When I command you to pleasure me, you obey without question. Now, when I ask you to obey this new command I want you to obey without question once more.'

Alex hesitated. He wanted to agree; he wanted to get on his knees and kiss her heels and swear that he would do whatever Mistress demanded of him. But what Patrick wanted went beyond anything he had imagined; it involved not just Master or Mistress and servant, it involved other people and other relationships.

'Will you obey?' Katerina demanded.

'I can't,' Alex replied miserably, unable to make the commitment that Mistress demanded.

Katerina smiled unexpectedly. She pushed her chair back away from the table and then, sitting on the very edge of the chair, she parted her thighs. Her skirt covered her to her knees and she gathered it up slowly, exposing her tanned flesh inch by inch. 'It's time you showed your Mistress the true value of your stubborn tongue,' she said sternly, passing her slim fingers through the dark mat of hair that fringed her exposed pussy.

He sank down quickly, on to his hands and knees where he knew he belonged. Mistress was waiting, her thighs parted and her fingers rubbing softly between her pussy lips. His confusion melted, transforming into the hardness of his desire as he gazed lovingly at his Mistress. Her black heels glinted in the sunlight and he knew that he had to kneel down and kiss them, to prove to Mistress that he was worthy despite all of her doubts.

'Pleasure me here,' Mistress ordered softly, pressing a finger between the dark lips of her sex. 'And then here,' she said, touching her fingertip between her bottom cheeks and stroking her anal hole.

'Yes, Mistress,' Alex whispered, thrilled once more to be serving his Mistress. He inched forward, grateful to be allowed the honour of pleasuring the goddess that he served so miserably.

Emily's feet ached as she waited to be called to serve. She stood in the far corner of the room, dressed in her uniform, with her feet together, back straight, chest thrust forward and head bowed respectfully. Her feet ached; the towering heels were uncomfortable to wear and she felt precariously balanced when she walked.

Occasionally, she glanced towards the other side of the

room, hoping in vain that Patrick, Katerina or their guest would deign even to notice her presence in the corner. Neil Anderson, the guest for whom Patrick had been training her, had hardly looked in her direction when she had welcomed him earlier. He had appraised her in an almost perfunctory manner, glancing over her with a cool, emotionally detached gaze before joining Patrick and Katerina for their meeting.

She had been slightly afraid of meeting Anderson. Patrick had primed her to such a degree of nervousness that she was certain he would turn out to be some sort of monster. In fact, he appeared to be more interested in his discussions with Patrick and Katerina than in anything else. He did not look like a monster; she had at least been pleasantly surprised when he had turned out to be in his thirties, conventionally dressed and quite good-looking, in a bland sort of way.

Her feet ached and yet she knew that she had to stand tall and straight, no matter how much it hurt. As before, the tightness of the black rubber uniform meant that every contour of her body was emphasised, from the curve of her tummy to the swell of her hips to the peaks of her breasts. She was there to serve in any way her Master desired, and she accepted the fact with a sense of pride that she could not quite understand. When she wore the uniform she felt that it suited her completely, that it represented a side to her personality that she could no longer deny.

Patrick's laughter rose above the muted level of conversation and was joined by a softer chuckle from Anderson. Emily glanced up surreptitiously, half hoping and half fearing that the meeting was over. The three of them had been poring over a set of plans that Patrick had spread across his desk, the discussion seemingly focused entirely on the documents. Katerina had been making corrections and changes as the discussion had progressed, marking the papers in vivid red ink, or else scribbling notes on a pad.

There seemed to be no sign of the meeting ending; Patrick unfurled another set of plans, adding another layer to the stack that already covered the desk. Emily sighed to herself; were they ignoring her for a reason? She began to feel doubts growing inside her. Didn't she look good enough? Was there something that she had done wrong, perhaps?

'Emily, some water please,' Katerina called suddenly, not even bothering to look up from the plans.

Emily moved quickly, anxious to please more than anything else and afraid, too, that failure would mean an instant and painful punishment. She went down to the kitchen for a jug of iced water and some glasses, which she carried back upstairs on a silver platter, as she had previously been instructed. The heels made it difficult to walk smoothly but she managed to carry the tray to the desk without spilling anything.

'Water, Mistress,' she whispered softly, standing obediently with her ankles together and her head bowed.

Katerina looked at her, sharply. 'Is this how well we've trained you?' she demanded, moving away from the plans she had been studying.

'I'm sorry, Mistress,' Emily replied, her face colouring red with shame and confusion. What had she done?

Patrick glared at her. 'It's not Mistress to whom you should be apologising,' he told her. 'You have compounded your error already. In this house, you serve guests first. To do otherwise is the height of bad manners or poor training.'

Emily swallowed hard and turned to Neil Anderson, who was watching her without emotion. 'I apologise, sir,' she whispered, avoiding the eyes that she could feel boring into her. She was shaking now, aware that she had done wrong and that it reflected badly on Patrick and Katerina.

'An apology is not enough in this sort of situation,' Anderson said, speaking not to Emily but to Patrick and Katerina. 'It's not that I take great offence at

203

her rudeness; rather, I feel it incumbent on someone to show her what happens when she lets her Master and Mistress down so badly.'

He spoke with an almost effortless sense of superiority, talking about Emily as though she were not there in front of him, red-faced and apologetic. She could sense the excitement in the air, an electric tension that was focused on her.

'I agree entirely,' Patrick concurred, walking around the table to casually put a hand under her dress and stroke her thigh possessively. 'She colours well when punished,' he explained, rubbing his hand insistently over the inside of her thigh, 'and she knows the value of obedience, even when she has done wrong.'

'Really?' Anderson asked, as though surprised. 'I had imagined that she would prefer the pleasures of the flesh to the value of discipline.'

Patrick smiled indulgently. 'I have no doubt that she'll be more than willing to give you the pleasure of her body after a taste of punishment. You're a good little bitch, aren't you, Emily?'

Emily felt her face burning with shame, her eyes filled suddenly with tears. 'Yes. I'm a good little bitch, Master,' she repeated, perplexed by the equally sudden surge of excitement that she had felt. Her nipples were hard points, pushing against the heat of the rubber uniform that clothed her tightly, constricting and constraining deliciously and adding to her arousal.

'May I suggest the crop?' Katerina offered politely. 'Emily, fetch the things from my room.'

'Yes, Mistress,' Emily said softly, obeying instantly. She crossed the room self-consciously, aware of the sexual figure that she cut in her uniform and aware also of the excitement in the eyes that watched.

Katerina had prepared things earlier; another silver platter had been laid out with a variety of disciplinary implements: whips, straps, a cane. Emily dared not think of the pain that each implement could impart on the soft flesh of her body; she hardly dared to look at the instruments as they lay on the polished metal ready to be used. She carried the platter back to the others, hurrying in case she earned another punishment or incurred even greater anger.

She presented the platter to Anderson, holding it up to him so that he might select the instrument which appealed to him the most. He seemed amused and excited by the choice, caressing each of the objects in turn, weighing each in his hand to see which would suit him best. The riding crop was tipped with a triangle of soft leather that flicked easily as he moved the implement casually through the air.

'I think you're right, Katerina,' he decided at last. 'The crop is an excellent choice.'

'You may put that down now,' Katerina instructed, referring to the platter which Emily gripped tightly, her knuckles showing white against the shiny metal.

Emily tried to set it down carefully on the desk, but the thickly scrolled plans obscured the true edge of the surface so that, when she let it go, the patter teetered precariously for a second and then, as if in awful slow motion, it toppled over. It crashed to the floor with a metallic clang which silenced everyone, its echo hanging like a question mark in the air. The various instruments of correction were scattered on the floor and Emily, panicking, bent down quickly to pick them up again.

'Stay there,' Katerina ordered, standing over her menacingly.

Emily did not dare to glance up, afraid of the anger that she knew she'd find in Katerina's dark eyes. She stayed on hands and knees, head bowed, trying not to think of the skirt of the uniform rising up at the back to reveal her rubber-clad backside and the tight latex stockings pulling on her creamy pale flesh.

'May I?' Emily heard Katerina ask Anderson.

'Of course,' he replied graciously, and Emily was easily able to imagine the smooth smile on his face.

'Emily, I want you to stand up and lean across the desk,' Katerina ordered, her voice carrying no hint of emotion, not even the anger that Emily knew seethed inside her dark-eyed Mistress.

She obeyed quickly, moving into place so that she was bent over the desk, her body pressed flat on the thick layer of plans that covered the polished wooden surface. The suspenders pulled tight against her bottom cheeks, stretching the stockings against her skin. The uniform was short enough for her to feel the frilled hem rise up, exposing the shiny strip of black rubber between her thighs and the pert curves of her rear.

She closed her eyes, imagining the enticing picture that her prone, uniformed body presented. It excited her to think of it, despite the apprehension that was making her heart pound. She inhaled sharply, the fear surging quickly when she felt Katerina's hand on her thigh. Katerina stroked her for a while, exploring the differing textures of bare flesh and smooth rubber with the tips of her fingers.

The first stroke came unexpectedly, Katerina bringing her palm down hard on Emily's right side. Emily winced but held her breath as the stab of sensation gave way to a glow of warmth on her flesh. The second stroke landed in the same place, smacking down with the sharp slapping sound of flesh on flesh. A third stroke landed on the other side, marking Emily's skin with red handprints that contrasted with the natural tone of her skin.

Katerina spanked hard, stroke following stroke in a smooth rhythm that seemed to touch every inch of Emily's posterior. Emily began to utter smothered cries of pain as the redness seeped into her body. Each time she was smacked hard she inched forward, pressing her body down on to the desk so that her nipples rubbed against the tightness of her dress. She tried to keep her long legs straight and her bottom pointing upward, afraid to let go in case Mistress punished her even more.

Her backside smarted painfully as Katerina's hand left its mark. Soon Emily's uttered cries of pain became softer, whispered sighs that signalled the subtle changes that she felt. The stinging pain had transformed into a red heat that glowed on her punished bottom cheeks, a glow that seemed to travel through her body, linking with the eddies of sensation that were rubbed on to her nipples and the savage fire that was ignited deep in her sex. She felt the wetness inside her cunt, a moisture that oozed as she pushed herself hard against the edge of the desk or when Katerina's hand landed violently on her backside.

'She's ready for the crop, I think,' Katerina concluded finally, stepping back to admire the deep blush that she had imprinted on Emily's pert rear cheeks. She stroked her fingers across the reddest part of the punished bottom and was rewarded with a long, slow sigh of pleasure from Emily.

'Thank you, Katerina,' Anderson responded, also stroking Emily's backside. Emily closed her eyes and let his hands explore her body; she lifted her bottom higher, parting her thighs as far as she could, in the vain hope that his fingers would brush against her pussy. He flattened his hand against her bottom cheeks, shaping his fingers around her firm punished flesh, but he seemed to be careful not to use his fingers where they might give her pleasure.

'Six strokes of the crop should suit her well enough,' Anderson suggested.

'Only six?' Patrick asked disappointedly.

'Six,' Anderson said. 'For the moment. I think perhaps I need to have some time alone with her. Is that acceptable?'

Patrick laughed graciously. 'Of course that's acceptable. Six strokes here and then you can continue as you like when you're alone.'

Emily shuddered. Having Katerina and Patrick around was reassuring in its own way – they at least knew her and her limits. But Anderson? She looked up at Katerina, trying to communicate the disquiet that she felt without speaking. Katerina looked at her and then deliberately looked away.

Emily winced and cried out sharply as the crop whistled viciously through the air and then snapped down hard across her stinging backside. The pain of contact was intense, an electric shock of sensation. She tried to stand up but Patrick forced her down, pressing on her shoulders so that she remained flat across the desk.

'I see you're not entirely happy with the crop,' Anderson remarked, nonchalantly. 'Never mind; I'm certain you'll learn to appreciate its finer qualities with a little more practice.'

The next stroke came down hard, the leather tongue on the end of the fine rod snapping down across her bottom. The smooth redness that had been imparted by the spanking receded quickly; it was nothing compared to the thin weals of the crop would leave. Emily yelped again, her knuckles white as she gripped the edge of the desk, bracing herself as the third stroke crashed down.

'She's a noisy little thing, isn't she?' Anderson commented, tracing with his fingers the three red lines he had marked on Emily's behind.

'Would you prefer her to be gagged?' Patrick offered.

'No,' Anderson chuckled, 'let her sing a little.'

Emily cried out again and again, her voice growing hoarse as she uttered a strangled cry of pain with each of the three hard strokes that followed. Everything else was blocked out; she thought of nothing, imagined nothing. The sharp strokes that burned on her backside became the only reality. When the crop bit down into her flesh it burned deep in her sex, on her nipples, all over her body. The concept of pain became one with the idea of pleasure; they merged and mixed completely so that, with the last stroke, she climaxed suddenly, her body exploding with pleasure. She felt more alive, more intense, more complete than she had done at any other time.

Still bent across the desk, unable to move because of the agony and the pleasure, she slowly became aware that Patrick had let go of her shoulders. She tried to turn but Anderson put a hand to her back and shook his head.

Katerina was watching, her eyes wide with excitement as Patrick moved into place.

Without a word, Patrick eased her panties down, tugging sharply so that the sticky garment was peeled away from her flesh. She knew that the inside of the shiny rubber panties glistened with the wetness of her sex. He pushed his fingers roughly into her pussy and she sighed hotly, the feel of his fingers inside her adding another layer to the swirl of pleasure sensations that seemed to tingle throughout her body.

Patrick finger-fucked her pussy quickly, using hard, swift strokes that had her panting breathlessly with excitement. When his fingers were soaked, he smeared her juices between the red heat of her bottom cheeks, sliding his fingers repeatedly between her cunt and her anal hole until she was wet all over. She moaned softly as his finger went into her rear opening, sliding in easily against her well-lubricated anal ring.

'She's ready,' Patrick announced.

'You first, old man,' Anderson insisted, grinning broadly as he brushed aside the hair that obscured Emily's half-closed eyes.

Patrick pressed his hard cock against Emily's anal opening and then speared her, forcing his massive hardness into the tight velvety passage of her behind. She inched forward, reaching round to pull her bottom cheeks open so that he could penetrate her deeply. She held her breath as his hardness cleaved her in two, driving into her anal passage so that he possessed her completely. He pushed his abdomen flat against the burning heat of her reddened buttocks, staying in place so that she could feel his cock deep in her rectum.

'Oh . . .' she whispered, uttering pleasure and surprise as Patrick began to fuck her hard, thrusting his cock in and out of her rear passage in a rhythm that made her swoon blissfully. The pleasure was unbearably sweet; it merged with the stinging that still marked her backside and the tingling of her clit as she was forced against the desk.

Patrick took his time, giving himself the maximum amount of pleasure as he fucked her anally, until, able to take no more, he uttered a strangled, guttural cry of pleasure and let go with his climax. He fell over her, his hardness pumping waves of spunk deep into her rear passage until he was sated. When he stepped away, his cock was still hard and he withdrew it slowly from her anus, leaving a wet, slimy trail of fluid leaking down between her rear cheeks.

Anderson took her by the waist, not bothering to wait. He had stripped while Patrick had been arse-fucking Emily and now his hardness slipped easily into her slick anal passage. She sensed him holding his breath as he fucked her slowly, as though he was too afraid to let go in case he climaxed instantly. She murmured softly as the pleasure filled her, bringing her to the edge of climax as he buried his cock deeply in her anus. She began to move back, pressing herself against the smooth muscles of his stomach as he thrust in and out.

They cried out together, his climax flooding into her and triggering her own shock of orgasm. He ground his crotch against her buttocks and she felt his cock flex and pulse inside her. When he let go and stepped back she relaxed at last, closing her eyes as the pleasure subsided into a warm, golden glow of satisfaction. Her thighs were smeared with her juices and the sticky trails of semen that leaked from her behind. She was dirty, disgusting, soiled beyond measure and yet immensely excited by it.

'Do I need to punish you first?' Katerina demanded, when Emily tried to stand up straight.

Emily looked round at the large black phallus that jutted from between Katerina's thighs. She felt the desire return instantly. 'No, Mistress,' she whispered softly, willingly. 'I'm ready.'

She lay back against the desk and reached round to hold her bottom cheeks open, knowing that her spunk-stained rear hole was going to be fucked once more.

* * *

Alexandra waited by the window, occasionally sneaking glances at her reflection in the mirror on the opposite side of the room. She had dressed according to Joanna's instructions – white trainers, short blue skirt, a tight white top and just a dab of colour on her lips. It was what Joanna wanted, even down to the shoes and the bare legs that were displayed to best effect by the flared skirt. Reflected back to Alexandra was a picture of young, female innocence; unsullied, virginal, naive. When asked, Joanna had explained it – and the other seduction games they had played previously – as recapturing her own seduction and self-discovery as a young adult.

'Are you sure this is safe?' Alexandra asked when Joanna arrived. Helen was down on the terrace, busy working, just as Joanna had been a minute earlier.

'Don't worry,' Joanna giggled softly, 'we're safe from the other girls here.'

Alexandra nodded. Joanna, dressed almost identically, had already started the game. As a young adult, Joanna had shown promise as a tennis player and it had seemed a good idea for her to join a college which had a good record in turning out tennis pros. It had been a female-only establishment, and Joanna had soon discovered more about her true nature than she had dared to imagine.

Joanna walked over to the window and kissed Alexandra on the lips, pressing her mouth forcefully to them so that Alexandra had to struggle for breath. They held each other close and Alexandra was tantalised by the feel of Joanna's large dark nipples as they embraced.

'This is lovely,' Joanna sighed dreamily when they parted. 'You look so good.

Alexandra blushed modestly. She loved to hear how good she looked, she loved the idea of being a beautiful and desirable young woman. She smiled shyly as Joanna touched her, reaching down to stroke her smooth bare thigh. 'That feels divine,' she whispered, leaning back against the wall as Joanna continued to caress her.

'You're such a bad girl these days,' Joanna teased, rubbing her fingers up and down the smooth, sensitive flesh of Alexandra's inner thigh.

'I can't help it,' Alexandra purred, as Joanna's fingers closed around her hard cock.

They kissed again, Alexandra closing her eyes to the pleasure and parting her thighs so that Joanna could do as she liked. Alexandra loved having her erection stroked softly and teased back and forth sensuously under her skirt. She reached out to touch Joanna's nipples, visible as hard dark rings beneath the pure white of her tight T-shirt.

'Let me fuck you now,' Joanna murmured hotly.

'But we'll get caught,' Alexandra said, trying to complain, but her voice became soft and indistinct as Joanna's fingers worked their magic on her cock.

Joanna knelt down in front of Alexandra, lifting the short blue skirt to expose the hard flesh that she had been stroking with her fingers. She kissed the glans softly, her full dark lips closing around the bulb of fluid that balanced on the end so that she could suck it in. She closed the fingers of one hand around Alexandra's cock and then slid her other hand under Alexandra's thighs, letting her middle finger press between the bottom cheeks.

Alexandra sighed deliriously as Joanna's finger began to explore the space under her balls. She saw Joanna wet her finger and then put it back, circling teasingly around the rear hole until she could stand it no longer. She uttered a sharp cry of pain and then relaxed into the pleasure as Joanna's finger sank in deeply. She moaned softly and almost buckled at the knees as Joanna begin to finger-fuck her, sliding her finger in and out, deliciously.

'You're such a bad girl,' Joanna whispered, smothering Alexandra's cock with soft kisses. 'Letting me finger your pussy like this.'

Alexandra uttered a sigh of pure pleasure and forced her cock deep into Joanna's welcoming mouth. The pleasure of being a bad girl was indescribable and she loved it more than anything. She wanted Joanna's finger inside her, she wanted to be finger-fucked in the arse and told she was a bad girl, she wanted it –

'You fucking bitch!'

Alexandra opened her eyes just as she climaxed, letting her semen spurt into Joanna's waiting mouth. There, in the doorway, was Helen, watching them with a look of pure disgust on her face.

Joanna stood up hurriedly, wiping Alexandra's come from her lips. 'Look,' she said, 'I can explain.'

'No you fucking can't,' Helen hissed. The colour had gone from her face, and the violence in her voice was so controlled that it made Alex fear the worst.

'Helen –'

'Shut up! You,' she said, pointing at Alex, 'get changed and get out. Now!'

Alex looked at Joanna, who merely nodded and then looked away, unable to say anything.

Fourteen

Helen stormed straight into the house as soon as
Katerina answered the door, leaving Alex to trail
helplessly in her wake. She went from room to room,
slamming doors and calling angrily for Patrick. Katerina
stood by and watched her, keeping her silence until Helen
finally realised that Patrick was out.

'Whatever it is,' Katerina told her calmly, 'you'll have
to talk to me about it first.'

Helen glared at her, eyes narrowed behind her glasses,
and then walked into Katerina's study. 'I was hoping to
talk to the boss,' she sneered, 'but I'll settle for second
best this time.'

Alex followed Katerina into the room, dreading the
scene that was to follow.

Katerina smiled sweetly. 'Do you really imagine that I'm
going to be angered by that? If you want to go back and wait
until Patrick returns, then do so; it's no concern of mine.'

'I didn't want him in the house in the first place,' Helen
snapped, pointing an accusing finger at Alex. 'I knew he
was bad news. That's why that bastard Patrick sent him
to stay with us.'

'Has he not worked well?' Katerina enquired calmly,
flicking her dark eyes towards Alex.

'He's worked too fucking well,' Helen replied acidly. 'I
caught him in bed with Joanna. The two of them were
fucking like animals,' she added, looking at him venomously.

'Isn't Joanna an adult?' Katerina asked. 'Is she not allowed to make love with whoever she pleases?'

'He was dressed like a girl! The freak was pretending to be a woman so that he could seduce Joanna. That's why he was sent to stay with us, isn't it? Patrick wanted to split Joanna and me up.'

Katerina sighed expressively. 'Sometimes the paranoia in this place astounds me,' she said. 'I repeat, Joanna is an adult. If she chooses to make love with Alex –'

'I don't fucking want to hear it!'

'As you wish,' Katerina agreed. 'In that case Alex will return to us until he can be assigned to some other task.'

'What's going on? Alex?'

All eyes turned to Emily, wrapped tightly in a pink towelling robe that matched the radiant tone of her freshly bathed skin. She ran to Alex and kissed him on the mouth quickly, wrapping her arms around him, completely ignoring the tense atmosphere in the room.

'Who the fuck is she?' Helen demanded, rounding on Alex with a look of pure fury.

'This is Emily,' he replied quietly. 'My girlfriend.'

'Hi! You must be Helen,' Emily said, beaming her a friendly smile.

'What are you doing here?'

Emily laughed softly. 'I'm staying here, of course,' she explained. 'Is something wrong?'

'What is she doing here?' Helen repeated slowly, turning on her heels to glare at Katerina.

'Emily and Alex arrived together,' she explained. 'She was assigned some work with us, which was why Alex was available for you.'

'I bet she was assigned work here,' Helen murmured darkly. 'Well, you can just unassign her from that and put Alex in her place.'

'What do you mean?' Emily asked, looking askance at Helen.

'I mean that your bastard of a boyfriend hasn't finished

215

the work I set for him. Now that he's screwed up big time, I think it only fair that you finish the job. Katerina?'

'It's not as simple as that –'

'Yes it is!' Helen insisted violently. 'It is very simple. You kept Emily's presence a secret from the rest of the community. You only told us about Alex because it suited your purposes to send him to us. You've abused the rules again, Katerina. You've ignored everything we set out to do because that's what Patrick bloody wants. Well, *I'm* bending the rules now, and I want to swap him for her. Is that okay? Him for her, and if you don't like it I'll cause such a stink that this whole bloody place will fall apart for good.'

Katerina and Helen glared at each other for a long, tense moment, and then Katerina looked away. 'Emily, go and pack,' she whispered.

'She can't do this,' Alex tried to argue, but he fell silent when Katerina looked at him.

'Emily,' she repeated, 'I want you to go and pack. You're going to stay with Helen and Joanna for a few days.'

'But what about Patrick?' Emily asked timidly.

'Don't argue,' Katerina told her, sounding tired. 'Please, go and get ready.'

Emily looked at Alex and then turned to go to her room.

'I'm going to enjoy seducing your little girlfriend,' Helen told him, grinning.

'Alex, I want you to wait outside,' Katerina instructed, before he had a chance to reply.

He walked to the door and then turned back to face the two women, who were still glaring at each other. 'Why is it,' he asked sadly, 'that you all hate each other so much?'

Alex watched the red tail lights of Helen's car tracing a path down the hill towards her house, as she went back home with Emily as her prize. He wanted to feel anger and rage, to match Helen's violence with his own, but instead he felt drained. Things were too complicated, too screwed up. Eden should have been a paradise instead of the hell that it was coming to resemble. His only hope was that Helen did not mistreat Emily, though he knew that Emily was more than capable of looking after herself.

And Joanna? He moved away from the window in what had been Emily's room but was now his own. Joanna should have been so strong but instead she had meekly assented to his being sent away; she had hardly dared look at him as he had left. It was as if she were exhausted by the sheer effort of just keeping going, as though she had decided that anything was better than arguing with Helen.

He lay back on the bed and closed his eyes, hoping that sleep would creep up to rescue him from his heavy thoughts and dark emotions. When he turned on to his side, he felt the frilly panties rubbing delightfully against his skin, reminding him that Joanna and he had shared something special. His cock hardened at the memories of what they had done, the images of him as a girl exciting him despite the heaviness of the mood that now affected him. Joanna and Alexandra – the games they had played had been the perfect escape from the dreary round of work and argument.

His thoughts were interrupted by a tentative knock on the door. For a moment he hoped that it was Emily – that Helen had changed her mind and left her behind – but he knew that Helen wasn't the type to give in.

'May I come in?' Katerina asked, opening the door but making no move to enter.

'I want you to know that I had nothing to do with us being caught,' he stated flatly, sitting up on the bed. He had steadfastly refused to obey Patrick's order, fearing precisely that which had come about.

'In that case you have nothing to feel guilty about,' she replied, managing a slight smile.

'You know,' he said, 'if I had known that Eden was like this, I would have stayed at home.'

Katerina stood by the door, her body framed by the pale light of the evening. 'Have you not learned much about yourself?' she asked softly. Her eyes were hidden, shielded by the shadows but Alex could guess at the intensity with which they regarded him.

'I have,' he admitted, 'but I've also leant a lot about how people live together.'

She laughed softly, moving at last into the room. 'We set a bad example,' she said, making it sound trivial. 'Do you think that Patrick and I are at fault? Or perhaps that Helen is the one who is in the wrong?'

'I'm not taking sides,' he told her, thinking back to what Joanna had said.

'Good, I am glad,' she assured him, sitting on the side of the bed close to him.

'Do you think that Emily's going to be okay?'

'Yes, I think she's probably ready to deal with living with Helen and Joanna. More to the point, do you feel ready to face Patrick when he returns?'

The question had not occurred to him, but now that he thought about it he realised that his rage and fury had not disappeared with Helen. 'Isn't this what he wanted? Didn't he want me to get caught with Joanna?'

'He did,' she agreed. 'But he did not imagine that he would lose Emily in the process. Nor did he imagine that you would be dressed as a girl when you were caught by Helen.'

Alex blushed furiously, the colour burning his face. He had hoped that the games he had played with Joanna would remain secret, from Katerina and Patrick and from Emily.

'I want you to be a girl for me now,' Katerina whispered. 'I want you to be a good little girl for your Mistress.'

Alex looked at her. There was no taunting in her eyes, no sign of sneering; instead, he saw the same look of

218

excitement that always touched him sexually. He looked at her and knew that Alexandra was still with him, still part of him and that now Mistress was ready to continue where Joanna had left off.

'Joanna gave me a girl's name,' he confessed. 'When we played I was called Alexandra.'

'Well, Alexandra, I think it's time you understood that every girl needs to have a Mistress to worship.' She stood up suddenly. 'Be ready for me in five minutes,' she ordered, her voice taking on a natural tone of command. 'There are clothes and cosmetics for you to use. If you are not ready by the time I return, Alexandra will also learn what it is to be punished by her Mistress.'

'Yes, Mistress,' Alex responded, his erection straining against the silky material of the panties he still wore.

Helen stopped the car in front of her house and switched the headlights off. 'Did you know,' she said, turning in her seat to face Emily, 'that your boyfriend was dressing up as a woman to have sex with my girlfriend?' They were the first words Helen had spoken since leaving Katerina's house.

'Pardon?' Emily replied, not quite able to believe what she had just heard.

'I said that he liked to dress up as a woman so that he could seduce Joanna,' Helen repeated, smiling grimly, as though enjoying the look of confusion on Emily's face. 'He liked to be called Alexandra when he was doing it; it gave him a thrill to have a girl's name when he was done up in drag.'

'Alex?'

Helen laughed. 'Alexandra. When I caught them together he was wearing a short skirt and tennis shoes. He'd even shaved his legs and was wearing lipstick and rouge.'

'That can't have been his idea,' Emily stated flatly. The notion sounded so outlandish – it was hard to picture Alex as a girl.

'You mean he's never done this before?'

'Never.'

Helen nodded. 'You're probably right,' she said. 'The idea's far too good to have come from him.'

'Then it must have been Joanna's idea,' Emily responded quickly. 'I guess she's probably done that sort of thing before.'

Helen smiled at the riposte. 'Maybe you're right. Anyway, now that you're here, things are going to be different.'

'So what do you want me for?'

'If Joanna's so eager to make it with boys,' Helen explained, 'then I think it's only right that we help her along.'

'I don't understand,' Emily admitted, feeling nervous because Helen was smiling even more broadly.

'You're into all that obedience stuff, aren't you? Well, all you've got to do is follow my example. Just do as you're told and everything will be fine.'

'What about Joanna?'

'Just do as you're told and she'll be okay. She's insisting on moving back into her own room, so you'll have to stay with me tonight. But that's okay. It'll be better all round like that.'

Emily followed Helen into the house, aware at once of the cold silence and of the darkness, as Joanna had switched all the lights off. The geography of the house was, however, familiar enough for Emily to know that she was being taken directly up to one of the bedrooms. At the top of the stairs she saw that one of the bedroom doors was shut tight and that a sliver of light was visible under it. Helen made them wait for a moment, but there was no sound coming from inside Joanna's room.

Emily dropped her heavy bag by the side of the sumptuous double bed in Helen's room and then turned to face her. Helen was smiling, her eyes sparkling with a feverish, almost childlike excitement. With her closely cropped hair and round glasses she looked both the picture of innocence and yet immensely tough.

'Aren't you pissed off at your boyfriend?' she asked, opening one of the wardrobes which lined the wall directly opposite the windows.

'No, why should I be?' Emily asked, leaning back against the wall rather than sitting on the edge of the bed. It was obvious that Helen was intensely pissed off with her own partner, probably more so than she herself was with Alex.

'Because he was getting into new stuff without you,' Helen explained, as she rummaged through the clothes which were racked tightly together.

'No. We're not like that. I was getting into new things with Katerina and Patrick that he didn't know about.'

Helen looked at her coldly. 'I suppose you're another one of those pathetic little girls who thinks Patrick's wonderful,' she sneered.

'Is there anybody that you're not angry with?'

'No, I hate everybody,' Helen said, laughing. 'How do you like the idea of playing your boyfriend's game for a while?'

'What game?' Emily asked suspiciously.

'Don't worry, I'm sure you're going to enjoy this . . .'

Joanna stretched sleepily, yawned and turned over. Hovering on the blurred border between sleep and consciousness, she wrapped herself tightly in the thin cotton sheet and exhaled softly as her eyes flickered open momentarily. She was vaguely aware that there was someone else in the room; a shadow standing by the bed, but the outline refused to sharpen and sleep felt too good to disturb. The room around her blurred again; her eyes closed and she drifted back to the dark sleep that kept her safe.

A light was flicked on in the corner of the room, and she became aware of the soft orange glow behind her eyes. Had Helen come back to make amends? The thought burst through the haze of sleep but she lay in silence, unwilling to abandon the coccooning warmth and comfort of her bed.

'Jo, baby,' came the whispered voice, low and breath-less into Joanna's ear. She made no reply, preferring the silence that still held hope of sleep.

The thin cotton sheet was pulled back gently, exposing the flawless brown of Joanna's back to the soft peach glow from the bedside lamp. She was naked, her dark body curled up tightly, her long limbs drawn up so that her backside was pertly rounded. She remained still as the warmth of her body was touched by the cool air that had settled in the room.

The steady rhythm of her breath was disturbed by the sudden touch of fingers against her skin; fingers that smoothed down the curve of her back with a silky, confident motion. She relaxed again, breathing softly as the unknown hand caressed her, trailing up and down her back with a slow, deliberate motion that scarcely disturb-ed her and yet felt beautifully sensual. She remained still, waiting patiently to see what would happen next.

The hand reached lower, tracing the tight curves of her bottom, inching down to explore the length of Joanna's thigh and then back up again. It felt like the most erotic massage, the fingers soothing away any disquiet that she felt. Gradually, she began to respond, her senses ignited by the slow, sensitive stimulation of her body. When she felt the fingers stroking her breasts, she knew that her nipples would be hardening little by little, as though awaking from a deep sleep.

Cool lips touched her on the shoulder, kissing tenta-tively as the fingers stroked her nipples. There was something odd, something that Joanna could not quite perceive as she lay half asleep and half aroused in her bed. She sighed as the skilful fingers reached down to tease her between the thighs, rubbing softly between the petals of her sex without venturing into the velvet heat within. The kisses grew more insistent, moving from her shoulder to her throat and then to her back.

There was a movement on the bed and suddenly Joanna realised that she was being kissed by two mouths.

She struggled against the pleasure to open her eyes, but again fingers stroked her breasts, thighs and pussy. When she finally opened her eyes, a hand was placed over them and she was kissed hard on the lips, her mouth opened and explored by another's tongue. Her mind reeled – doubts rose quickly to the surface – but the pleasure of being kissed and touched was too strong to resist.

When the hand was taken from her eyes, she let herself glimpse those around her, but in the weak light she could not make out who her companions were. The person who had kissed her on the lips had not been Helen; of that she was sure. She moaned softly as the person behind her pressed a single finger deep into the wetness of her sex. She arched her back instinctively, pushing out her backside so that she could be fingered properly. The reactions of her body merged with the feeling of not being quite awake, so that everything felt like a secret and sexy dream.

She responded to another kiss on the lips, opening her mouth to the invasive, mobile tongue. Her hard nipples were being massaged, squeezed and stroked by loving hands that sent tendrils of pleasurable sensation through her body. She turned slightly so that she could part her thighs. Her pussy was slick with her honey and she sighed deliciously as two fingers were pushed into her and moved rhythmically.

Dreamily, she reached out to touch her unknown lover, wanting to caress the person who teased her nipples while kissing her so passionately. Her hand was gripped tightly and then moved down into place, and held against the rough denim that her lover wore. Her hand pressed down, her fingers finding the bulging hardness that she had suspected. Who was the strange man in her bed? And whose fingers were bringing her ever closer to climax as they thrust quickly into her pussy?

The questions were stifled quickly, a hand covering her eyes once more as she was kissed passionately on the mouth. She tried to struggle, to push away the hand that blinded her, but the pleasure in her sex was insistent. When a finger eased between her bottom cheeks to caress her rear hole, she arched her back and cried out her pleasure, climaxing quickly as a mouth closed tightly over a nipple.

'Don't talk,' a voice hissed in her ear.

'Who are you?' she whispered, blinded still by the hand over her eyes.

'Keep your mouth shut,' came the voice from behind her. Male or female? In the near darkness Joanna could not even be sure about the gender of her unknown lovers. True, her fingers had closed tightly around a hard prick, and the shadows she had glimpsed seemed to outline young men, but the voices were strange, alien.

She was pushed on to her stomach, turned over roughly by unseen hands. A frisson of fear sparked deep inside her as a scarf was tied quickly around her head, blindfolding her completely. The pleasure of orgasm still buzzed through her body, but now she could feel a colder tension settling over the room.

'Do you think she sucks cock?' one of the voices asked, speaking with a guttural, menacing hardness.

'She'll take it any way we want,' came the reply.

Joanna cried out as she was penetrated again, rough fingers pushing deep into her pussy without warning. She lifted her backside high, opening herself as three fingers slipped in and out of her wetness. The sudden pain of penetration gave way to an intense pleasure that made her gasp. Vaguely, she was aware that one of her unseen companions was getting undressed; she could hear him tugging down sharply at his denims.

The feel of a stiff cock against her skin made her catch her breath – the hard flesh stroked by accident against her thigh, giving her a warning of what she should expect. Her hands were free and she tried to undo the blindfold, but she was easily caught out; her hands were seized and stretched over her head. She tensed but the pleasure in her sex was growing and she could not help but move with the rhythm of the fingers fucking her beautifully.

A belt was used to bind her hands together, tightening around her wrists and then pulling them hard against the top of the bed. When she was tightly bound her head was pulled around – her hair gripped painfully tightly in a fist – and she was kissed again, her complaints sucked easily away. She was being used, her body explored with impunity and there was nothing she could do to fight the pleasure that was her response.

'Please – who are you?' she begged, but even her questions were punctuated by her sighs of pleasure.

Her breasts were pushed flat under her weight, but two hands slid round to massage her nipples, pulling at the bullets of flesh with playful roughness. Again and again she was tantalised by the caress of an erect hardness, touching her across the thigh or in the side or against her calves. She climaxed again, lifting herself high so that one set of the fingers could go deep into her pussy, while the other hand toyed with her clit.

'Do you think she's ever been fucked here?'

Joanna tensed as a slick finger rubbed her pussy juices against her tight, rear hole. She struggled quickly, pulling hard against the leather belt that gripped her wrists together. The hard slap against her bottom resounded through the room and the brief but intense pain settled into a warm glow that warned her of more to come.

She lay still as her bottom was massaged with the slippery juices that poured from her pussy. Each time she felt a finger trace a circle of wetness around her anus she tensed, afraid that it signalled an attempt to fuck her there. The dimensions of the cock she had felt seemed to grow in her mind; the thought of the massive shaft pressing into the tightness of her anal hole made her tense even more.

She uttered a brief cry of pain as a finger was pushed against the ring of muscle, entering her slowly. She held her breath, afraid to let go in case it hurt even more. The tension was broken only by the spasm of pleasure as her nipples were stroked again. She relaxed, slowly becoming

225

used to the intrusive presence pushed deep into her anal passage. When she felt the finger begin to move, frigging her gently, she sighed softly. The pleasure was intense, different from the pleasure of having her pussy fucked, but it was pleasure all the same.

Soon she was murmuring softly, opening herself to the thrusting exploration of her anus. The wetness that poured from her was licked up softly as her pussy was mouthed from behind. She managed to get up on to her hands and knees so that her backside was displayed to its best advantage, and, her legs parted so that she could be entered from behind while her pussy was sucked. She climaxed quickly as a tongue snaked into her cunt and then lapped playfully at its apex.

One of her mysterious lovers slid under her completely to suckle at her large breasts, which swayed as she moved with the rhythm of the fingers that explored her pussy and her arsehole. She cried out in pain and pleasure as teeth closed around her engorged nipples and when the thrusting in her rear grew faster and deeper. Suddenly, she felt the belt seeming to work free of the bed, coming away so that her wrists were still bound tight but she was no longer tied to the headboard. She squatted down quickly, forcing her backside down on to the hands that explored her.

'Sit up!' the person under her ordered, roughly. She obeyed instantly, moving her bottom down on to the hardness that she longed for. The pleasure of being impaled on the immense prick made her gasp repeatedly as her pussy was forced open by the thick, meaty cock.

She began to buck and writhe, moving the hardness deeper into her sex as her lover held her by the waist. They fucked together, Joanna writhing deliriously on the penis so that the pleasure was intense for both of them.

'Two at once,' the other man laughed, pushing a finger into her rear hole again. She screamed her orgasm at that instant, driven into pure bliss by the feel of a cock in her pussy and of a finger inserted deep into her anus.

She fell forward, her body pressing down on the man under her as he jerked his rod deep into the slick folds of her pussy. They were both completely still for a moment and then she moaned softly. The other man was pushing the bulging head of his erection into her slippery anal hole – he held the position for a moment and then pushed it in. The feel of two cocks inside her was too much for Joanna to take – she shuddered and felt herself grow dizzy with pleasure.

The cock in her anus seemed to fill her up, to cleave her in two, but she felt, too, an intense pride that she could take such hardness from behind. She knew also that each man could feel the other's prick inside her, that each time they moved the two cocks were almost rubbing together. When they began to fuck her, it was with a slow, unsteady motion but she felt the double pleasure bubbling inside her. She squirmed and began to respond furiously, matching their thrusts, eager to have both men take her hard. She wanted them to fuck her with a violence that would make her pleasure molten.

All three moved together, their bodies working as one until Joanna screamed her climax and then felt her two partners shuddering with pleasure. They fell into a bundle of bodies, arms and legs everywhere as they sprawled helplessly on the bed.

Joanna lost track of time; she felt as though she had blacked out, come round and then blacked out again. She opened her eyes and realised that the blindfold had slipped free. In the pale orange light she looked down and saw the glistening cock that stood proud from between the legs of one of her two lovers. The leather harness that held the dildo in place contrasted with the creamy white of her skin. Beside her lay Helen, also wearing a strap-on cock that jutted manfully from between her thighs.

'Suck me,' the first woman demanded, looking at Joanna with a predatory smile.

'You must be Emily,' Joanna guessed.

'Don't call me that,' Emily replied. 'I like the idea that

I've just fucked a woman the way a man does. Now, are you going to suck my cock or do I have to take you the way he did?'

Helen smiled. 'I think she loves having a prick up the arse, don't you?'

Joanna closed her eyes and nodded. Her hands were still bound and she knew that she was helpless to resist the two 'men' who had invaded her room. She sat up with difficulty, trying to get into place to suck the cock that glistened with her pussy juices. When she felt Emily's fingers seek her anal hole she responded at once, offering her backside meekly.

Alexandra sat passively on the floor, her short skirt in disarray, her reddened backside striped with six distinct lines, cut by the riding crop that Mistress still held. The crumpled folds of her skirt covered her thick erection, cased in the skimpiest layer of a white G-string. The pain that smarted on her backside had been an intense sea of sensation but had now receded into a warm glow that tingled like her arousal.

Mistress was dressed in a short leather skirt, black high heels and a leather corset that cinched her waist and pushed her breasts up enticingly. Black elbow-length gloves completed her outfit, the glossy fingers closed tight around the handle of the crop she had used so elegantly on her slave.

'You've got to get her back,' Patrick demanded. He had returned to find Mistress beating the last stroke against Alexandra's proffered backside. His reaction had been instant anger, directed not at Helen, nor Joanna or Emily, but at Mistress.

'This is what you wanted, Patrick,' Katerina replied calmly, ignoring his anger. 'Emily has served her purpose; Neil Anderson used her the way he wanted to.'

Patrick laughed bitterly. 'Do you really think he's going to be satisfied with one session? I dropped him off at his hotel and then he said that he needed to see us

228

again tomorrow. He made it clear that he wants to see Emily again.'

'Then you'll have to tell him that he can't,' Katerina replied simply.

'Don't be so stupid,' Patrick hissed. 'You know that without him the deal's off.'

'He can't come round tomorrow, anyway,' Katerina announced, with a slight smile.

'Why not?'

'Because I've called a meeting of the community.'

For a moment Alexandra was certain that Patrick was going to explode – his face turned red and then deathly white. 'For what reason?' he asked, his voice barely a whisper.

'Because many of us are unhappy with the way things are being run.'

'Is it that bitch Helen? Is this her idea?'

Katerina shook her head sadly. 'No, she hasn't been told yet.'

'Then who the hell are you to do this?'

'Joanna and I have spoken to everybody apart from you, Helen and Oliver. We feel that the time has come to sort things out for good.'

Patrick sat down in the nearest chair, his look of anger giving way to one of shock. 'But what about our plans?' he asked, numbly.

'We'll discuss that tomorrow,' Katerina told him, 'with everybody else.'

She reached down and tapped Alexandra with the riding crop. 'You'll spend the night with Mistress tonight,' she said softly. 'I want to see what a good girl you are with that pretty little mouth of yours.'

'Yes, Mistress,' Alexandra replied and she bent down to kiss Mistress's shiny high heels. Suddenly she felt immensely proud of her Mistress, and she knew that she had been honoured in being allowed to serve her.

229

Fifteen

Mistress had woken up early that morning, and though the day ahead was obviously going to be fraught with confrontation she looked radiant. She had lain naked on the bed, the bright sunshine streaming across her tanned, golden body. Alexandra had never seen Mistress looking so relaxed, the haunted look that she habitually wore had cleared, as though a great weight had been lifted from her shoulders. Her dark eyes had sparkled when Alexandra had crawled on to the bed beside her to kiss her hand meekly.

'What's going to happen, Mistress?' Alexandra asked softly, her eyes travelling across the sleek curves of Mistress's naked body.

'I don't know,' Mistress admitted, stroking Alexandra absently. 'Perhaps it's time to finish the experiment. In many ways, Eden has failed our expectations.'

Mistress had spoken without sadness, but the idea that Eden had failed was one that made Alexandra feel depressed. 'No,' she said, 'perhaps it's time to clear the air and start again.'

Mistress smiled, 'Perhaps,' she agreed. 'Now, I'd better get ready. I think it would be best if you remain here, today.'

'Yes, Mistress,' Alexandra agreed softly, kissing her on the hand once more. She could not take her eyes from Mistress's body; from the dark nipples that peaked on the fullness of her breasts, or the jet black curls that framed the opening of her sex, or the long, supple thighs that were stretched out so elegantly.

'What is it that you want, Alexandra?' Mistress asked, sensing her growing excitement.

'To give you pleasure, Mistress,' Alexandra replied shyly. Mistress looked at her gravely, and then, just when Alexandra was certain that she had done wrong, Mistress smiled. 'When I return,' she said, turning over on to her stomach, 'I want to find you dressed completely as a girl.' She arched her back and lifted her bottom high, presenting her backside to her adoring slave.

Alexandra's heart beat faster, pounding the excitement deep in her chest. She gazed at Mistress, bent over on the bed, her backside high and her face pressed into the soft folds of a pillow. The deep cleft was parted slightly so that Alexandra was presented with the perfect picture of her Mistress's pussy lips and the darker anal ring that puckered enticingly.

Her Mistress was a goddess and Alexandra a slave fit only to worship with her mouth. She kissed Mistress gently under the thigh, trembling slightly as her lips touched the smooth golden flesh of her idol. She nuzzled along the thigh and then kissed the delicate petals that were Mistress's labia. She kissed softly, hardly daring to press herself closer, letting her tongue move back and forth slowly. She lapped teasingly before slipping her tongue between the pussy lips to touch at the first dew drops of feminine nectar.

Mistress sighed softly and Alexandra's heart thrilled with delight. Eden had taught her so much – she had discovered many selves in her time there and the ways of pleasure had been the key to them all. She pressed her tongue deep into Mistress's body and Mistress responded with a flow of honey and a deep, satisfied sigh of pleasure. Alexandra sucked deeper, pushing her face directly against Mistress's bottom so that her tongue could lick slow and deep. She dared use her fingers at last, prising open Mistress's pussy lips gently so that her tongue could lap against the pink walls of her sex.

She sought Mistress's pussy bud, seeking it with the wet tip of her tongue before sucking on it directly. Mistress squirmed and her ecstatic sighs voiced the pleasure that Alexandra, too, felt stirring deep inside her. She sucked harder, putting her lips to Mistress's sex and pushing her tongue into the velvet delight of her goddess's body.

Mistress climaxed moments later and Alexandra moved back to admire the radiance of her naked body. She longed to touch and stroke Mistress's breasts, to suck on the hard nipples or to kiss her lovingly on the mouth – but these delights were forbidden to her. As a slave she was honoured enough merely to be allowed a glimpse of Mistress's beauty.

'Alexandra,' Mistress murmured sleepily, 'you neglect your duties. Do not think that I will forget this.'

'I'm sorry, Mistress,' Alexandra whispered, brought back to earth by the honeyed words which concealed the bitter threat of punishment within the sweetness with which they had been uttered.

She leant forward again and put her lips to Mistress's pussy, which was still swimming with the sweet juices of her orgasm. Alexandra licked them into her mouth, her quicksilver tongue making Mistress whisper her pleasure. In moments her mouth was suffused completely with the very essence of her Mistress's pleasure.

Mistress pushed her backside high again, parting her thighs so that her anal opening was exposed completely. Alexandra felt a surge of excitement as she realised what it was that her Mistress desired still. She touched her tongue to the tightly puckered hole and felt Mistress respond with a swooning sigh.

'That's it – Good girl,' Mistress whispered, lifting herself higher, opening herself so that her rear hole was a stretched, tight ring of pure muscle.

Alexandra used the tip of her tongue to circle Mistress's rear hole, wetting and teasing it at the same time. The thought that she was sucking on the forbidden anal hole only made her feel more excited, so that under her flimsy skirt her cock bulged hard. Soon she was pushing her tongue into the dark opening, pressing against the delicious resistance of the anal ring and then probing deep inside.

Mistress began to slide her fingers into her pussy, stroking her pleasure bud with each thrust of Alexandra's tongue until she tensed, arched her back and gasped her climax. She rolled over and parted her thighs instinctively, making way for Alexandra to continuing licking at the rear hole, as her pleasure subsided from an intense peak into a sated glow of delight.

'I want you to be here for me when I return,' Mistress murmured softly, running her long fingers through Alexandra's hair.

'I will, Mistress, I promise.'

'Expect to be punished,' Mistress added, her smile edged with darkness.

'Yes, Mistress,' Alexandra sighed submissively.

It was the high heels that caused Alexandra most excitement. Mistress had provided everything: seamed stockings, suspender belt, pretty black panties, and a lacy slip top that was pure heaven against her skin. With the underwear, Mistress had provided a short, flared skirt that reached down to barely cover the black stocking-tops, and a white blouse that contrasted with the black skirt and the lacy underthings. But it was when Alexandra picked up the shiny patent high heels that her heart really skipped a beat.

The sleek curve of the heel narrowed down to a point that was tipped with steel. For a moment, Alexandra just held the shoes close to her face, her lips barely touching the curving heel, her breath misting on the shiny surface. Could they really be for her? It seemed too much to hope for; with her own shiny high heels Alexandra's transformation would be complete. The thought of it aroused her instantly, making her cock stiffen in her lacy panties as she pictured herself balanced on feminine heels.

Finally she put the shoes down on the floor, in front of the full-length mirror on the open inner door of the wardrobe. She looked down on her shoes, balanced side by side, the patent surface a flawlessly glossy black. Inhaling sharply, she dared to put her right foot to its shoe, slipping it into the tight, welcoming leather pocket. Her toes were squeezed together as her heel slipped into the back of the shoe; her foot was constrained, enclosed and contained by the snug fit. In a moment she was standing in front of the mirror, balancing precariously – beautifully – in her own pair of black high heels.

For a while Alexandra did not dare to move. She did not want to spoil her reflected image, she wanted to capture the moment, the look, forever. The stiletto heels forced her to stand straight, making her muscles tense so that her backside, her thighs and her calves were taut. The shoes shaped her body, creating the feminine contours for which her clothes were designed. The question came suddenly, making Alexandra sigh contentedly. 'Am I beautiful?' she asked herself, and for the first time the question was not ridiculous.

The reflection before her was a new self, an image that had been created to match the creature that had emerged from within. Long limbs, smooth skin, eyes that were mysteriously enigmatic, full lips that were glossed – Alexandra stared at herself and, for the first time, did not see Alex at all.

She tried to walk and at first she could not bear to watch herself. She was fumbling, clumsy, unbalanced. Her feet were unused to the discipline of stiletto heels and, for a long while, she struggled to walk at all. However her body adjusted and a feminine, elegant gait was imposed from below, as though the stamping of her heels snapped the life back into her. Soon, she dared to look at the mirror image, surprised to see that not only could she walk in her heels, but that her body moved with a natural sway of the hips.

When she looked at herself over her shoulder, she saw reflected the swish of her loose skirt and noticed that with each step the dark upper band of her stockings was revealed. Even more exciting was the realisation that, if she bent over a little, the pale whiteness of her thighs could be glimpsed between skirt and stocking. She bent over fully, locking her legs so that the seams of her stockings were straight and pointing from her ankles to her bottom. The lower she bent the more flesh she displayed, until she could see the suspender belt pulling at the stockings and could even glimpse the dark lacy material that was pulled tight between her rounded bottom cheeks.

'That's quite a display.'

Alexandra looked up sharply to find that Emily was standing at the door, looking at her sideways and smiling. She felt the colour rush to her face – the burning fire of shame at being caught admiring herself in the mirror combined with the embarrassment of being dressed as a girl in front of Emily. She felt rooted to the spot, as though her widely-spaced heels had sunk deep into the ground. Her skirt had ridden up completely, exposing the pretty lace thong that divided her bottom cheeks and the suspenders which stretched tightly down to her stockings.

'I didn't quite believe Katerina when she told me that you'd been a bad girl,' Emily continued, 'but now that I see it for myself, I can see why she needs to punish you so much.'

Alexandra found the power to move again and she straightened up quickly, smoothing down her skirt modestly to cover up her panties and the glimpse of bare white thigh. When she looked again she saw that Emily was still smiling but when their eyes met the smile seemed to melt away.

'What else did she tell you?' Alexandra asked, her voice

a low, husky whisper of sound. She looked away from Emily's eyes, disturbed by the dark, threatening expression she saw there. Emily was wearing a pair of faded Levi's, trainers and a white T-shirt, which combined with her short hair and stark expression to create a cold, threatening aura about her.

'Do you know what's happening in the meeting?' Alexandra asked, when Emily made no reply. She stepped back towards the bed as Emily walked casually into the room. Her hands were pressed deep into her pockets and the insolent look in her eyes was making Alexandra feel increasingly nervous.

'We're on our own here, aren't we?' Emily remarked, ignoring Alexandra's question.

Alexandra moved back, slightly afraid of the predatory tone of voice that she detected. 'What are you doing?' she asked, stepping back again as Emily approached closer.

'You've been a bad girl, haven't you?'

'Emily –'

'Don't call me that!' she snapped, angrily. 'Now, hasn't anyone ever told you that showing your legs like that is slutty?'

Alexandra swallowed hard. She sat on the bed, her eyes averted, aware only of the way in which Emily was standing so close to her. 'I didn't know you were looking,' she replied meekly.

'No? You mean you were bending over like that for yourself? That makes you an even bigger slut.'

'That's not what I meant,' Alexandra complained.

'What did you mean? Do you know what I think? Do you?'

'What?'

'I think you like teasing cock,' came the hissed reply.

'No . . .' Alexandra whispered. Her pulse was racing and she felt a thrill of fear deep inside her.

'You've been a dirty, slutty little girl.'

Alexandra tensed as Emily sat down beside her. Even the way she sat seemed different; she seemed to occupy

236

more space, her legs were parted wide and her feet planted flat so that she carved out a territory – a male territory – that was aggressive and threatening. Alexandra drew in on herself, yielding the space meekly.

When she was touched on the knee Alexandra almost jumped. She held her breath, hardly daring to look at Emily as her thigh was stroked slowly with an almost possessively sensual touch. Her inner thigh was squeezed softly but firmly, and then she felt fingers moving over the stocking-tops to stroke bare flesh. Her cock strained against the thin lacy covering of her panties, the feel of the flimsy material tantalising on the sensitive flesh of her hardness.

'Don't talk,' Emily whispered softly, her fingers beginning to inch closer to Alexandra's aching cock.

Alexandra shivered and sighed as she felt Emily's probing fingers slide under her panties. She turned to speak but her mouth was covered by Emily's, her lips crushed in a hard kiss that sucked the air from her lungs. She felt helpless against the pleasure; her mouth was taken, her lips pushed open by Emily's voracious tongue. At the same time she felt Emily's fingers inside her knickers, stroking the base of her hardness gently before sliding down between her thighs. Unable to resist, Alexandra lifted herself slightly, implicitly allowing Emily to explore further.

'This is what you want, isn't it?' Emily breathed, pushing her finger directly against Alexandra's puckered anal hole.

Alexandra sighed, her eyes were half closed and she felt dizzy with excitement. She could not answer; she didn't know what she wanted. All that she knew was that it felt too good to stop.

'And this is what you want, too,' Emily added, leaning back to unzip her jeans, slowly. Alexandra's eyes opened wide as she saw that dark bulge that emerged from between Emily's thighs. She watched with horror and fascination as Emily slowly eased the hard black erection out of her jeans, until it jutted obscenely from her body. Sleek, hard, slightly curved and tipped with a smoothly shaped glans, the fake cock looked dangerously real.

'Isn't this what you want, slut?' Emily hissed through gritted teeth.

'I don't know what I want.' Alexandra whispered, her eyes still fixed on the thick erection that Emily stroked softly with her fingers.

'Don't give me that! I know what you *need*, girl . . .'

Suddenly, Alexandra was pushed back on the bed, her skirt riding up above her waist so that her stockings and her black panties were partially exposed. She was breathing hard, her heart thumping as the adrenaline rush tore through her body, bringing with it fear and excitement and the explosive promise of danger.

'Suck on it!'

Alexandra turned away from the dark latex phallus that was pushed into her face. Up close, she could see a tiny slit in the fake glans and the shape of a thick vein running on the underside of the shaft.

'Want to play rough?' Emily laughed harshly.

'This isn't what I want,' Alexandra complained weakly, knowing that what she was saying was only half true.

'No, but it's what I want,' Emily responded, and for a moment she was her old self again, her eyes filled with concern and excitement. 'Now, turn over you little bitch,' she commanded, snapping back into her game so that even her voice sounded viciously male.

Alexandra resisted for a moment, but a hard slap in the face brought fire to her cheek and a surge of sexual excitement. She turned over on to her stomach, pushing her cock down hard so that it rubbed deliciously against her tight panties. Her skirt was lifted quickly and she sensed Emily's eyes on her backside, enjoying the view.

'So this is what you've been hiding from me,' Emily whispered.

Alexandra cried out when the first hard stroke landed

on her backside; Emily's hand landing with a crack of sound and a sharp pain that made Alexandra squeal.

'It's your choice, slut; learn to suck cock or take a few more of these,' Emily threatened and then began a slow, methodical spanking. Her strokes fell evenly on each side of Alexandra's bottom, marking her flesh so that its redness could clearly be seen, even through the black lacy panties.

Alexandra writhed and struggled, trying to escape the hard smacks that fell across her behind. The sharp pain of impact mounted and merged with the vivid red glow that seeped through her body. She felt the wetness pour from her glans, the fluid excitement leaking into her panties and smearing on to her abdomen until she felt close to orgasm.

'I'll do it – don't spank me any more . . .' she begged, finally, looking up in anguish at a cool and triumphant Emily.

'That's it, suck it well.'

Alexandra turned on to her side and moved her head closer to the hardness that Emily sported like a trophy. She eyed it warily before putting her lips to it, kissing the very tip of it softly. She kissed it for a moment more and then traced its length with her tongue, moving from the bulbous glans down to the thickest part of the base. She could see that there was another end to the dildo and that this was pushed deep into Emily's pussy. As she kissed it reverently, she glimpsed Emily's pussy lips bulging around it. There were tell-tale signs of wetness and Alexandra guessed that the pleasure Emily felt was physically real and did not derive solely from their game.

'Suck it harder,' Emily urged. 'Take it into your mouth, bitch.'

Alexandra opened her mouth and took the glans between her lips, licking the underside and then taking it deeper into her mouth. She moved up and down, slowly, extravagantly, sucking and kissing, licking and biting at the hardness that fucked her mouth. She used her hands to masturbate it, rubbing it up and down as she sucked, playing with the cock that she knew gave Emily so much pleasure.

When Emily began to touch her again, Alexandra moved closer. Her skirt was in complete disarray but she knew that her panties still covered the redness of her punished bottom cheeks. The cock in her mouth added to her excitement; the harder it fucked her the better it felt. Her panties were pulled aside suddenly, the thin material was almost torn from her body.

'Finger yourself,' Emily demanded. 'Fuck yourself for me while you suck my cock.'

Alexandra licked her fingers quickly, wetting them in the same way that she had wetted Emily's hard prick. She reached down slowly and pulled her panties down to her knees, exposing her hardness to full view before letting the skirt cover most of it again. She lay back so that her arsehole was exposed, lifted slightly from the bed. Her fingers were cool and wet on her thigh and, when she touched her rear hole, the feelings of shame burned strongly inside her.

'Do it; fuck yourself. That's it – nice and deep for me.'

She held her breath and pushed her spit-soaked finger against her anal hole, circling it for a moment before applying more saliva. She repeated the process several times, rubbing her anal ring and then putting her finger to her mouth to wet it again. Finally, she pressed her finger into herself, pushing against the resistant play of muscle until she relaxed enough to take it. For a moment she looked away as she did it – as though too ashamed of herself to view what she was doing – but when she glanced at her reflection in the mirror she felt a thrill of excitement. Her finger was disappearing into her anal hole; she could see the tight ring of muscle clenched around her digit as it moved in and out of her body.

Emily took her by the hair and guided the hard cock into her mouth again, forcing it deep this time. Alexandra sucked deliriously as she fingered herself, taking pleasure from both actions. She glimpsed herself in the mirror, her skirt around her waist, her backside exposed. Fingering her arse-hole while sucking on the big black phallus that filled her mouth.

'That's it.' Emily gasped, shuddering her climax and forcing her cock deep into Alexandra's throat.

Alexandra lay back, her thighs parted and her knees pulled up so that her backside was utterly exposed. She continued to fuck herself with her finger, probing deep and hard and gasping with the sharp pleasure of it all. Emily sat back, watching for a moment, recovering from her sudden climax.

'You're a dirty slut,' she whispered, 'but I wouldn't want you any other way.'

Alexandra smiled, breathlessly. She held her bottom cheeks open as Emily positioned herself so that the head of the latex cock was pressed into place. When Emily was ready she pushed down, forcing the massive erection into Alexandra's back passage. There was a sharp pain that made Alexandra gasp, but it was nothing compared to the thrill of being fucked. She closed her eyes as the cock slid deep into her arsehole, filling her, opening her, taking her completely. Emily pressed down until her abdomen was pushed flat against Alexandra's spanked bottom cheeks.

'I've always wanted to fuck you,' Emily whispered.

Alexandra sighed, swooning ecstatically as the tip of the hardness touched her deep inside. She pulled her knees further back, wanting Emily to take her as completely as possible. When Emily began to thrust and withdraw, Alexandra felt the world give way. No other pleasure had been so pure. She writhed and moaned, crying and whimpering as she was fucked with a hard, swift rhythm.

She was beautiful; she was desirable; she was a woman. Her body took the hardness that was plunged into her, and responded to the pain with pleasure. She cried out once and felt her cock exploding, its seed bursting out in burning spasms, so that it felt as though it were being pumped into her body by Emily.

Alexandra wept with pleasure.

Sixteen

Emily had changed out of her Levis and was wearing a short cotton slip dress that emphasised the curve of her breasts and showed off her long, smooth legs. She had also glossed up her lips and painted her eyes, making herself look feminine and sexy once more. Dressing up like a man had been exciting but it had frightened her, too. As a man she felt angry, vicious and predatory and, though that added spice to her sex play, it also made her feel nervous.

Alex had changed out of the clothes that Mistress had selected for him – he was wearing jogging bottoms and an old sweatshirt. Emily had been fascinated to see him shedding his other persona, transforming himself from sweet, submissive Alexandra back into plain old Alex. When they had both been in drag fucking together had been intense – Alexandra had sobbed her heart out after her climax and Emily, too, had been shaken by the power of the moment.

The sun was setting over the horizon, casting a glow across the world that touched gold on the peaceful expanse that was Eden. Emily contrasted the serene landscape with the psychic slaughter that she knew was occurring at the big meeting. It wasn't just the future of Eden that was at stake; it was the whole idea of living apart from the rest of the world.

'They're on their way back,' Alex reported, joining Emily out on the terrace.

'Isn't it lovely?' she whispered, looking out across the sloping greenery to the blurred horizon. There was a silence over the land that was deeply attractive and Emily hoped that it was a good omen. Having a place apart from the rest of the world was good – it created a space to act out the fantasies and desires which were nourished by the harshness of reality.

Minutes later, Katerina arrived home, accompanied by Joanna but not by Patrick.

'Did Alexandra cry?' was Katerina's first question. She looked tired and, in the fading light of evening, Emily could not tell what her mood was.

'Yes, she cried,' Alex admitted quietly, as though speaking of some third party and not another part of himself.

'And Emily?'

'I felt stunned,' she admitted. 'Just like you said I would.'

'And is Alexandra still with us?' Joanna asked, a slight smile on her face.

Alex inhaled sharply and then nodded, his eyes closed as though he were holding back a flood of emotion.

'But what about you?' Emily asked urgently. 'What's happened?'

Joanna looked at Katerina and smiled. 'Eden still stands,' she said. 'There are going to be changes – big changes – but we're going to carry on with it.'

'And Patrick?' Alex asked.

'Patrick has decided that he cannot live the way the rest of us want to,' Katerina told him. 'It's his own decision; we gave him the choice. He's talking now about going to the States for a while, but first he needs to find someone to sell his share of Eden to. I have suggested that he speak to Robert, who has often expressed an interest in joining us here.'

'It's hard to believe that he gave up so easily,' Joanna remarked. She was, evidently, still trying to get her head around the speed and the ease with which things had changed.

244

'No,' Katerina disagreed. 'You see, Patrick is guilty of confusing fantasy and reality. He mistook the dominance of our sexual play for dominance in the real world – in the end he started to believe his own propaganda. When I refused to continue he was suddenly faced with the real world again. At the moment he is in shock, but in time he will recover. I know him well enough to be certain of that.'

'And Helen?' Emily asked.

'Helen is staying,' Katerina replied. 'But she has decided that she and Joanna should live apart for a while.'

Alex looked at Joanna sharply. 'Is that what you want?' he asked.

'Yes, I think we'll work together much better if we don't have to live together as well. So, for the time being, I'm going to be staying here with Katerina, Emily and Alexandra.'

Emily smiled. 'Alexandra? I think she needs time to get ready again.'

'Just one more thing,' Alex said quietly. 'What about the plans you had for extending this place? I thought you were keen to expand.'

Katerina shook her head. 'No. That's my present to Patrick; he can have the plans to take with him to America. Things are going to be changing here but there's no point in growing until we know ourselves exactly how we want to live.'

'What about you two?' Joanna asked suddenly. 'Now that things are changing do you still want to stay?'

Alex looked at Emily and she looked back. Their eyes met and they both knew the answer: 'Yes.'

Katerina smiled. 'Alexandra can expect to be punished tonight,' she reminded everyone. 'And with three of us here to keep her in check I am sure she's going to learn to be a good girl.'

Alex blushed. With Mistress, Joanna and Emily to serve he knew that Eden had taken a step closer to becoming Paradise.

NEW BOOKS

Coming up from Nexus and Black Lace

Intimate Games by Julia Marlowe
January 1997 Price £4.99 ISBN: 0 352 33138 0

After meeting the enigmatic and persuasive Gilles at a party, the sexually adventurous Arianne Fontaine takes him on board as a partner in the exclusive club she has created at her luxury home in Paris; a place where the rich and ribald can indulge their most daring fantasies. When they meet Fleur – a novice to lascivious behaviour – Gilles and Arianne draw her into a life of bizarre sex and ritual discipline.

Molten Silver by Delaney Silver
January 1997 Price £4.99 ISBN: 0 352 33137 2

This is the first collection of short stories by one of Nexus's best-selling authors. In these stories of fetishism and unusual behaviour, characters live in a world where decadence and depravity are never far away – and naughty behaviour never goes unpunished. Each story is flavoured with a liberal amount of deviance.

Candida's Secret Mission by Virginia Lasalle
February 1997 Price £4.99 ISBN: 0 352 33141 0

Candie has a new job at a secret government establishment high in the Bavarian Alps. However, this is no ordinary employment; top-secret investigations are being conducted to measure female arousal and highly-sexed young women are needed to help research. If all goes well, Candie could be in for a big reward. There are so many tempting distractions: Sister Serena, who performs the intimate medical examinations, and Herr Direktor, who oversees the delectable lovelies in his charge.

New Erotica 3 – Extracts from the Best of Nexus

February 1997   Price £4.99   ISBN: 0 352 33142 9

This is the third volume of extracts from the best-selling and most well-liked Nexus books of the past couple of years. The settings are as eclectic as the sexual peccadilloes of the characters. Emma, for instance, in *Emma's Secret World*, who gives up her life of privilege to become the slave of the cruel lesbian mistress. And Constance, employed as a Cornish Governess, who soon finds herself administering discipline to the local gentlemen – including the vicar! These are just two of the stories featured in this anthology which reflects the diverstiy of the Nexus imprint.

BLACK
lace

Nadya's Quest by Lisette Allen
January 1997   Price £4.99   ISBN: 0 352 33135 6

Empress Catherine of Imperial Russia was notorious for her sexual appetite and unusual pastimes. In this story, she is on the look-out for a new lover, who must be handsome, virile, and able to satisfy her lust for flesh. When the young Nadya, who comes to St Petersburg in the year of 1788, finds Swedish seafarer, Axel, she wants him as a lover. But so too does everyone else, including the Empress. Against a backdrop of unbridled decadence, the Imperial Court is soon to erupt with jealousy and sedition.

Desire Under Capricorn by Louisa Francis
January 1997   Price £4.99   ISBN: 0 352 33136 4

1870s Australia. The feisty Dita Jones is engaged to Jonathon Grimshaw, the most eligible bachelor in Sydney's polite society. But when the young couple are shipwrecked, they are thrown into a world where survival instincts and natural urges triumph over civilised values. Jonathon is appalled at his fiancée's overtly sexual behaviour and fellow castaway Matt Warrender cannot resist Dita's ample charms. After they're rescued, things will never be the same again and Matt cannot forget the woman who has so inflamed his lust.

The Master of Shilden by Lucinda Carrington
February 1997   Price £4.99   ISBN: 0 352 33140 2

When successful interior designer Elise St John is offered a commission at a remote castle, she isn't prepared for some of the more curious terms of her employment. She has been chosen to create rooms where guests will be able to realise their most erotic fantasies. She soon finds herself indulging in some fantasies of her own – which soon become reality. Max Lannsen – the owner of the castle – is dark and mysterious while Blair Devlin – the riding instructor – is overtly confident. Both have designs on Elise. Designs which manifest themselves in bizarre and very sexual ways.

Modern Love – a Black Lace Anthology

February 1997   Price £4.99   ISBN: 0 352 33158 5

Black Lace is the leading imprint of erotic fiction for women and the publishing sensation of the decade. This is the first anthology of the series with an exclusively comtemporary theme. Seduction and mystery and darkly sensual behaviour are the key words to this unique collection of writings from the female perspective. Worlds of passion collide with unbridled erotic exploration and scintillating characters delight in the thrill of total surrender to pleasure and decadent indulgence.

Please send me the books I have ticked above.

Name ....

Address ....

....

....

.... Post code ....

Send to: **Cash Sales, Nexus Books, 332 Ladbroke Grove, London W10 5AH**

Please enclose a cheque or postal order, made payable to Virgin Publishing, to the value of the books you have ordered plus postage and packing costs as follows:

UK and BFPO – £1.00 for the first book, 50p for each subsequent book.

Overseas (including Republic of Ireland) – £2.00 for the first book, £1.00 for each subsequent book.

If you would prefer to pay by VISA or ACCESS/MASTER-CARD, please write your card number and expiry date here:

....

Please allow up to 28 days for delivery.

Signature ....